John Heneage Jesse

Memoirs of King Richard the Third

And Some Of his Comtemporaries, Volume I

John Heneage Jesse

Memoirs of King Richard the Third
And Some Of his Comtemporaries, Volume I

ISBN/EAN: 9783743401440

Manufactured in Europe, USA, Canada, Australia, Japa

Cover: Foto ©Raphael Reischuk / pixelio.de

Manufactured and distributed by brebook publishing software (www.brebook.com)

John Heneage Jesse

Memoirs of King Richard the Third

MEMOIRS

OF

KING RICHARD THE THIRD

AND SOME OF HIS CONTEMPORARIES

With an Historical Drama on the Battle of Bosworth

BY

JOHN HENEAGE JESSE

A New Edition

IN TWO VOLUMES—VOLUME I.

NEW YORK

FRANCIS P. HARPER

1894

PREFACE.

THE character of this work seems to demand some explanation from the author. Had he commenced his labours with the original and definite purpose of writing Memoirs of Richard III. or of his times, the reader would have been spared these observations. But such was not the case. This volume, in fact, emanated indirectly in the drama which forms a portion of its pages. The necessity of acquiring a knowledge of the characters and motives of action of the different historical personages, whom the author proposed to introduce among his *dramatis personæ*, entailed on him some amount of literary research. The author found his task an agreeable one. By degrees he collected the materials which constituted the groundwork of the several memoirs in this volume. That which pleased himself, he thought, might possibly please others. As fresh facts and anecdotes increased on his hands, he had, of course, the option of reconstructing his labours, and substituting a more regular, and perhaps a more ambitious plan. But it is not always that a literary work is improved by being diverted from its original design, and accordingly the author decided on adhering to the plan which he had at first adopted. To the merit of novelty, whether of facts or arguments, he can prefer but a very trifling claim. To compress scattered and curious information, and, if possible, to amuse, have been the primary objects of the author. If he shall in any degree have succeeded in this latter object, the thanks of the reader are mainly, if not entirely, due to those harvest-lords in the field of old historical literature, whose learned and diligent researches have left but little to be gleaned by those who follow in their footsteps. The obligations under which the author lies to the labours of Mr. Sharon Turner, Dr. Lingard, Miss Halsted, Sir N. Harris Nicolas, Sir Henry Ellis, Mr. Bruce, and Mr. John G. Nichols, he would indeed be ungrateful if he omitted to acknowledge. To Mr. T. Duffus Hardy and Mr. James Gairdner, he takes this opportunity of expressing his thanks, as well for the courtesy which he personally experienced from them, as for the valuable assistance which he has derived from their literary publications. To such other persons who have kindly responded to his inquiries, or who have in any way aided the performance of his task, the author also begs to tender his thanks.

John Heneage Jesse.

London.
September 1861.

CONTENTS

OF

THE FIRST VOLUME.

MEMOIRS OF KING RICHARD THE THIRD.

CHAPTER I.

CHAPTER II.

CHAPTER III.

CHAPTER IV.

CHAPTER V.

CHAPTER VI.

CHAPTER VII.

CHAPTER VIII.

King Richard the Third

King Richard the Third

MEMOIRS OF KING RICHARD III.

CHAPTER I.

THE WARS OF THE ROSES.

AT the time when Richard Duke of Gloucester won his first laurels in high command at the battle of Barnet, he was only in the nineteenth year of his age. Few, however, as were the years which had passed over his head, he was old enough to have witnessed the commencement of that fierce and memorable contest between the houses of York and Lancaster, which deluged the battle-field and the scaffold with blood, and which, fourteen years after the battle of Barnet, was destined to be brought to a close by his own violent death on the field of Bosworth.

In the course of that long and terrible contest, thirteen pitched battles were fought; three kings met with untimely ends, and twenty-six knights of the Garter perished either by the sword or by the hand of the executioner. The ancient nobility of England was almost entirely annihilated. Of the royal house of Plantagenet, Richard Duke of York, and his son the Earl of Rutland, were slain at the battle of Wakefield; the Duke of Clarence died the death of a traitor; Edward V. and his brother the Duke of York were murdered in the Tower of London; and lastly, their uncle, Richard III., was killed at Bosworth. Of the house of Lancaster, King Henry VI. perished mysteriously in prison; his son, Edward Prince of Wales, was slain at Tewkesbury. Of the kindred of Queen Elizabeth Woodville, the consort of Edward IV., her father, Richard Earl Rivers, and her brother, Sir John Woodville, were beheaded at Northampton; her husband, John Lord Grey of Groby, fell at the second battle of St. Albans; her son, Sir Richard Grey, was beheaded at Pomfret, and on the same scaffold perished her brother, the accomplished Anthony Woodville, Earl Rivers. Of the royal house of Beaufort, Edmund Duke of Somerset, formerly Regent of France, was slain at the first battle of St. Albans; Henry, the second Duke, was beheaded after the battle of Hexham; Edmund, the third Duke, was beheaded after the battle of Tewkesbury; and in the same battle was slain Sir John Beaufort, son of the first Duke. Of the great house of Stafford, Humphrey Earl of Stafford fell at the first battle of St. Albans; his father, Humphrey Duke of Buckingham, fell at the battle of Northampton; Henry, the second Duke, was beheaded at Salisbury; and, of another branch of the Staffords, Humphrey Earl of Devon perished on the scaffold at Bridgewater. Of the house of Neville, Richard Earl of Salisbury was beheaded after the battle of Wakefield; his sons, Richard Earl of Warwick, the "Kingmaker," and John Marquis of Montagu, fell at Barnet; a third son, Sir Thomas Neville, fell at Wakefield; Sir John Neville was killed at the battle of Towton; Sir Henry Neville, son and heir of Ralph Lord Latimer, was beheaded after the battle of Banbury, and Sir Humphrey Neville and his brother Charles, after the battle of Hexham. Of the Percies, Henry second Earl of Northumberland, one of the heroes of Agincourt, fell at the first battle of St. Albans; two of his gallant sons, Henry, the third Earl, and Sir Richard Percy, was slain at Towton; a third son, Thomas Lord Egremont, perished at the battle of Northampton, and a fourth son, Sir Ralph Percy, at Hedgeley Moor. Of the house of Talbot, John second Earl of Shrewsbury, and his brother Sir Christopher Talbot, were slain at Northampton; their kinsman, Thomas Talbot, Lord Lisle, fell in a skirmish at Wotton-under-Edge. Of the Courtenays, Thomas sixth Earl of Devon was beheaded after the battle of Towton; Henry, the seventh Earl, was beheaded at Sarum; and at Tewkesbury was slain their only remaining brother, John, the eighth Earl. Of the De Veres, John twelfth Earl of Oxford, and his eldest son Sir Aubrey de Vere, perished together on the scaffold on Tower Hill. Of the Cliffords, Thomas, the eighth Lord, was slain at the first battle of St. Albans, and his son John, the ninth Lord, at the battle of Towton. Of the house of Hungerford, Robert third Baron Hungerford was beheaded after the battle of Hexham; and his heir, Sir Thomas Hungerford, was beheaded at Salisbury. Of the Bourchiers, Humphrey Lord Cromwell was slain at the battle of Barnet, and Sir Edward Bourchier, brother of Henry Earl of Essex, at Wakefield. Lastly, of the house of Welles there perished the representatives of three generations: Leo Lord Welles was slain at the battle of Towton; his son, Richard Lord Welles and Willoughby, and his grandson Sir Robert Welles, severally perished by the axe of the executioner.

Long as is this catalogue of slaughtered heroes, there might be appended to it many other, and no less illustrious names. At the battle of Blorcheath was slain James Touchet, Lord Audley; at the battle of Northampton, John Viscount de Beaumont; at Wakefield, William Bonville, Lord Harrington; at Tewkesbury, John Lord Wenlock; at Towton, Ranulph Lord Dacre of Gillesland; and at Bosworth, John Howard, Duke of Norfolk, and Walter Devereux, Lord Ferrers of Chartley. Lastly, on the scaffold perished William Herbert,

Earl of Pembroke; John Tiptoft, Earl of Worcester; James Butler, Earl of Wiltshire; William Bonville, Lord Bonville; William Lord Hastings; and Sir Owen Tudor, grandfather of King Henry VII.

Although the tender years of Richard of Gloucester had prevented his bearing a part in the earlier struggles between the houses of York and Lancaster, he had not been exempted from the extraordinary vicissitudes which for so many years had befallen his race. He had shared their flight when capture would probably have been death. He had worn the garb of woe for many a near and illustrious relative, and had doubtless personally witnessed many of those disasters, which desolated alike the hall of the baron and the cottage of the peasant. As associated, therefore, with the story of his boyhood,—and also as throwing a light on the motives which subsequently influenced his conduct in manhood, and the circumstances which incited him to seize a crown,—it may not be inexpedient to introduce a brief summary of the stirring events, which immediately preceded the first appearance of Richard Duke of Gloucester on the great stage of the world.

When the misconduct and misgovernment of Richard II. induced his indignant subjects to rise in rebellion against him, it proved to be a great calamity to England that the prince of the house of

Plantagenet whom they elected to reign in his stead was not also, by the laws of lineal inheritance, the nearest in succession to the throne. Henry Bolingbroke, Duke of Lancaster, who succeeded by the title of King Henry IV., was descended from John of Gaunt, Duke of Lancaster, *fourth* son of Edward III. But that monarch had also left descendants by his *third* son, Lionel Duke of Clarence, which descendants, on the eve of the Wars of the Roses, were represented by the house of York. Thus the parliamentary title to the crown appertained to the house of Lancaster; the hereditary right belonged to the house of York.*

So long as the sceptre of England was swayed by the strong grasp of Henry IV., and afterwards by that of his son Henry V., the scions of the elder branch of the line of Plantagenet were reduced to figure at the court of their rivals as simple princes of the blood, with little prospect of recovering their inheritance. But to the wise and vigorous rule of the victor of Agincourt, had succeeded the dominion of a prince whose piety and chastity justly obtained for him the admiration of the wise and good, but who, on the other hand, was lamentably deficient in that firmness and energy of mind which,

---

* The annexed genealogical table will explain the descent from King Edward III., as well as the relationship by blood or marriage, of some of the principal persons subsequently mentioned in these memoirs.

EDWARD III. = PHILIPPA of Hainault.
EDWARD the Black Prince.
WILLIAM of Hatfield: D.S.P.
LIONEL Duke of Clarence.
BLANCH PLANTAGENET = JOHN of Gaunt, Duke of Lancaster = CATHERINE SWYNFORD.
HENRY IV.
JOHN Earl of Somerset.
RICHARD II.
PHILIPPA = EDMUND MORTIMER, Earl of March.
HENRY V. = CATHERINE, daughter of CHARLES VI., King of France = SIR OWEN TUDOR.
ROGER Earl of March.
PHILIPPA = Sir HENRY PERCY (Hotspur).
HENRY VI. = MARGARET of Anjou.
EDMUND Earl of Richmond = MARGARET, daughter of JOHN Duke of Somerset.
ANNE MORTIMER = RICHARD Earl of Cambridge.
ELIZABETH = JOHN Lord Clifford.
EDWARD Prince of Wales: D.S.P.
HENRY VII.
RICHARD Duke of York.
THOMAS Lord Clifford.
EDWARD IV. = ELIZABETH WOODVILLE.
RICHARD III.
JOHN Lord Clifford.
ELIZABETH = HENRY VII.
HENRY Lord Clifford.
JOHN Duke of Somerset.
EDMUND Duke of Somerset.
MARGARET = EDMUND Earl of Richmond.
HENRY VII.
MARGARET = HUMPHREY Earl of Stafford.
HENRY Duke of Buckingham = CATHERINE WOODVILLE.

especially in fierce and turbulent times, are required in those who are called upon to govern kingdoms. Taken from a cradle to sit upon a throne, the imbecile Henry VI. had reigned nearly thirty years over England, when the continued maladministration of his affairs by incompetent ministers at length raised such an amount of indignation in the breasts of his subjects, as to threaten the subversion of the throne of which he was the innocent usurper. Seldom had the royal treasury been known to be in a more exhausted state. Seldom had the administration of justice been more tardy. Never, perhaps, had the sheriffs of counties, and the collectors of taxes, been more arbitrary in their proceedings, or more extortionate in their exactions. Never, perhaps, had the arrogance and the luxurious habits of the prelates, as well as the scandalous immoralities and negligence of the clergy in general, entailed greater disrepute upon the Church. The great barons, too, had their especial grounds for complaint. Deeply they resented the influence which William de la Pole, Duke of Suffolk, a man of plebeian origin, had acquired over the weak king and his accomplished consort. Deeply they felt the loss of the rich provinces of Anjou and Maine, by which Henry had far too dearly purchased the hand of the beautiful Margaret of Anjou. Moreover, the ancient glory of England had been tarnished by the disasters and defeats, which she had encountered in her recent contest with France. It was felt by all classes that, since the Conquest, no greater misfortune had befallen England than the loss of Normandy with her seven bishoprics and one hundred churches. All ranks of society admitted the existence of intolerable grievances. In all quarters there was a cry for redress.

Unfortunately for the house of Lancaster, the head of the rival house of York happened, at this crisis, to be a prince eminently qualified to carry on a successful competition for empire, whether the occasion might require wisdom in the closet, or personal valour on the battle-field. Richard Plantagenet, Duke of York, was the grandson of Edmund of Langley, Duke of York, fifth son of Edward III. It was not, however, from his paternal descent, but from being the representative of Philippa, daughter and heiress of Lionel Duke of Clarence, the *third* son of Edward III., that he founded his title to the throne. Brave, discreet, and gifted with abilities considerably above the ordinary standard,—possessed, moreover, of vast wealth and of princely territories,—beloved by the people, and allied, by blood or by marriage, to the most powerful barons of England,—so powerful a subject as the Duke of York might well have been regarded with apprehension and jealousy by a monarch far more energetic than the spiritless

Henry, and far better capable of coping with an ambitious rival. While yet a boy, Richard had distinguished himself by his personal valour and military ability. Before he was eighteen years of age he had been preferred before the Duke of Somerset to be Regent of France.

The Duke of York was apparently in his thirty-third year, when the spirit of disaffection which pervaded England naturally revived the long dormant hopes of the elder branch of the Plantagenets. At the period of which we are speaking, he was holding his court in Ireland, of which island he had rendered himself the idolized governor. But though absent, his friends in England had kept him constantly supplied with intelligence, and had assiduously watched over his interests. Their primary object had been to familiarize the public mind with his claims, and gradually to prepare the people to receive him as their ruler. Accordingly, his subordinate partisans received instructions to discuss and maintain his claims in all public places, to extol the services which, as a soldier and a statesman, he had rendered to the State, and especially to draw invidious comparisons between the eminent administrative abilities of the duke, contrasted with the misgovernment of the queen and the imbecility of her consort.

By these means the party of the Duke of York was daily becoming more formidable in the State,

when the breaking out of the formidable popular
tumult, known as Jack Cade's insurrection, seemed
to invite the duke openly to espouse the cause of
the people, and, at the same time, to assert his
legitimate rights. Tempting, however, as the
opportunity appeared to be, he allowed it to slip
by. Not improbably he may have shrunk from
the responsibility of being the first to entail on his
country the horrors of civil war, or, not impossibly,
he may have imagined that, sooner or later, the
imprudent conduct of the queen must lead to his
being called to the throne by the general voice of
the people, and thus relieve him from the hateful
necessity of unsheathing the sword. He returned
from Ireland, indeed, and assumed the attitude of
an armed dictator, but without advancing any title
to the throne. His only motive, he said, in ap-
pealing to arms was to procure redress for notorious public wrongs, and more especially to obtain
the dismissal from the king's councils of the
queen's unpopular favorite, Edmund Duke of Somerset. At first success attended his measures.
Alarmed at the approach of an army equal if not
superior to its own, the court entered into a solemn
engagement to take measures for the redress of
grievances, and to commit Somerset to the Tower.
No sooner, however, had York disbanded his
forces than the promise was broken, and Somerset
reinstated in all his former authority. Accord-

ingly, disgusted with the insincerity of the court.
and probably apprehensive of personal danger, the
duke retired for a season to his castle of Wigmore,
on the borders of Wales, where his retainers were
numerous, and his influence paramount.

For two years from this period the public tranquillity remained undisturbed, but, at the end of
that time, Henry VI. was seized by one of those
attacks of mental aberration by which he was peri-
odically afflicted.   The star of York was now again
in the ascendant.   The queen, to her excessive
mortification, found herself incapable of contend-
ing with the first prince of the blood; the Duke of
Somerset was arrested in her apartments and sent
to the Tower; the Duke of York was declared by
parliament to be protector of the realm during
pleasure.   Still the cautious prince of the blood
shrank from seizing the sceptre.   In the mean time
the king gradually recovered from his dreadful
malady; Somerset was released from the Tower,
and resumed his seat at the king's councils; York
was deprived of his important post of governor of
Calais, and once more flew indignantly to Wigmore.

The contention between Somerset on the one side,
and the Duke of York on the other, had now
become a war to the knife.   The latter, indeed, still
shrank from advancing his title to the crown, but
he no longer hesitated to appeal to arms.   His

friends were entreated to meet him in the marches of Wales. The Earls of Salisbury and Warwick and Lord Cobham speedily joined his standard. He had soon the satisfaction of seeing himself at the head of three thousand men. In the mean time Somerset had not been idle. Having collected a force nearly equal to that of the Yorkists, he induced the king to accompany him on his march, and boldly advanced to give battle to the insurgents.

Thus commenced the terrible and bloody struggle between the houses of York and Lancaster. The first blood was shed at the battle of St. Albans, on the 22nd of May 1455. The Yorkists proved victorious. On the side of the king were slain the Duke of Somerset, the Earl of Northumberland, the Earl of Stafford, eldest son of the Duke of Buckingham, and Thomas Lord Clifford. The king himself was wounded in the neck with an arrow, and fell into the hands of the Yorkists. Signal, however, as was the duke's success, he still continued to exercise that moderation and caution which ever characterised his policy. Incontrovertible as were his claims to the throne by right of hereditary descent, he probably felt that unless his title were also solemnly recognized by parliament, his triumph must necessarily be but brief. Accordingly parliament was appealed to by him, and, to his disappointment, was appealed to in vain. The barons, instead of inviting him to ascend the throne, solemnly renewed their oaths of fealty to the king; the lords spiritual laying their hands upon their breasts, the lords temporal placing their hands within those of the king. But, unhappily for Henry, he had scarcely received the congratulations of his friends when he relapsed into his former state of mental incapacity. Again the Duke of York was invested by parliament with the protectorship. Again the kingly power seemed to be within his grasp.

There was at this period an exalted personage in the State, whose high spirit, united to the fascinations of wit and female beauty, very nearly proved a match for the vast influence, the wary genius, and long political experience of the over-cautious chief of the house of Plantagenet. That person was the famous Margaret of Anjou, now in her twenty-seventh year, and in the zenith of her loveliness. Hitherto the only talent which she had displayed was for intrigue. Indeed, so far from her having afforded any evidence of that indomitable fearlessness for which her name has since been rendered famous in history, it was notorious that, at the time of Cade's insurrection, the beautiful girl had not only flown terrified from the scene of danger, but had tarnished the honour of the house of Plantagenet, by inducing her uxorious consort to become the companion of her flight. But, since then, an event had occurred which necessarily influences the character of all women, but which completely revolutionized that of Margaret of Anjou. Eighteen months before the battle of St. Albans, at the time when the king was prostrated by his distressing mental malady, the queen had given birth to a son, her first-born child and her last. From this period, all her hopes, all her interest in life, seem to have been centred in her beloved offspring. It was evident to her that, so long as the influence of the house of York prevailed, she had reason to tremble for the birthright of her child, if not for his very existence. To recover her husband, therefore, from his mental disorder,—to arouse him to a sense of the utter ruin which impended over himself and his line,—became the all-absorbing object of her life. No sooner, then, did he partially rally from his distemper, than every expedient calculated to amuse or to beguile him was called into play. The pious king, it seems, confidently believed in the efficacy of being prayed for by others; and accordingly applications, real or fictitious, were read to him from his nobles, soliciting permission to visit the shrines on the continent for the purpose of praying for his recovery. Again, his mind having become harassed by thoughts of the exhausted state of his treasury, he was not only deluded with assurances that it was in a satisfactory condition, but that it was about to be replenished

with inexhaustible gold.   Lastly, music was found
to soothe his distemper, and forthwith the sheriffs
of counties were directed to look out for beautiful
boys skilled in minstrelsy, and to despatch them
to the court.

At length the clouds which had darkened the
king's mind passed completely away.   It happened
that business had called the Duke of York away
from court, and accordingly the queen resolved to
take every advantage of his absence, in order to
accomplish the favourite object which she had at
heart.   Without having given any previous notice
to parliament, she unexpectedly produced her royal
consort before the House of Lords, and induced
him to address them from the throne.   By the
blessing of God, said the king, he had been restored
to health; he believed that the realm no longer required a protector.   His improved appearance, as
well as the dignified composure with which he
addressed them, satisfied the barons of his recovery.
Accordingly, an order was sent to the Duke of
York to resign the protectorship, and the king
resumed the reins of empire.

But though the device of the young queen had
proved a master-stroke, it was evident that so long
as the powerful leaders of the Yorkist party were
at liberty, peril still threatened her husband and
her child.   The Duke of York, by his marriage
with Cecily, daughter of Ralph Earl of Westmore-

land, had closely allied himself with the great family of the Nevilles, of whom no fewer than six of that name were at this period barons of England. Of these, the two most powerful, and the most devotedly attached to the house of York, were Richard Earl of Salisbury, and his eldest son, Richard Earl of Warwick, afterwards designated the Kingmaker. Salisbury, on account of his having fought and vanquished at St. Albans, where the queen's favourite Somerset fell, appears to have been regarded by her with especial aversion. To secure the persons of these three powerful barons was now the paramount object of Margaret. In order to effect her purpose, she announced that the king's health required the diversions of hunting and hawking, and on this pretext withdrew with him to Coventry. From thence she caused letters, under the privy seal, to be addressed to the duke and the two earls, intimating that the king urgently required their advice in certain important matters, and inviting them to his court. The invitation was accepted by all three of them. On the road to Coventry, however, they were met by a secret emissary, who informed them of the trap which had been set to ensnare them. The Duke of York flew to his stronghold on the borders of Wales; the Earl of Salisbury to his princely castle at Middleham, in Yorkshire; and the Earl of Warwick to his government at Calais, where he was the idol of the formidable garrison.

Still both parties shrank from reviving the horrors of civil war, and subsequently, through the good offices of Bourchier, Archbishop of Canterbury, a temporary reconciliation was effected between them. It had been agreed upon, as a preliminary step, that the leaders of the rival factions should repair to London; the partisans of the house of York to take up their quarters *within*, and those of the house of Lancaster *without*, the walls of the city. Accordingly the Duke of York took up his residence at his mansion of Baynard's Castle on the banks of the Thames; the Earl of Salisbury repaired to his stately palace, the Erber, lying further eastward; the Earl of Warwick also took up his quarters at his own house, Warwick Inn, Newgate. The leaders of the Lancastrian party, including the Dukes of Somerset and Exeter, were quartered without Temple Bar, and in other parts of the suburbs. The former party held their councils at the Black Friars, near Ludgate; the latter in the Chapter-house at Westminster. The king and queen held their court in the palace of the Bishop of London, close to the great cathedral of St. Paul's. Never perhaps had London presented so brilliant and so exciting a scene as during the great congress of the barons. Each baron, apprehensive of treachery, had brought with him a gallant, though limited number of retainers.* Day and night the lord-mayor, Sir Godfrey Boleyn, patrolled the streets with a guard of five thousand armed citizens. It had been decided that the solemn ceremony of reconciliation should take place before the high altar in St. Paul's. Accordingly, on the appointed day, the feast of the Annunciation, the king, arrayed in his royal mantle and with the crown on his head, issued from the bishop's palace, and bent his steps towards the cathedral. In the procession which accompanied him, the rival barons walked two and two, each with his hand in that of an enemy. The Earl of Salisbury walked with the Duke of Somerset, whose father he had discomfited and helped to slay at St. Albans; Warwick walked with the Duke of Exeter; in the hand of her deadliest foe, the Duke of York, was that of the beautiful and high-spirited queen. Fortunately this memorable "love-day," as the chronicler Fabyan styles it, passed off without disturbance. York and Salisbury returned to their several castles, and Warwick to Calais.

But the demon of hatred and revenge rankled

* "The Duke of York came this time to London with 400 men, and was lodged at his place of Baynard's; the Dukes of Exeter and Somerset, each of them with 400 men; the Earl of Northumberland, the Lord Egremont, and Lord Clifford, with 1500. The Earl of Warwick came from Calais with 600 men to London, with red liveries, embroidered with ragged staves."—*Leland, Collect.* vol. ii. p. 496.

far too deeply in the breasts of both parties to admit of the truce becoming a lasting one. It required, indeed, no great discernment to foretell that the slightest provocation on either side would infallibly be followed by an appeal to arms; that a single spark might kindle a conflagration which blood alone could extinguish. And so, before many months had elapsed, it came to pass. A servant of the king having insulted a retainer of Warwick in the court-yard of the palace at Westminster, an encounter took place between them, in which the aggressor was wounded. The king's servants naturally took the part of their comrade, and accordingly, pouring forth in great numbers from the palace, they not only fell with great fury on the earl's retinue, who were awaiting his return from the king's council-chamber, but even beset Warwick himself, who with difficulty fought his way to his barge at the river stairs. Warwick either believed, or affected to believe, that the attempt on his life had been a premeditated one. York and Salisbury were only too ready to resent the insult offered to their kinsman. Both parties hastened to arm their retainers, and mutually agreed on referring their cause to the arbitration of the God of battles.

The first engagement which was fought after the renewal of hostilities, was at Bloreheath in Staffordshire, on the 23rd of September 1459, when the

Earl of Salisbury, at the head of the Yorkists, obtained a complete victory over the royal forces, under the command of James Lord Audley, who, with many gallant knights, was slain in the encounter. This engagement was followed, on the 10th of July 1460, by the still more important battle of Northampton. On this occasion the royal army was commanded by the Dukes of Somerset and Buckingham; Warwick, the great Earl, led the Yorkists. His orders were to respect the person of the king and to spare the common soldiers, but to give no quarter to baron or knight. During the battle, which was long and fiercely fought, the intrepid Margaret of Anjou stood with her beloved child, the heir of England, upon a commanding spot, from whence she could point out to him the pomp and circumstance of war, and, as she fondly hoped, the utter discomfiture of his foes. It was the first battle witnessed by the ill-fated Edward of Lancaster, the first fought by Edward of York, afterwards King Edward IV. Although the latter was only in his nineteenth year, such confidence had Warwick in the son of his old companion in arms, that he gave him the command of the centre of his army; he himself engaging at the head of the right wing, and Edward Brooke, Lord Cobham, commanding the left. And nobly did the young Earl of March fulfil the expectations which Warwick had conceived of his valour. A splendid charge which he made scattered havoc and dismay among the Lancastrians. Treachery completed their discomfiture. Edmund Lord Grey de Ruthyn, who held an important command in the royal army, deserted in the heat of the battle to the Yorkists. Dearly were the earldom of Kent and the seignory of Ampthill purchased by the stain which is attached to his memory. The Yorkists were completely successful. The Duke of Buckingham, the Earl of Shrewsbury, and many other gallant nobles and knights, were slain either in action or in flight. With difficulty Queen Margaret contrived to escape with her idolized son into the fastnesses of Wales, from whence she subsequently fled into Scotland. Once more King Henry found himself a prisoner in the hands of the enemies of his house.

At length the time had arrived when, in the opinion of the Duke of York and his friends, he might with safety prefer his claims to the crown. Accordingly, on the 16th of October 1460, three days after the parliament had assembled, the duke alighted from his horse at the entrance of the great hall at Westminster, through which he passed to the House of Lords. A blast of trumpets notified his approach; a sword of state was carried naked before him. His reception by the barons was apparently very different from what he had anticipated. Amidst a dead silence, and with every eye fixed upon him, York advanced to the throne upon

which, with the exception of an interval of the last
sixty years, his forefathers had sat from the days
of the Conqueror. Standing under the canopy of
state, with his hand resting on the throne, he si-
lently awaited the result of his boldness. He had
expected, perhaps, that the barons would, with one
accord, have invited him to ascend the chair of the
Confessor. But not a voice rose in advocacy of
his claims; no look of encouragement met his eye.
At length Bourchier, Archbishop of Canterbury,
broke the silence. Approaching the duke, he
coldly intimated to him that the king was in the
royal apartments, and inquired whether it was not
his intention to visit his sovereign. "I know no
one in this realm," replied the duke haughtily,
"whom it doth not rather beseem to visit me."
With these words he descended the steps which led
to the throne, and indignantly quitted the assembly.

But, cold as was the reception which the duke's
pretensions had met with from the barons, his position in the State was too formidable, and the validity of his claims too incontestable, not to secure
them a patient investigation. Accordingly several
deliberations subsequently took place in the House
of Lords; the most eminent men in the Commons
were invited to take part in them, and they consented. An extraordinary compromise was the result. The title of the Duke of York to the throne

was declared to be certain and indisputable; but inasmuch as King Henry had swayed the sceptre for thirty-eight years, it was decided that the empty title and mock dignity of king should be guaranteed to him for the remainder of his days. The Duke of York thereupon was declared to be the true and rightful heir to the throne of his ancestors, the peers solemnly swearing to maintain his succession.

Sick of the cares of royalty, and fatigued by the weight of a crown, the probability is. that, had Henry been childless, he would have succumbed to the decision of parliament, not only without a struggle, but without a sigh. But when he also signed away the birthright of his child in favour of his hereditary foe, it could scarcely have been without a pang. On Margaret, the tidings of her consort's pusillanimity, and of the proscription of her child, produced an effect which seems to have been almost infuriating. The energy and resources of this remarkable princess appear by this time to have been fully appreciated by friend and foe, and accordingly, the Duke of York sent her a peremptory order, in the name of the king, to return immediately with her son to London, threatening her with the penalties of treason in the event of her refusal. This mandate she not only treated with becoming scorn, but, having obtained a loan of money from the Scottish court, she boldly crossed the borders, and entered England at the head of a small band of gallant followers.

Her success in the northern counties was rapid and triumphant. Her youth and beauty, as well as her heroism, her insinuating address, and the compassion which is ever felt for fallen greatness, excited an admiration and sympathy for which it would be difficult to find a parallel. It was afterwards said of her by Edward IV. that he stood in more apprehension of Margaret of Anjou when she was a fugitive and an outcast, than he did of all the princes of the house of Lancaster in the plenitude of their power. The warlike chivalry of the north rallied round the banner of the Red Rose almost to a man. In an incredibly short space of time the qeeen found herself at the head of an army amounting to 20,000 men.

The next event of importance which followed was the battle of Wakefield, which was fought on the 30th of December 1460. So energetic and expeditious had been the proceedings of Margaret, so unlooked for the success she had met with in arming the people of the north, that when the Duke of York marched forth to give her battle, he could muster only 6000 men. His friends exhorted him to shut himself up in his castle of Sandal, where he might have awaited in security the arrival of his gallant son the Earl of March, who was actively engaged in collecting reinforcements. The duke, however, obstinately refused to listen to the entreaties of his followers. Whatever hesitation he might have betrayed in the cabinet, on the field of battle he was ever undaunted. He scorned, he said, to retreat before a woman; he was resolved to triumph or to die. Considering the odds against which he had to contend, the result may be readily imagined. The Lancastrians obtained a signal victory; York himself was killed in the battle. His head was carried to the queen, who is said to have burst into an hysterical laugh on beholding the bloody trophy. Pity had ceased to find any place in her breast. The executions which she ordered after her victory were cruel and excessive. Among other gallant men whom she handed over to the executioner was Warwick's father, the stout old Earl of Salisbury, whose head, with that of his brother-in-law the Duke of York, she ordered to be affixed to the gates of York; the latter, in derision of his royal title, being circled with a paper diadem. "Leave room," said the exasperated heroine, "for the heads of March and Warwick, for they shall soon follow."

Elated with her victory, Margaret of Anjou decided on the bold step of marching to London at the head of one division of the army, while she despatched the other division, under the command of Jasper Tudor, Earl of Pembroke, to give battle to the young Earl of March, now Duke of York, who was advancing from Wales at the head of a formidable force, in the hope of speedily avenging the death of his father. The two armies, commanded by March and Pembroke, met at Mortimer's Cross, in Herefordshire, on the 2nd of February 1461. The Lancastrians suffered a signal defeat. Pembroke had the good fortune to effect his escape, but his father, Sir Owen Tudor, who had married Katharine of Valois, the beautiful widow of Henry V., was taken prisoner, and with several others beheaded. Queen Margaret was in the first instance more successful than her discomfited general. At St. Albans she encountered the army of the Yorkists, commanded by the Earl of Warwick, whom she completely defeated. Thus the unhappy king, whom Warwick had forced to attend him to the field of battle, was now once more restored to his friends. The victory was no sooner completed than Margaret, leading the young Prince of Wales by the hand, was conducted by Lord Clifford to his tent, in which the agitated monarch was waiting to embrace his heroic consort, and the fair boy whom he had been prevailed upon to deprive of his birthright. The "meek usurper" kissed and embraced them both with great gratitude and joy. He then conferred on his child the honour of knighthood, after which the royal party repaired to the abbey church of St. Albans, in which they solemnly returned thanks to Heaven for the victory which had been vouchsafed to them.

To enter London, and to restore her consort to his palace and his throne, were the paramount objects of Margaret. The citizens, however, refused to admit her within their gates; the lord-mayor sending her word that he only was her friend. In the mean time, the Duke of York had succeeded in uniting his army with the scattered troops of Warwick, and was rapidly advancing from Herefordshire with a far superior force. Under these circumstances the queen had no choice but to retrace her steps to the north, whither she accordingly retreated with her husband and child. There, as we have seen, her adherents were both numerous and devotedly attached to her cause, and there she hoped again to make head against her adversaries.

In due time the new Duke of York made his appearance before the gates of London, which he entered amidst the joyful acclamations of the people. His youth, the fiery valour which he had displayed in battle, his recent victories at Northampton and Mortimer's Cross, the irresistible fascination of his address, and lastly his stately height and the singular beauty of his countenance, excited a feeling of enthusiasm in his favour which it would be difficult to exaggerate. With one accord, the crowds which visited his camp in St. John's Fields, Clerkenwell, acknowledged and greeted him as their king. In the mean time a meeting, consisting of the lords spiritual and temporal and of the chief magistrates of London, had been convened in Baynard's Castle, for the purpose of solemnly discussing his claims. The determination at which they arrived was an unanimous one. They declared that King Henry, by breaking his recent compact with parliament, had forfeited all royal authority and power; further pronouncing that the title to the crown of England lay incontestably in Edward Earl of March, son of the late Duke of York, whom they therefore elected and asserted to be king and governor of this realm. On the following day Edward was conducted in great state, and amidst masses of shouting citizens, from Baynard's Castle to Westminster. In the great hall of Rufus, seated on the throne of the Plantagenets, and holding the sceptre of Edward the Confessor in his hand, his claims to the crown were recited by the Archbishop of Canterbury, who inquired of the assembled multitude whether Edward of York should be their king. The vast hall rang with an universal acclamation of assent, whereupon, according to ancient usage, the new king was conducted to the shrine of the Confessor in Westminster Abbey, where he offered up his devotions. This ceremony being over, the barons and prelates knelt one by one to him, and did homage to him as their sovereign. On the 4th of March 1461, he commenced his reign as King Edward IV.

In the mean time Queen Margaret had succeeded in levying an army of 60,000 men. The force at Edward's command is said to have consisted of 48,000 men, at the head of which he marched northwards to give her battle. Fortune, at the outset, seemed inclined to favour the Lancastrians. A success which was obtained at Ferrybridge by Lord Clifford, over an advanced body of the Yorkists under Lord Fitzwalter, raised immoderate hopes in the hearts of Margaret and her friends. They were destined, however, to meet with signal disappointment. On Palm Sunday the two armies came in sight of each other in the open country between Saxton and Towton. As Warwick surveyed the superior force with which he was about to contend, the stout heart of the great earl seems almost to have failed him. The weakness, however, was but a momentary one. Ordering his charger to be led to him, he stabbed it in the face of the whole army, at the same time solemnly swearing, on the cross which formed the hilt of his sword, that on that day his hazards and those of the common soldier should be the same, and that, though the whole of the king's army should take to flight, he would oppose himself alone to the swords of the Lancastrians.

Of all the battles between the rival Roses, none

was more fiercely contested, none lasted for a greater number of hours, than that of Towton. At length the fiery valour of Edward, and the military experience of Warwick, prevailed over superior numbers, and the Lancastrians were totally routed. No quarter was given; the carnage was terrific. The buriers of the dead counted 38,000 corpses. Among the slain were discovered the bodies of the Earls of Westmoreland and Northumberland, of the Lords Welles and Dacre of Gillesland. The Earl of Devon was beheaded after the battle. Immediately after his victory the young king proceeded to York, where he removed the heads of his father and of his kinsman the Earl of Salisbury from the gates of the city, setting up in their stead the heads of the Earl of Devon, and of others whom he had caused to be decapitated after the battle. In one respect the hopes of the young king were sadly disappointed. He had trusted, by obtaining possession of the persons of King Henry, and especially of Queen Margaret and her child, to crush for ever the hopes of the house of Lancaster. The energetic queen, however, contrived to escape with her husband and son to Berwick, from which place they subsequently fled to Scotland.

For three years after the battle of Towton, Edward was permitted to continue in quiet possession of his throne, and in the entire enjoyment of his voluptuous pleasures. The spirit of the indefatigable Margaret, however, remained unsubdued by defeat or disaster, and accordingly, having obtained the aid of two thousand men from Louis XI. of France, she summoned her Lancastrian partisans to repair to her standard, and once more took the field. Fortune, on this occasion, scarcely even smiled on her. She was speedily encountered by the Marquis of Montagu, brother of the Earl of Warwick, who signally defeated her at Hexham. Her partisans, the Duke of Somerset, and the Lords Hungerford and Ross, were taken prisoners and immediately beheaded.

The romantic adventures which befell Margaret of Anjou after the battle of Hexham are well known. Flying with her beloved child from the scene of slaughter and defeat, her only hope of escaping from their foes lay in the darkness of the night, and in being able to penetrate the gloomy mazes of Hexham Forest. But scarcely had the forest been gained, when the royal fugitives were beset by a band of robbers, who, besides stripping them of their jewels and costly upper garments, treated them with much indignity. Fortunately the richness of the booty, and the difficulty which the brigands found in partitioning it to the satisfaction of all, induced a quarrel, and then a conflict, among the band. The queen took advantage of the confusion, and fled with her child to a denser part of the forest. Without food, and without sufficient raiment to protect them from the chills of the night, they were wandering they knew not where, when suddenly, by the light of the moon, they beheld a man of giant stature, and of forbidding aspect, approaching them with a drawn sword. Fortunately the courage of the intrepid Margaret rose with the occasion; her resolution was formed on the instant. Advancing towards the robber, for such he proved to be, she presented to him the young prince, exclaiming,—"My friend, to your care I commit the safety of the son of your king." It happened providentially that the man was by nature of a generous and humane disposition. Impulsively he knelt to her, and even shed tears. Margaret, in fact, could scarcely have met with a more valuable protector. Carrying the way-worn Prince of Wales in his arms, he led the way to his place of concealment, a retreat still pointed out as "Queen Margaret's cave." Subsequently the generous robber performed further good service, by conducting to the queen more than one unfortunate Lancastrian gentleman who had contrived to escape the slaughter of Hexham. Among these were Henry Holland, Duke of Exeter, and Edmund Beaufort, now Duke of Somerset. By the assistance of the freebooter, not only the queen and the prince, but the other hunted fugitives, were enabled to reach the sea-coast, from whence they obtained shipping to Flanders. De Commines tells

us that some time afterwards he saw the Duke of
Exeter running barefooted after the Duke of Burgundy's train, begging in the name of God for
bread to satisfy his hunger. The fate of the last
of the Beauforts was yet more miserable. After
the battle of Tewkesbury, where he commanded
the Lancastrian army, he was dragged from a
church where he had sought refuge, and immediately beheaded.

In the mean time the escape of the unhappy
Henry VI. had been even a more narrow one than
those of his wife and child. In the flight after the
battle, "King Henry," according to the chronicler
Hall, "was the last horseman of his company."
So hot was the pursuit that an attendant who rode
behind him, bearing the royal cap of state, was
overtaken and made prisoner. For about a year,
the hunted king remained concealed in different
hiding-places in Westmoreland and Lancashire.
At length, his retreat having been betrayed by a
monk of Abingdon, he was arrested as he sat at
dinner at Waddington Hall, in the latter county,
and again committed a prisoner to the Tower. According to the prejudiced accounts of the Lancastrian historians, when the pious monarch made his
entry into London, it was with his legs strapped
under the belly of his horse, and with an offensive
inscription placarded on his back, in which de-
graded condition, we are told, he was conducted

through the populous district of Cheap and Corn-hill to his former apartments in the Tower. The account, however, of a more faithful contemporary, the chronicler of Croyland, in no degree substantiates the assertion that Henry was subjected to this ignominious treatment. On the contrary, Edward, we are told, gave orders that "all possible humanity," not inconsistent with safe custody, should be shown to the illustrious and afflicted prisoner.

The motives which, in 1469, induced the Earl of Warwick to rebel against his sovereign and friend, and the Duke of Clarence against his brother, will probably never be satisfactorily explained. Their treason, for a time, was eminently successful; Edward was eventually compelled to fly from his kingdom. This flight of his rival once more opened for the unfortunate Henry the door of his prison-house. He was waited upon in his solitary chamber in the Tower by the Duke of Clarence, the Earl of Warwick, Lord Stanley, and other noblemen, who, with great ceremony and respect, conducted him to the royal apartments in the palatial fortress. Once more, and for the last time, he wore the trappings of monarchy, and listened to adulations and professions of loyalty of which he had long since learned the hollowness. Arrayed in a mantle of blue velvet, and wearing the kingly crown upon his head, he proceeded in solemn state to St. Paul's

Cathedral, where, amidst the empty shouts of the
fickle populace, he returned thanks to Heaven for
a deliverance which was destined to be followed by
worse sorrows, and for the recovery of a crown
which doubtless he secretly regarded as a burden.

Leaving King Edward for a time in poverty and
exile, and King Henry in the possession of his brief
authority, let us now revert to the extraordinary
prince whose story forms the principal subject of
these memoirs.

CHAPTER II.

BIRTH, PARENTAGE, AND EARLY LIFE OF RICHARD
OF GLOUCESTER.

RICHARD Duke of Gloucester, afterwards King
Richard III., was born in the princely castle
of Fotheringay in Northamptonshire on the 2nd of
October 1452.* He was the eleventh child of Richard
Plantagenet, Duke of York, and was sixth in de-
scent from King Edward III. His mother was
Cecily, daughter of Ralph Neville, Earl of West-
moreland, by Joan Beaufort, daughter of John of
Gaunt, Duke of Lancaster.

The Duchess of York—or the " Rose of Raby,"
as she was designated in the north of England—
was, by the death of her husband, left a widow
with a numerous offspring. Only a year or two
previously,—happy in the society of her illustrious
lord, and watching the sports of her young children in the noble halls of Middleham or Baynard's
Castle,—how little could she have anticipated the
bloody wars which were about to devastate her
native country, and the misfortunes which impended
over her house! Seldom have greater sorrows

* William of Wyrcester's Annals, Liber Niger Scaccarii, vol. ii. p.
477.

fallen to the lot of woman, and never perhaps were sorrows borne with greater magnanimity. Her beloved husband perished at the battle of Wakefield.* For months his severed head remained a ghastly object on the gates of York. In the same battle was slain her third son, the young Edmund Earl of Rutland. Her fourth surviving son, George Duke of Clarence, died a traitor's death in the dungeons of the Tower. Her eldest son, afterwards King Edward IV., died from the effects of intemperance and sensuality, in the prime of his days. She lived to see the sons of this mighty monarch miserably immured in the Tower, destined to carry with them to their early graves the awful secrets of their prison-house. Lastly, she survived to see her son Richard close his errors or his crimes by a bloody death on the field of Bosworth. It was the singular fortune of this illustrious lady to have lived in the reigns of five sovereigns, to have been the contemporary of six queens of England, and of five princes of Wales.†

The character of this beautiful woman was in many respects peculiar to the high-born matrons of the middle ages. Inheriting the lofty spirit of the Nevilles and of the Plantagenets, she entered fully into the ambitious projects of the powerful lord with whom her fate was united. From the day on

* 30th December 1460.
† Archæologia, vol. xiii. p. 16.

which he had demanded the head of the obnoxious
Somerset at the gates of London till he himself
perished by the sword at the battle of Wakefield,
she seems to have been his constant companion in
the day of adversity, the willing sharer of his
perils. If, on the one hand, her ambition was un-
bounded, and her pride of birth so overweening as
almost to amount to extravagance, she nevertheless
figures as an affectionate and discerning mother,
and a pious Christian. If scandal whispered that
in her youth she had been unfaithful to her lord,
her widowhood, at all events, was an exemplary
one. For her sons she secured the best education
of which the age would permit, devoting herself
with unwearying care to the advancement of their
spiritual as well as their temporal welfare, and pre-
paring them to play a part in the world suitable to
their royal birth and the stormy times in which they
lived.

The princely fortune enjoyed by the widowed
duchess was in accordance with her exalted rank.
At the several patrimonial residences of the house
of York—at Middleham, Fotheringay, Sandal, and
Berkhampstead, at each of which she occasionally
resided with her youthful family,—the magnificence of her mode of living was surpassed only by
the decorum which ever prevailed in her household.
" She useth," writes a contemporary, " to arise at
seven of the clock, and hath ready her chaplain to

say with her matins of the day and matins of our Lady; and when she is full ready she hath a low mass in her chamber; and after mass she taketh something to recreate nature, and so goeth to the chapel, hearing the divine service and two low masses. From thence to dinner, during the time whereof she hath a lecture of holy matter. After dinner she giveth audience to all such as have any matter to show unto her by the space of one hour, and then sleepeth one quarter of an hour, and after she hath slept she continueth in prayer unto the first peal of even-song; then she drinketh wine or ale at her pleasure. Forthwith her chaplain is ready to say with her both even-songs; and after the last peal she goeth to the chapel, and heareth even-song by note. From thence to supper, and in the time of supper she reciteth the lecture that was had at dinner to those that be in her presence. After supper she disposeth herself to be familiar with her gentlewomen, to the season of honest mirth; and one hour before her going to bed she taketh a cup of wine; and, after that, goeth to her privy closet and taketh her leave of God for all night; making end of her prayers for that day, and by eight of the clock is in bed." * Such is the curious picture which we possess of the manner in which an illustrious lady passed her hours in the fifteenth century. Such was the household which

* Ordinances for the Government of the Royal Household, p. 37.

sheltered the boyhood of the celebrated Richard of Gloucester; such the mother from whom he alike derived the good qualities which were the ornament of his youth, and inherited the ambition which, at a later period, incited him to the commission of crime.

Though at the time a mere child, Richard of Gloucester was a witness of those early struggles between the houses of York and Lancaster which hurried his father York to the grave, and eventually raised his brother Edward to the throne. At the period when the loss of the battle of Bloreheath compelled his father to fly for shelter in the fastnesses of Ireland, Richard was in his seventh year. When, shortly after the battle, King Henry entered Ludlow Castle in triumph, he found there the Duchess of York, whom, with her two younger sons, he committed, in the first instance, to the charge of her sister, Anne Duchess of Buckingham.* For nearly a year Richard remained a prisoner with his mother in the hands of the Lancastrians, till at length the victory obtained by the Yorkists at Northampton restored them to liberty. Three months after the battle we find the " Rose of Raby " in London with her young children George and Richard, afterwards Dukes of Clarence and Gloucester, and her daughter Margaret, afterwards Duchess of Burgundy. But though the metropolis was now

* Leland's Collect. vol. ii. p. 497 ; Hearne's Fragment, pp. 283-4.

in the hands of the Earl of Warwick and of her victorious son the Earl of March, there seem to have been reasons why London was still no secure place of retreat for the high-born lady and her children. Accordingly, instead of taking up her abode at the celebrated Baynard's Castle, the London residence of her lord, we find her concealed with her children in an obscure retreat in the Temple. The chambers which sheltered the illustrious party were those of Sir John Paston, a devoted partisan of the house of York, who was at this time absent at Norwich. The important event of their seeking shelter under his roof is thus communicated to Sir John in October 1460, by his confidential servant Christopher Hansson.

" To the Right Worshipful Sir and Master John Paston, Esquire, at Norwich, be this letter delivered in haste.

" Right worshipful Sir and Master, I recommend me unto you. Please you, to weet, the Monday after our Lady-day, there come hither to my master's place my Master Bowser, Sir Harry Ratford, John Clay, and the harbinger of my Lord of March, desiring that my Lady of York might be here until the coming of my Lord of York, and her two sons, my Lord George and my Lord Richard, and my Lady Margaret, her daughter, which I granted them in your name, to lie here till Michaelmas.

And she had not lain here two days, but she had tidings of the landing of my Lord at Chester. The Tuesday after, my lord sent for her that she should come to him to Hereford; and thither she is gone; and she hath left here both the sons and the daughter, and the Lord of March cometh every day to see them."*

A few days afterwards, the Duke of York entered London in triumph, and restored his wife and children to the condition which was due to their exalted birth.

But though the house of York was destined finally to be triumphant, many reverses and misfortunes were still in store for its numerous members. The return, indeed, of Margaret of Anjou from Scotland, and the fatal result of the battle of Wakefield, seemed to threaten a total annihilation of their hopes. In that battle the "Rose of Raby" lost not only her husband, but also her young and beautiful son the Earl of Rutland. She now began to tremble for the safety of her younger sons, whose lives, had they chanced to have fallen into the power of the implacable Margaret, would in all probability have been sacrificed to her revenge. Happily for the house of York, their great kinsman, the Earl of Warwick, still held the command of the seas. Accordingly, with the aid of the earl, the Duchess of York contrived to effect the removal

* Paston Letters, by Fenn, vol. i. p. 199.

of her children to the Low Countries, where they had the good fortune to meet with a kind and generous reception from Philip Duke of Burgundy. It happened that the court of that accomplished prince was no less distinguished for the encouragement of literature and the fine arts, than for the due maintenance and exercise of the ancient laws and customs of chivalry. Examples, therefore, were constantly before them, which were calculated to produce a beneficial and lasting effect on the minds of the young princes. During a part of their stay in the Low Countries, we find them pursuing their studies under able instructors in the city of Utrecht.*

In the mean time, the struggle in England between the rival Roses had been renewed with unabating vigour and fury. The young Earl of March had succeeded to his father's title of Duke of York, and with it to his father's claims to the throne. Those claims, though only in his twentieth year, he proceeded to assert and uphold with an ability, enterprise, and fearlessness, which would have reflected credit on the wisest statesmen and ablest generals of the age. At Mortimer's Cross he gave battle to, and defeated, the army of King Henry, and, though his troops under the Earl of Warwick were repulsed at St. Albans, he nevertheless pushed

* Buck's Life and Reign of Richard III. in Kennet's Complete History, vol. i. p. 516; Sandford, Gen. Hist. book v. p. 430.

forward to London, which, as we have previously recorded, he entered amidst the acclamations of the people, and a day or two afterwards mounted the throne by the title of King Edward IV.

Edward no sooner found the sceptre secure in his grasp than he recalled his younger brothers from the Low Countries. On George, now in his twelfth year, he conferred the title of Duke of Clarence; Richard, who was only in his ninth year, he created Duke of Gloucester.* It may be mentioned that, in the days of chivalry of which we are writing, whenever a royal or noble youth had arrived at an age when it was considered no longer desirable that he should be kept in the society and under the care of women, it was customary to obtain his admission into the establishment of some powerful baron, in order that he might duly acquire those accomplishments which were presumed to be necessary to support the knightly character. That Edward should have selected the establishment of his re-nowned kinsman, the Earl of Warwick, as offering the most eligible school for training up his younger brothers to distinguish themselves in the tilt-yard and the battle-field, is not only not unlikely, but the following circumstances render it extremely probable. Edward himself would seem to have been indebted for his military education to War-wick †; we have evidence of the anxiety of the

* Dugdale's Baronage, vol ii. pp. 162, 165.

† Mémoires de P. de Commines, tome i. p. 232. Paris, 1840.

young king to render his brothers as accomplished
soldiers as he was himself; there is extant, in the
archives of the exchequer, a contemporary entry of
moneys "paid to Richard Earl of Warwick for
costs and expenses incurred by him on behalf of
the Duke of Gloucester, the king's brother,"[*]
besides other evidence showing that Gloucester was
at least once a guest at Middleham [†]; and, lastly,
we find the future usurper retaining an affectionate
partiality for Middleham to the close of his eventful career.[‡] Under these circumstances, to what
other conclusion can we arrive than that Middleham
was once the home of Gloucester? And, if such
was the case, with what other object could he have
been so domesticated but for the advantages to be
derived from the precepts of the renowned Warwick, and being educated in the vast military
establishment which was supported by the most
powerful of the barons? The mention of Middleham
recalls to us the romantic attachment which Richard
subsequently conceived for Anne Neville, the
youngest and fairest daughter of the "Kingmaker," an attachment which would of itself have
been a subject of no mean interest, even had Shakspeare not invested it with immortality. Anne was
his junior only by two years. May it not, then,

* Halsted's Richard III. vol. i. p. 113.
† Buck in Kennet, vol. i. p. 516.
‡ Whitaker's History of Richmondshire, vol. i. p. 335.

have been at Middleham, in the days of their childhood, that Richard was first inspired by that
memorable passion which was destined to triumph
over all human opposition,—which continued to
nerve his arm, and to fire his soul, even when Anne
Neville had become the betrothed, if not the bride,
of another, and which was eventually rewarded by
her becoming his wife, and finally his queen.

Of the boyhood of Richard of Gloucester, unfortunately but few particulars have been handed down to
us. The diligent inquirer, Hutton, could discover no
more important facts than that the wisest, wiliest,
and bravest prince of his age, "cuckt his ball, and
shot his taw, with the same delight as other lads."*
Only on one occasion, in his boyhood, we find him
playing a prominent part on the stage of the world.
From the day on which the Red Rose had proved
triumphant at Wakefield, till that on which victory
again decided in favour of the White Rose on the
field of Towton, the ghastly head of Richard Duke
of York had been allowed to disfigure the battle-
ments of the city from which he had derived his
title. In the mean time his headless remains had
rested at Pontefract, where they had been hurriedly and ignobly committed to the grave. Young
Edward no sooner found himself triumphant over
his adversaries, than he performed the pious duty
of causing his father's head to be removed from

* Hutton's Battle of Bosworth Field, Introd. p. xvii.

the gates of York, preparatory to reinterring the
great warrior with a magnificence suitable to his
rank. Descended from, and destined to be ancestor of kings, the remains of Richard of York
might without impropriety have been awarded a
grave in the memorable burial-place of the sovereigns of the house of Plantagenet, in Westminster
Abbey. To that deeply interesting group of monuments, which surround the shrine of Edward the
Confessor, the effigy of the illustrious chieftain
would have formed no unworthy addition. But
the young king preferred for the mightiest of the
barons a baron's resting-place. In the chancel of
the collegiate church of Fotheringay, near the remains of his father Edward Duke of York, who
was slain at Agincourt, Richard of York was reinterred, on the 29th of July 1466, with a magnificence befitting the obsequies of kings. Followed
by an array of nobles and pursuivants, Richard
Duke of Gloucester rode next after the corpse of
his father, in its melancholy journey from Pontefract to Fotheringay. Awaiting its arrival in the
churchyard of Fotheringay, stood the king and
queen in deep mourning, attended by the two eldest
princesses and the principal nobles and ladies of
the land. The ceremony of reinterment must have
presented a striking and deeply interesting scene.
On the verge of the vault were to be seen the lofty
form of King Edward, the handsomest prince of

his age*; his beautiful queen, Elizabeth Woodville;
their infant daughter, Elizabeth, who was destined
to succeed her father on the throne; the slight figure and thoughtful features of Richard of Gloucester; and, lastly, the mild and melancholy face
of Margaret Countess of Richmond, who, like the
illustrious dead upon whose coffin she was gazing,
was also destined to be the ancestor of kings.† Of
that memorable party, Margaret alone outlived the
prime and vigour of life, and enjoyed a tranquil
and respected old age.

Richard, even in early boyhood, appears to have
enjoyed the confidence and affection of his brother
Edward. The wealth and estates which the king
from time to time put him in possession of, seem
almost incredible. In 1462 he conferred on him a
large portion of the domains of John Lord Clifford,
who was killed at the battle of Towton.‡ The same

* Mémoires de Commines, vol. i. p. 239.

† Sandford's Genealogical Hist. of England, book v. pp. 391-2. At
the same time with those of York were reinterred the remains of his
third son, Edmund Earl of Rutland, who was killed by Lord Clifford at
the battle of Wakefield, and whose head had also disfigured the battle-
ments of York. Thirty-one years afterwards, the remains of the " Rose
of Raby" were laid, according to a desire which she had expressed in
her will, by the side of her husband. When, in the reign of Queen
Elizabeth, her coffin happened to be opened, there was discovered, we
are told, " about her neck, hanging on a silk riband, a pardon from
Rome, which, penned in a fine Roman hand, was as fair and fresh to be
read as if it had been written but the day before." The duchess died
in Berkhampstead Castle on the 31st of May 1495. Sandford, Gen.
Hist. book iv. p. 387; book v. pp. 391-2.

‡ Cal. Rot. Pat. p. 304, m. xiii.

year he gave him the castle and fee-farm of the
town of Gloucester, and the castle and lordship of
Richmond in Yorkshire, lately belonging to Edmund Earl of Richmond; also no fewer than forty-
six manors which had lapsed to the crown by the
attainder of John de Vere, Earl of Oxford.*   In
1464 he granted him the castles, lordships, and
lands of Henry de Beaufort, Duke of Somerset, as
well as the castle and manors of Robert Lord Hungerford, both of which noblemen had been beheaded
after the battle of Hexham.†   Again, when the
part which the Nevilles took at the battle of Barnet
deprived them of their magnificent estates, Edward
conferred on his brother, for his " great and laudable
services," Warwick's princely castles of Middleham and Sheriff-Hutton, together with other lands
which had belonged to the earl's brother, the Marquis of Montagu.‡   In 1465 Edward created his
brother a knight of the Garter, and, in 1469, caused
him to be summoned to parliament.

Not satisfied with heaping wealth and honours
on his favourite brother, Edward also selected him
to fill appointments, the responsible duties of which
prove how entire was the confidence which he
placed in his judgment and abilities.   In 1461 he
appointed him high admiral of England.§   On the

* Rotuli Parliamentorum, vol. vi. p. 228.; Cal. Rot. Pat. p. 304, m. v.
† Cal. Rot. Pat. m. i. p. 314.
‡ Rot. Parl. vol. vi. pp. 124-5; Cal. Rot. Pat. p. 316, m. xviii.
§ Dugd. Bar. vol. ii. p. 165.

27th of October 1469, he made him constable of England, and justice of North and South Wales.* The following year he nominated him to be warden of the Western Marches, bordering on Scotland.† On the 18th of May 1471, he was made lord-chamberlain.‡ In 1472 he was appointed to the lucrative situation of keeper of the king's forests beyond Trent §; and, lastly, in 1474, he was re-appointed to the office of lord-chamberlain. ∥

Such were the high offices and appointments which King Edward conferred upon his brother Richard, almost before the latter had completed his twentieth year. It must be remembered that not only did more than one of these appointments require that the person holding them should be gifted with singular ability, firmness, and judgment, but that they also conferred on him an authority which rendered him the most powerful subject in the realm. That a monarch, therefore, so notoriously jealous as Edward IV., who, moreover, had already been deceived by a favourite brother, the fickle and ungrateful Clarence, should have conferred on a third brother wealth so vast and powers so great,

* Sandford, Gen. Hist. book v. p. 430; Dugd. Bar. vol. ii. p. 165.

† Ibid.

‡ This appointment he surrendered to his brother, the Duke of Clarence, on his being appointed a second time constable of England, viz. 29th February 1472. Sandford, Gen. Hist. book v. p. 431; Dugd. Bar. vol. ii. p. 166.

§ Cal. Rot. Pat. m. x. p. 317.

∥ Dugd. Bar. vol. ii. pp. 166.

evinces not only how high was the opinion he had formed of Richard's talents, but also how great was the confidence which he placed in his loyalty and integrity. Indeed, that Richard of Gloucester was to the last the faithful and loyal subject of Edward IV., we are as much convinced as that he was afterwards a disloyal subject to his nephew Edward V.

A conjecture has already been hazarded in these pages, that it was as long since as when Richard was learning the use of arms and the accomplishments of chivalry in the halls of the renowned Warwick, that he first became enamoured of the youngest and gentlest of the two daughters of the Kingmaker. It was destined, indeed, that they should hereafter be united by indissoluble ties. As yet, however, many and apparently insurmountable obstacles interposed between Richard and the realization of the hopes of his boyhood.

A singular and romantic interest attaches itself to the story of Isabel and Anne Neville. Born to a more splendid lot, and to greater vicissitudes of fortune, than commonly fall to the lot of women, the career of both was destined to be a brief and a melancholy one. At the period of which we are writing, nine months had elapsed since the Lady Isabel had given her hand, in the church of Notre-Dame at Calais, to George Duke of Clarence, at that time the nearest male heir to the throne of

England.* The Lady Anne, at this time, was on the eve of being betrothed to Edward Prince of Wales, the ill-fated son of Henry VI.

When, in the month of April 1470, Warwick and Clarence, flying from the rapid and victorious pursuit of Edward, set sail from Dartmouth, the Lady Isabel accompanied her husband and her father. The voyage proved to be a singularly hazardous and inauspicious one. After a narrow escape from having been captured by the royal fleet, commanded by Earl Rivers, the ship in which they were embarked was overtaken by a violent tempest, in the midst of the perils and discomforts of which the young duchess was seized in labour of her first child. Mishap followed mishap. On reaching Calais, John Lord Wenlock, the deputy-governor of the town in the absence of Warwick, not only positively refused them permission to land, but fired his "great guns" at them. The only favour which they could obtain from him was a present of two flagons of wine for the use of the duchess and her ladies.† Accordingly Warwick set sail for Dieppe, in which port the duchess and her new-

---

* The marriage ceremony was performed, on the 12th of July 1469, by her uncle, George Neville, Archbishop of York, in the presence of her father the Earl of Warwick, then governor of Calais, her mother, and her sister the Lady Anne.

† De Commines, tome i. p. 235.

born infant were safely landed.*   From Dieppe the earl, accompanied by his daughter and son-in-law, proceeded to Amboise, in which town the cruel and crafty Louis XI. of France was at this time holding his court.†

Warwick, incensed against the prince whom he had formerly so loved, and whom he had laid under so many obligations,—ambitious, moreover, of securing a second chance of founding a kingly dynasty for his descendants,—had for his chief object at this period the union of his younger daughter Anne with Edward Prince of Wales, the only child of Henry VI. and Margaret of Anjou. By this expedient, should King Edward, on the one hand, die without leaving a male heir, the children of Isabel would fill the throne; while, on the other hand, should the house of Lancaster succeed in triumphing over the house of York, the hopes of the Kingmaker would have every prospect of being realized by the Lady Anne becoming the mother of kings.

* According to Monstrelet, it was at Honfleur and not Harfleur that the fugitives disembarked. "They found there the lord high admiral of France, who received the Earl of Warwick, the Duke of Clarence, and the Earl of Oxford, and their ladies, with every respect. Their vessels were admitted in the harbours; and after a short time, the ladies, with their trains, departed, and went to Valognes, where lodgings had been provided for them."—*Montstrelet's Chronicles*, vol. iv. p. 304. The Hearne Fragment also mentions Honfleur as the port at which Warwick and his family landed (pp. 302-3).

† Hearne Fragment, p. 303.

It was apparently in pursuance of this ambitious project that Warwick sought the presence of the French king. Louis received him with every mark of respect and friendship. From the time when the earl had formerly been ambassador at his court, the French king had not only retained an extraordinary affection for him, but they had ever since carried on a secret correspondence.* Louis, on one occasion, told Queen Margaret of Anjou that he was under greater obligations to the English earl than to any man living.† Thus, "no less enamoured and delighted with the presence of his friend than with his renowned fame."‡ Louis received the great earl with open arms, and bade him heartily welcome to his court.

From Amboise the French court removed to Angers, whither Warwick and his daughters also repaired. The dethronement of the English monarch, a reconciliation between Margaret of Anjou and Warwick, and the re-establishment of the house of Lancaster on the throne of England, were the projects which the French king and the English earl were constantly engaged in discussing, and which each of them had deeply at heart. The principal difficulty lay in the implacable disposition

* De Commines, tome i. p. 433.   Warwick had been ambassador to France in 1467.

† Sharon Turner's Hist. of the Middle Ages, vol. iii. pp. 261-3.

‡ Polydore Virgil, lib. xxiv. p. 660 (ed. 1651), and Camden Soc. Transl. p. 131.

of Margaret, and in the great improbability, which they foresaw, of her being induced to consent to so unnatural a marriage as that of the heir of Lancaster with the daughter of the arch-enemy of his house. Many grievances, moreover, had to be forgotten on both sides, many wrongs forgiven. Warwick had to forgive the remorseless woman who had sent his father Salisbury to the block; while Margaret was called upon to forgive still deeper wrongs. Warwick had not only given her the deepest offence by aspersing her fair fame as a woman, but he had also disputed the legitimacy of her darling son. He had caused to be put to death, either on the field of battle or on the scaffold, the bravest and wisest of the partisans of the Red Rose. Twice he had thrown her royal consort into a dungeon. More than once she herself had been driven by him into exile; more than once, a fugitive with her beloved child, they had been compelled to owe their daily bread to the charity of the stranger. Warwick, she said, had inflicted wounds on her which would remain unhealed till the day of judgment, and in the day of judgment she would appeal to the justice of Heaven for vengeance against her persecutor.*

Difficult, however, as was the task of appeasing the haughty Margaret, it was cheerfully under-

* Chastellain, Chroniques des Ducs de Bourgogne, par Buchon, tome ii. p. 242.

taken by the French king. Without delay, he invited to his court the persons principally interested in the memorable treaty which his talents and subtlety subsequently enabled him to accomplish. It was indeed a remarkable party whom he assembled around him in the old palatial fortress of Angers. At the time when Margaret made her tardy appearance in its halls, there were already met there the renowned Warwick, the false and fickle Clarence, and his beautiful duchess, Isabel Neville. Thither subsequently repaired two of the bravest warriors of their age, John de Vere, Earl of Oxford, and Jasper Tudor, Earl of Pembroke. Thither also came René, King of Sicily, father of Queen Margaret, the Countess of Warwick with her gentle daughter, the Lady Anne, and lastly Margaret herself, accompanied by the gallant and beautiful boy in whose welfare every wish of her heart was centred, he who from his infancy had been the occasion of her heroism, her self-devotion, and her crimes.

As may be readily imagined, it was not till after urgent and repeated entreaties, and after almost fruitless endeavours on the part of King Louis, that Margaret was induced to confront Warwick face to face, and to confer with him on the means of re-establishing her husband on his throne. When at length the meeting took place, the scene must have been a singularly striking one. Warwick, we are told, falling on his knees before the queen, solemnly "offered himself to be bounden by all manner of ways to be a true and faithful subject for the time to come:" Margaret, on her part, compelling the proud earl to remain in this humiliating posture for a quarter of an hour, before she could be prevailed upon to pronounce his pardon.* At length a treaty was concluded, which was sworn to by each of the contracting parties on the true cross in St. Mary's Church at Angers. On their part, Warwick and Clarence engaged themselves on no account "to surcease the war" till they should have restored the kingdom of England to the house of Lancaster. On the other hand, Queen Margaret and the Prince of Wales solemnly swore to appoint the great earl and his son-in-law protectors of the realm, till such time as the youthful prince should be "meet and fit by himself to undertake that charge." † Lastly, the French king guaranteed to furnish Warwick with a supply of "armour, men, and navy," to enable him to effect a successful landing on the shores of England. ‡

* Chastellain, Chron. par Buchon, tome ii. p. 243.

† Polydore Virgil, lib. xxiv. p. 680, and Camd. Soc. Trans. p. 131.

‡ Louis kept his word. Monstrelet tells us that the manning and victualling of Warwick's fleet was extremely expensive to him. Chronicles, vol. iv. pp. 306–7. For an account of this remarkable conference, see a very curious document entitled "The Manner and Guiding of the Earl of Warwick at Angers," Harl. MS. 543, fol. 169b, printed in Ellis's Original Letters, vol. i. p. 132, &c., Second Series. See also De Commines, tome i. p. 238.

The article in the treaty which Margaret naturally regarded with the greatest dissatisfaction was that which gave the hand of Anne Neville to her son. "What!" said the haughty queen, "will Warwick indeed give his daughter to my son, whom he has so often branded as the offspring of adultery and fraud?" When at length she gave her consent to the unnatural union, it was accompanied by a very important article which has been overlooked by most of our historians. By a clause in the marriage treaty it was provided that not only should Anne Neville remain "in the hands and keeping" of the queen, but that the marriage should not be *perfected* till the earl had recovered the kingdom of England, or the greater portion of it, for the house of Lancaster.* Accordingly, inasmuch as the death of Warwick, which took place a few months afterwards, prevented his fulfilling his part of the agreement, the great probability seems to be that the marriage of the Prince of Wales and Anne Neville was never consummated. The facts, indeed, are unquestionable, that they were not only solemnly affianced to each other, but that, at the French court, Anne was called by the title of, and received the homage due to, a Princess of Wales.† But, on the other hand, when we consider the re-

* "Manner and Guiding of the Earl of Warwick," Ellis's Orig. Letters, vol. i. pp. 134–5, Second Series.

† Montstrelet, vol. iv. p. 309.

pugnance with which Queen Margaret regarded
their union, and the singular proviso introduced
into the marriage treaty, we may reasonably doubt
whether they were ever united to each other by
any more binding obligation than that of a marriage contract, the future confirmation of which was
dependent on the fulfilment of certain specified
conditions.   It has even been asserted by a modern
historian that no contemporary writer speaks of the
marriage as having been actually celebrated.*   But
whatever the nature of the ceremony may have
been, it took place at Amboise, about the end of
July, in the presence of Louis XI., King René,
Queen Margaret, the Duke and Duchess of Clarence, and the Earl of Warwick.   The youth and
beauty of the contracting parties must have added
considerably to the interest of the scene.   Edward
was but seventeen, Anne Neville only fourteen
years of age.†   Already they had been introduced

---

*Sharon Turner's Hist. of the Middle Ages, vol. iii. p. 323, note.
Ed. 1830. This would seem to be almost too sweeping an assertion.
The continuator of the Croyland Chronicle certainly, in one place,
merely speaks of "espousals" between Prince Edward and Anne as
having been "contracted" (p. 462). Further on, however, we read:
"After, as already stated, the son of King Henry, to whom the Lady
Anne, the youngest daughter of the Earl of Warwick, *had been married*,
was slain at the battle of Tewkesbury, Richard Duke of Gloucester
sought the said Anne in marriage," &c. (p. 469).

† Edward Prince of Wales was born at the palace of Westminster on
the 13th of October 1453; Anne Neville was born in Warwick Castle
in 1456. The young prince is said to have been eminently accomplished and handsome; "the composition of his body," according to

to each other at Paris, where, if any trust is to be
placed in contemporary gossip, her charms had
kindled a violent passion in the heart of Edward.*
A sad reverse awaited each of them. Before many
months had elapsed, Edward lay a mangled corpse
in the abbey of Tewkesbury; while the beautiful
girl to whom his troth was pledged was compelled
to secrete herself, in the garb of a waiting-maid, in
an obscure quarter of London.

Faithfully and energetically Warwick proceeded
to carry into effect his engagements with Margaret
of Anjou. The powerful fleet of the Duke of Burgundy, superior at this time to the united navies
of England and France,† happened to be blockading
the mouth of the Seine, and accordingly it was not
till after a delay of some weeks that Warwick was
enabled to quit the shores of France. At length, a
violent tempest compelled the blockading ships to
seek shelter in the ports of Scotland and Holland,
and the sea was once more open to Warwick. On
the 4th of August he quitted Angers, and on the
13th of September disembarked the small force

Habington, "being guilty of no fault but a too feminine beauty."—
Kennet, vol. i. p. 453. According to Shakspeare's description of him,—

> " A sweeter and a lovelier gentleman,
> Framed in the prodigality of nature,
> Young, valiant, wise, and, no doubt, right royal,
> The spacious world cannot again afford."
>
> *King Richard III.*, Act i. Sc. 2.

* Hist. de Marguérite d'Anjou, par l'Abbé Prévost, p. 344.
† De Commines, tome i. p. 239.

under his command at Plymouth and Dartmouth. His return to his native country was hailed by the great mass of the people with extraordinary enthusiasm.   In an almost incredibly short space of time he found himself the leader of 60,000 men.   The sorrows and wrongs of the unfortunate Henry VI. were descanted upon from the pulpit; the wandering minstrel never failed to delight his audiences in town or in village, so long as the virtues and valour of Warwick were his theme; no ballad of the day, we are told, was popular, but such as redounded to the glory of the "Kingmaker."*

In the mean time, sunning himself in the smiles of beauty, and sauntering in an atmosphere of voluptuous sensuality, King Edward persisted in underrating his enemy, even though that enemy was Warwick.   In vain his brother-in-law, the Duke of Burgundy, urged him to make preparations for repelling the invader.†   Trusting to his own superior military genius and dauntless personal valour, and, as De Commines tells us, affecting to despise and laugh at danger as affording evidence of his resolution and courage, Edward pertinaciously persisted in pursuing his course of sensual inactivity.   Let Warwick, he said, land on English soil; there was nothing he wished better.

Dearly as Edward prized the smiles of woman

---

* Lingard's Hist. of Engl. vol. iv. p. 178.   Ed. 1849.
† De Commines, tome i. pp. 239, 242.

and the pleasures of the banquet, no less grateful to him was the bray of the clarion when it proclaimed the approach of danger. No sooner, then, did his subjects break out into armed revolt, than, with his usual promptitude and vigour, he sallied forth to grapple with the enemy. But the time for action had been allowed to glide unprofitably away. The wrongs and exile of Warwick had excited an enthusiasm in his favour which, for a season, proved irresistible. Treason was rife, moreover, among those whom Edward had most trusted and loved. When, in the gloomy apartments of the Tower, the sanguine and chivalrous king took leave of his lovely queen, then on the eve of becoming a mother, little could he have imagined that, within a few short weeks, he himself would become a miserable exile. Little could he have believed that, during his eventful absence, his hunted queen would give birth to a male heir to the throne in the prison sanctuary at Westminster; indebted to the monks for procuring her an ordinary nurse in her travail, and to a butcher, more tender-hearted or more loyal than his fellows, for the common food by which she and her female attendants supported existence.

Edward, as he himself afterwards related to De Commines, was at dinner in a fortress near Lynn, when suddenly the astounding tidings were brought to him that the Marquis of Montagu, his personal friend and favourite, with other influential barons in whom he had blindly confided, were tampering with his forces. Notwithstanding he had long been accustomed to encounter treachery and ingratitude, he at first refused to credit such shameless apostasy. Nevertheless he sent forth messengers to investigate the truth of the rumours, and in the mean time rapidly arrayed himself in his armour. The intelligence which the messengers brought back was sufficiently disheartening. Not only had the soldiers been induced to shout " God bless King Henry," but the rebels were advancing in overwhelming numbers. Fortunately the only access to the fortress was by a bridge which Edward had taken the precaution to guard with a few of his most devoted followers. Accordingly, without a moment's delay, he leaped into the saddle, and, dashing along the bridge with a few followers, made the best of his way to the neighbouring seaport of Lynn. Hastings, alone, remained behind for a few minutes, in order to urge his friends to consult their safety by pretending submission to Warwick, and then, putting spurs to his horse, galloped off in the direction of Lynn, where he had the satisfaction of rejoining his royal master.*

At Lynn, Edward had the good fortune to find shipping for himself and his followers in an Eng-

* De Commines, tome i. pp. 244, &c.; Croyland Chronicle Continuation, p. 462, ed. 1854.

lish brig of war and two Dutch merchant vessels, which were on the point of putting to sea. On the waters, however, perils awaited the fugitives, almost as imminent as those from which they had had the good fortune to escape on land. Chase was given them by a formidable fleet of the Easterlings, or Hanse Towns, then at war with England; and only by running his ship on shore near Alkmaar, on the coast of Holland, with the risk of being drowned, was Edward enabled to evade his pursuers. So rapid had been his flight, so destitute was the victor of Towton of the common appurtenances of royalty, that his ordinary robe, lined with rich sables, was the only guerdon with which it was in his power to remunerate the captain of the vessel who had delivered him from a dungeon, and not impossibly from death.*

Richard of Gloucester was the companion of his brother in his flight, and landed with him at Alkmaar.† For some months, utter ruin seemed to stare them in the face. A great revolution had taken place in England. King Henry—"who was not so worshipfully arrayed and not so cleanly kept as should seem such a prince"‡—was taken from his "keepers" by Warwick, and once more sat, with the crown on his head, on the marble seat of the Confessor at Westminster. Warwick and

* De Commines, tome i. p. 248.

† Ibid. p. 248.   ‡ Warkworth Chronicle, p. 11.

Clarence were declared to be the protectors of the realm during the minority of Edward Prince of Wales. In the event of his dying without issue, the crown was entailed upon Clarence. The exiled Edward, lately so envied and so feared, was denounced by parliament as an usurper; Richard of Gloucester was attainted and outlawed. But the daring and indomitable spirit of King Edward and his brother, Gloucester, was destined to triumph over every difficulty. Having obtained from his brother-in-law, the Duke of Burgundy, a loan of fifty thousand florins,* Edward, early in the month of March 1471, set sail from the port of Vere, in the island of Walcheren, with about two thousand men, and, on the 14th of that month, disembarked at Ravenspur, in Yorkshire, the same place at which, seventy-two years previously, Henry of Lancaster had landed to depose Richard II. Like Henry, he disclaimed having any design upon the crown. His object in returning to England, he said, was merely to recover the inheritance to which he was entitled as Duke of York.† He even carried this dissimulation so far, as to cause his followers to shout " Long live King Henry," in the different towns and villages through which they passed. He himself wore in his helmet an ostrich-plume, the device of his rival, Edward Prince of Wales.‡

* De Commines, tome i. p. 257.
† Fleetwood Chron. p. 4.   ‡ Leland's Collect. vol. ii. pp. 503–4.

The Duke of Gloucester accompanied his brother to England; the young prince landing about four miles from Ravenspur, at the head of three hundred men.* Together, the brothers commenced their desperate march towards the south,—for almost desperate it must have seemed even to themselves. For the first few days Edward's progress was discouraging in the extreme. Scarcely a single individual joined his standard. But though the men of the north kept aloof from him, he was everywhere allowed to pass without molestation. Within four miles of his line of march stood Pomfret Castle: but though Warwick's brother, the Marquis of Montagu, occupied it with a superior force, he made no effort to check the invader. Fortunately for Edward, the city of York had been induced to open its gates to him, and from that time his circumstances began to improve. At Nottingham he was joined by Sir William Stanley and Sir William Norres, the former bringing with him four hundred men.† Three thousand more flocked to him at Leicester, and at Warwick he had the satisfaction of being joined by his brother, the Duke of Clarence, who deserted to him with four thousand men.

Confiding in his own military genius and desperate valour, Edward appears to have ardently desired to

* Fleetwood Chron. p. 3.
† Leland's Collect, vol. ii. p. 504.

bring his enemies to battle on the first possible occasion. Success, he felt, could be obtained only by intrepidity and vigour. To obtain a victory early in the day he knew to be of the most vital importance. He was aware that sooner or later his enemies would be enabled to concentrate their forces, and accordingly, though Warwick lay at Coventry with an army much superior to his own, he determined not only to risk an engagement, but, if possible, to force it upon the Kingmaker. Warwick, however, whatever may have been his reasons, declined the combat. The young king therefore resumed his march towards London, of which city he confidently hoped to obtain possession. So rapid had been his march, and so skilfully had it been conducted, that he seems to have made his way far into the midland counties before the intelligence of his landing had reached the metropolis.

Had London refused to receive Edward within its walls, there can be little doubt that his discomfiture would have been complete. But with the citizens he had ever been an especial favourite. The city dames were enthusiastic in their admiration of a prince at once so beautiful and so affable. Many of them are said to have been liberal in their favours to him; many others were probably ready to follow their example. Their wealthy husbands, moreover, had their reasons for wishing well to the invader. They were grateful to him for the encouragement he had extended to commerce; nor was it a trifling circumstance in his favour that he was indebted to many of them for large sums of money, which his restoration only would enable him to repay.* Lastly, former gracious presents of royal venison were perhaps not altogether forgotten, nor the peaceful days when, in the green glades of Hainault and Windsor forests, they had been regaled and flattered by the most gallant and most fascinating monarch of his age.†

In the mean time, Warwick had intrusted the safe-keeping of the city of London to his brother,

* De Commines, tome i. p. 259.

† A contemporary, Fabyan, thus describes a banquet given by Edward to the lord-mayor and aldermen of London, after a day's hunting in Waltham Forest:—"And after that goodly disport was passed, the king commanded his officers to bring the mayor and his company into a pleasant lodge made all of green boughs, and garnished with tables and other things necessary, where they were set at dinner, and served with many dainty dishes, and of diverse wines good plenty ; as white, red, and claret; and caused them to be set to dinner before he was served of his own ; and, over that, caused the lord-chamberlain, and other lords to him assigned, to cheer the said mayor and his company sundry times while they were at dinner, and at their departing gave unto them of venison great plenty."—*Chron.* p. 667.

From the pen of Sir Thomas More we have an account of a similar scene at Windsor:—"In the summer, the last that ever he saw, his highness being at Windsor hunting, sent for the mayor and aldermen of London to him, for none other errand but to have them hunt and be merry with him. He made them not so stately as friendly and familiar cheer ; and sent them venison from thence so freely into the city, that no one thing, in many days before, gave him either more hearts, or more hearty favour among the common people, which oftentimes more esteem, and take for greater kindness, a little courtesy than a great benefit."—*Sir T. More, Hist. of Richard III.* p. 5. Ed. 1821.

George Neville, Archbishop of York, who was secretly Edward's friend.* Under these circumstances the young king had only to present himself before the gates of London to find himself invited to come within the walls. On the 10th of April the Tower was taken possession of in his name, and on the following day he rode through the city amidst the enthusiastic acclamations of the people, and took up his abode in the bishop's palace. Never, perhaps, had so hazardous, and apparently desperate, an enterprise been crowned with more signal success. Six months only had elapsed since he had escaped a fugitive to Holland; twenty-eight days only since he had landed at Ravenspur. Yet Edward was again in possession of the capital of his kingdom; his rival, King Henry, was again a prisoner in his hands.

In the mean time, if, as there is reason to believe, Richard of Gloucester was really enamoured of Anne Neville, greatly must his exile have been embittered by the reflection that she was not only united to another, but that his fortunate rival was the heir of the detested house of Lancaster. Not impossibly, indeed, he may have been aware of the existence of that special article in the marriage-treaty, which delayed its *perfecting* till such time as Warwick should have completed the recovery of the sovereignty of England for the Red Rose. If

* Fleetwood Chron. p. 16; Paston Letters, by Fenn, vol. ii. p. 65.

such was the case, Richard doubtless resolved that, as far as depended upon his own indomitable energy and valour, the marriage of Anne Neville should remain unconsummated. Looking forward to the inevitable time when the banner of York must be again confronted with that of Lancaster, he probably panted for the occasion when haply his sword or his lance might leave Anne Neville a widow, yet still a maid. When a few months afterwards, he made his famous onslaught into the ranks of the Duke of Somerset at Tewkesbury, it may have been this passionate feeling, added to his knowledge that Anne Neville was an actual spectator of the scene, which, on that memorable day, lent such resolution to his soul and vigour to his arm.

The deference which Edward ever paid to the advice of his younger brother, the Duke of Gloucester, affords further evidence how high was the opinion he had formed of his judgment and abilities. But the day was fast approaching when Richard's reputation for sagacity in the cabinet was destined to be eclipsed by his valour on the field of battle. Edward had scarcely time to receive the congratulations of the citizens of London, when intelligence reached him that not only was Warwick approaching with a powerful army, but that Queen Margaret and her son, Prince Edward, were daily expected to land in the south. It was clearly the policy of the king to encounter Warwick

before Margaret could come to his assistance. Warwick had also his reasons for hazarding a battle,
and accordingly, on the 14th of April, Easter Sunday, the two armies confronted each other on the
field of Barnet, about ten miles from London.
Though Gloucester at this time was only in his
nineteenth year, the confidence Edward placed in
his brother's discretion and courage was so great,
that he intrusted him with the command of the
right wing of his army.* The post was rendered
the more important in consequence of Gloucester's
forces being immediately opposed to the veteran
forces of Warwick, headed by the mighty baron in
person.   And valiantly, on that memorable day,
did the young prince fulfil his brother's expectations.   Bearing down all before him, he fought his
way, we are told, "so far and boldly into the
enemies' army," that two of his esquires, Thomas
Parr and John Milwater, were slain by his side.†
For six hours the battle was furiously and obstinately contested.   In order to inspire confidence
in his men, Warwick dismounted from his charger
and fought on foot.‡ Observing that his followers
faltered, he flung himself into the thickest of the
fight, and, by his exhortations, and the example

* Harl. MSS. No. 543, quoted in S. Turner's Middle Ages, vol. iii.
p. 296.

† Buck's Life and Reign of Richard III. in Kennet, vol. i. p. 517.

‡ King Edward IV., the victor of so many battles, always fought on
foot. De Commines, tome i. p. 234.

of desperate valour which he set them, restored confidence in his ranks. According to tradition, Gloucester and Warwick encountered each other in the last charge, when the great earl, remembering an affecting promise which he had made to his friend the late Duke of York, spared the life of his son. The field of Barnet was the death-scene of Warwick. A thick fog obscured the part of the field in which he fought; his followers mistook friends for foes; and in the midst of the terrible confusion, attacked by overpowering numbers, the "Kingmaker" met his death.* His fall decided the fate of the day. His fate was shared by his brother, the Marquis of Montagu. The same evening Edward and Gloucester returned to London in triumph. In their train was the ill-fated Henry VI., whom, at the commencement of the battle, Edward had placed in front of the Yorkist ranks, exposed to imminent peril from the arrows of his own friends. When the victors and the vanquished parted company on reaching London, the captive monarch was conducted back through silent streets to his miserable apartment in the Tower, from whence, five weeks afterwards, he was carried to his grave. Edward and Gloucester, in the mean

* The old chroniclers differ in their accounts of Warwick's death. According to the Fleetwood Chronicle (p. 20), " In this battle was slain the Earl of Warwick, somewhat fleeing." The chronicle, printed in Leland's Collectanea (vol. ii. p. 505), also implies that he was slain in flight.

time, passed through admiring masses of people to
the great cathedral of St. Paul's, where, in gratitude for the victory which had been vouchsafed to
him, Edward offered up, "at even-song," his own
standard and that of the great baron who had
formerly raised him to a throne.   Thither also were
brought the bodies of Warwick and Montagu,
which for three days "layid nakid in St Paul is
Chirch to be seene." *

In the mean time, Queen Margaret had for weeks
been prevented by contrary winds and tempestuous
weather from quitting the shores of France.   At
length, on the 13th of April, she was enabled to set
sail from Harfleur, and, on the following day,—the
very day on which the great battle was raging at
Barnet,—she landed with a few but intrepid followers at Weymouth.   Relying on the resources
and the military genius of Warwick, as well as on
the enthusiasm which her presence in England had
hitherto never failed to excite among her partisans,
the high-spirited queen appears to have entertained
a confident hope that at length the cause, for which
she had so long and so heroically struggled, was
about to be triumphant.   When, therefore, a few
hours after her landing, she was informed of the
defeat and death of the mightiest of her champions,
and of the re-committal of King Henry to the
Tower, her grief and disappointment were over-

* Leland's Collect. vol. ii. p. 505 ; Fleetwood Chron. p. 21.

whelming. For the first time, in the course of her many misfortunes and reverses, she appears to have been overwhelmed by despondency, and to have almost yielded herself up to despair. The time had arrived when King Edward might have said of the royal heroine, as John Knox afterwards said of Mary Queen of Scots,—"I made the hyæna weep." While in this distracted state, she was discovered by the Earls of Pembroke and Devonshire, in the sanctuary of the abbey of Beaulieu in Hampshire, where the widow of Warwick had also found shelter.* Tradition still points out an apartment in that interesting ruin, in which the descendant of Charlemagne anathematized the enemies of her husband's house, and in which, in her softer moments, she wept over the ruined fortunes of her accomplished and idolized son. It was not without much difficulty that the devoted barons, who waited on her at Beaulieu, succeeded in inducing her to shake off her dejection. But when, at length, she was induced to take the field, her former heroism returned. By her exertions and those of her friends, a large army, consisting principally of her adherents in the west of England, and the survivors of the battle of Barnet, was assembled at Tewkesbury on the banks of the Severn. Thither King Edward advanced to meet her, and there, on the 4th of May 1471, was fought that memorable battle

* Fleetwood Chron. p. 22.

which was destined, for years to come, to crush the hopes of the house of Lancaster.

At the battle of Tewkesbury, Richard of Gloucester not only increased the reputation for valour which he had won at Barnet, but, by an able strategical movement, he was mainly instrumental in winning the day for the White Rose. Placed by his brother Edward in command of the van, he found himself confronted by the Duke of Somerset, who commanded the advanced division of the Lancastrian forces. So advantageously had the latter taken up a position, surrounded by dykes and hedges, that, had it not been for his own rash and impetuous nature, he might have set at defiance a much more formidable force than that which Gloucester was able to oppose to him. "It was," we are told, "a right evil place to approach as could well have been devised." To entice Somerset from his vantage-ground was therefore clearly the policy of his antagonist. Accordingly, after maintaining a conflict for a short time with brisk discharges of arrows, Gloucester made a movement as if he had been worsted, and commenced a feigned retreat.* The manœuvre was completely successful. Somerset eagerly led his men from their intrenchments, for the purpose, as he thought, of pursuing the Yorkists, when Gloucester suddenly faced about and attacked the Lancastrians in his

* Habington in Kennet, vol. i. p. 452.

turn with impetuous fury. In vain Somerset endeavoured to regain his vantage-ground. Together Gloucester and Somerset entered the encampment; the forces of the latter in full flight, those of Gloucester in eager pursuit. At this moment an incident occurred which was singularly characteristic of the fierce vindictiveness of the age. Had Lord Wenlock, it seems, hastened to Somerset's assistance, the fortunes of the day might have been reversed. Enraged by Wenlock's delay, and at his own discomfiture, the duke no sooner regained his intrenchments, than, riding furiously up to his noble comrade in arms, he denounced him in the most opprobrious terms as a traitor and a coward. The probability is that Wenlock recriminated. It is only certain, however, that Somerset's battle-axe descended on the head of Wenlock, and dashed out his brains.* This remorseless act was followed by the promiscuous slaughter of the flying Lancastrians by their victorious foes. The carnage, more especially on a narrow bridge which spanned a millstream, is described as terrific. The Earl of Devonshire and Sir John Beaufort, brother of the Duke of Somerset, were slain in the battle. The duke himself, the Grand Prior of the order of St. John, and several other persons of distinction, were taken prisoners and beheaded; the Duke of Gloucester, as High Constable, and the Duke of Norfolk, as Marshal of England, sitting as their judges.†

* Habington in Kennet, vol. i. p. 452.　† Fleetwood Chron. p. 31.

Thus, by his valour and generalship, was the young Duke of Gloucester mainly instrumental in winning for his brother Edward the great victory which secured him on his throne. Thus, "wrought high in the opinion of the king by his wisdom and valour,"* we find him, at the early age of eighteen, filling with credit the most important and responsible offices; respected at the council-table for his wisdom, and admired for his chivalry on the field of battle. We might search in vain, perhaps, in the annals even of the wisest and the best, for a more illustrious boyhood! And yet, even at this early period of his life,—a period when youth is usually actuated by the purest and most generous motives,—we find him charged by the prejudiced chroniclers, who wrote under the dynasty of the Tudors, with the commission of the most atrocious crimes. True it is, that the time was destined to arrive when ambition, and events almost beyond human control, tempted him to become an usurper and a murderer. As yet, however, not only, we think, can no offence be with justice laid to his charge, but on the other hand, his conduct appears to have been eminently distinguished by integrity, loyalty, and honour. Less resemblance, indeed, is to be traced between Richard in youth, and Richard in manhood, than between the Richard of Shakspeare and the Richard of true history.

* Habington in Kennet, vol. i. p. 456.

The earliest crime, in point of date, which the old chroniclers have attributed to Richard of Gloucester, is his presumed share in the murder of Edward Prince of Wales after the battle of Tewkesbury. According to the common version of this pitiable tragedy, Edward IV., on the young prince being brought into his presence, haughtily asked him how he dared to take up arms against his lawful sovereign. If Edward, as is probable, anticipated a submissive answer, he must have been disappointed as well as astonished. With a boldness and a dignity, such as became the grandson of Henry V., the royal youth replied that he was in arms to rescue a father from miserable oppression, and to recover a crown that had been violently usurped.* Incensed at his hardihood, the king is said to have struck him with his gauntlet; on which the Dukes of Clarence and Gloucester, the Marquis of Dorset and Lord Hastings, are affirmed to have hurried him from Edward's presence, and to have despatched him in an adjoining apartment with their poniards.†

> * "*K. Edw.* Peace, wilful boy, or I will charm your tongue.
> *Clar.* Untutored lad, thou art too malapert.
> *Prince.* I know my duty, you are all undutiful.
> Lascivious Edward, and thou perjured George,
> And thou misshapen Dick, I tell ye all,
> I am your better, traitors as ye are,
> And thou usurp'st my father's right and mine."
> *King Henry VI.* Part III. Act v. Sc. 5.

† Habington in Kennet, vol. i. p. 453; Polydore Virgil, lib. xxiv. p. 672.
"Tradition still points out a house in Church Street, nearly opposite

The earliest writer, we believe, who has chronicled this affecting story is Polydore Virgil, whose authority, inasmuch as he had conversed with, and drew many of the materials of his history from, the actors in the scenes which he described, must certainly be received with some deference.   But, on the other hand, Polydore Virgil was not only notoriously infected with Lancastrian prejudices, but it must be borne in mind that he wrote his history expressly at the desire of Henry VII., and consequently with every inducement to malign the character and actions of Richard III.   Moreover, we have the accounts of still older writers than Polydore Virgil, not one of whom charges Richard of Gloucester with being an actor in this detestable crime.   Buck, on the authority of a faithful contemporary MS., asserts that when the bloody attack was made on the young prince, "the Duke of Gloucester only, of all the great persons, stood still, and drew not his sword."*   Fabyan, an alder-

to the market-place, in Tewkesbury, as that in which the young prince was stabbed in the presence of King Edward.   In the abbey church of that ancient town, nearly in the centre of the choir, may be seen a brass plate, beneath which lie the remains of the fair boy for whom such torrents of blood were shed,—the last earthly hope of the pious King Henry and of his heroic consort."—*Bennett's Hist. of Tewkesbury*, p. 176. In the same venerable edifice lie buried the false and perjured Clarence, as also those two devoted adherents of the Red Rose, Edmund Duke of Somerset, who was beheaded after the battle of Tewkesbury, and John Earl of Devon, who was slain while gallantly fighting at the head of the rear-guard.

  * Buck's Life and Reign of Richard III. in Kennet, vol. i. p. 549.

man of London and a contemporary, though he
describes the murder as having taken place in the
presence of the king, in no way inculpates Richard
of Gloucester. The king, he says, "strake him
(the prince) with his gauntlet upon the face, after
which stroke, so by him received, he was *by the
king's servants* incontinently slain."* Great
doubt, indeed, seems to exist, whether the story of
the young prince having been assassinated in the
presence of King Edward is not altogether a fiction.
Certainly there appears to be quite as much reason
for presuming that he was slain either in the battle or in flight. Of three contemporary writers, De
Commines clearly implies that he fell on the field
of battle;† another observes,—"and there was slain
in the field Prince Edward, which cried for succour
to his brother-in-law, the Duke of Clarence;"‡
while the third positively states that the prince
"was taken fleeing to the townwards, and slain in
the field."§ Lastly, Bernard Andreas, who wrote
in 1501, and whose prejudices were all arrayed

* Fabyan's Chronicle, p. 662.

† Mémoires de Commines, vol. i. p. 262. " Et fut le prince de Galles
tué sur le champ et plusieurs aultres grans seigneurs," &c.—*Ed.* 1841.

‡ Warkworth Chronicle, p. 18. The term "brother-in-law" has
reference to Clarence and Prince Edward having married two sisters,
the daughters of the Earl of Warwick.

§ Fleetwood Chronicle, p. 30. The statement of the Croyland chronicler (p. 466) is too obscurely worded to be received as evidence either
on one side or the other.

against Richard, clearly implies that the prince was slain in fight.*

The accounts which have been handed down to us of the fate of the heir of the house of Lancaster, being thus contradictory and confused, we may fairly inquire with what justice Richard of Gloucester can be arraigned as one of his murderers. Certainly no evidence can be more unsatisfactory than that which has been hitherto advanced to convict him of the charge. The young and the brave are seldom cold-blooded assassins. Richard, moreover, is known to have been sensitively alive to the good opinion of the world; and accordingly, when we consider how indelible a stain, even in that remorseless and unscrupulous age, the perpetration of so cowardly a murder would have affixed on the perpetrator of it, we may safely ask whether it is probable that he would have sullied the knighthood which he valued so highly, by staining his sword with blood which he had no personal interest in shedding, and by committing an act which might have been delegated to the common headsman.†

* "Is enim ante Bernardi campum in Theoxberye prælio belligerens ceciderat."—*Vit. Hen. Sept.* pp. 21-2.

† Of our modern historians, Carte, apparently with little reason, intimates that the Prince of Wales was assassinated by Dorset and Hastings. Hist. of Eng. vol. ii. p. 790. Hume, on the contrary, who quotes the prejudiced authority of Polydore Virgil, Hall, and Holinshed, confidently lays it down that the assassination took place in the presence of the king, and that Clarence and Gloucester took part in the murder. Hist. of Eng. vol. iii. p. 244. Lingard's account is more

From the story of Richard of Gloucester let us briefly revert to the fortunes of the unhappy Margaret of Anjou. It was doubtless with a mother's pride, not unmingled with a mother's fears, that, on the morning of the battle of Tewkesbury, she had beheld her gallant son arraying himself for his first and last fight. When the mother and son parted on that fatal morning it was for the last time. Having witnessed the total defeat of her army, Margaret fled with the ladies of her suite to a church near Tewkesbury, in which edifice, two days afterwards, she was arrested by Sir William Stanley, who conducted her to King Edward at Coventry. Here she first received the afflicting intelligence that she was no longer a mother. But other sorrows awaited her. The haughtiest princess of her time was compelled to figure in her enemy's triumphant progress to London, where on her arrival she was committed to the Tower. Within these walls languished her unhappy consort; but strict orders had been given that they should be kept asunder. Only a few hours, indeed, elapsed after her admission into the Tower, when

guarded. "Edward," he says, "had the brutality to strike the young prince in the face with his gauntlet; Clarence and Gloucester, *or perhaps the knights in their retinue,* despatched him with their swords."—*Hist. of Eng.* vol. iv. p. 189. Lastly, Sharon Turner, who had access to better sources of information, differs altogether from his predecessors; his opinion agreeing with the contemporary account which we have already quoted, that the prince "was taken as flying towards the town, and was slain in the field."—*Middle Ages,* vol. iii. p. 313.

it was announced to Margaret that she was a widow. The question whether King Henry died a natural death, or whether he fell by the hand of an assassin, we shall presently have to consider. Of Margaret of Anjou it remains to be said, that, after having been detained a prisoner in different fortresses in England for nearly five years, she was ransomed and released on the 13th of November 1475, for the sum of fifty thousand crowns. She then returned to her native country. But life had long since ceased to possess any charms for her. Old age seems to have crept prematurely over her. Disease ravaged the beauty which had formerly dazzled kings. Her days were passed in tears and lamentations. At length, on the 25th of August 1480, the afflicted queen breathed her last in the château of Dampierre, in the fifty-second year of her age.*

On the night of the 21st day of May 1471, the same day on which King Edward returned to London, and seventeen days only after the battle which lost him his crown, perished, in durance and misery, the last king of the house of Lancaster,— the pious, the gentle, and most unfortunate king, Henry VI. The following day, we are told,† being Ascension Eve, the body of the late king, " borne barefaced on the bier," and surrounded by

* Strickland's Queens of England, vol. ii. pp. 311-2.
† Fabyan, p. 662; Leland's Coll. vol. ii. p. 507; Warkworth, p. 31.

"more glaves and staves than torches," was carried from the Tower to St. Paul's, where it remained for some time exposed to the public view, the "face open that every man might see him." * "To satisfy the credulous," writes a modern historian, " it was reported that he died of grief. But though the conqueror might silence the tongues, he could not control the belief nor the pens of his subjects; and the writers who lived under the next dynasty, not only proclaimed the murder, but attributed the black deed to the advice, if not to the dagger, of the younger of the three brothers, Richard Duke of Gloucester." † According to Shakspeare, who follows the accounts of Hall and Sir Thomas More, Richard killed the unhappy king with his own hand.

" *K. Henry.* Men for their sons', wives for their husbands',
And orphans for their parents' timeless death,
Shall rue the hour that ever thou wast born.
The owl shrieked at thy birth, an evil sign ;
The night-crow cried, aboding luckless time ;
Dogs howled, and hideous tempests shook down trees ;
The raven rook'd her on the chimney's top,
And chattering pies in dismal discords sung.
Thy mother felt more than a mother's pain,
And yet brought forth less than a mother's hope ;
To wit, an indigest deformed lump,
Not like the fruit of such a goodly tree.
Teeth hadst thou in thy head when thou wast born,
To signify thou cam'st to bite the world ;

---

* Warkworth Chronicle, p. 21 ; Leland's Collect. vol. ii. p. 507.
† Lingard's Hist. of England, vol. iv. p. 192.

> And, if the rest be true which I have heard,
> Thou cam'st——
>   *Gloucester.* I'll hear no more:—Die, prophet, in thy speech.
>   [*Stabs him.*"*

That King Henry met his end by foul means, there is unhappily only too much reason for conjecturing. To the house of York, his life or death unquestionably involved consequences of considerable importance. So long as he lived, it was certain that he would be a rallying point for the house of Lancaster; while, if he died, it would leave Edward without any formidable competitor for the throne. Edward, then, had powerful motives for getting rid of his rival. Moreover, not only had he the mere motive, but we have evidence that he projected, if he did not actually contrive, the death of Henry. "It was resolved in King Edward's cabinet council," says Habington, "that, to take away all title from future insurrections, King Henry should be sacrificed."† This assertion, if true, certainly gives a peculiar importance to certain instructions given by Edward to the Archbishop of York, "to keep King Henry out of sanctuary."‡ Yet more indicative of Edward's anxiety to rid himself of the deposed monarch, is the fact of his having placed him in the front of his army at the recent battle of Tewkesbury. Surely this

* King Henry VI. Part III. Act v. Scene 6.
† Habington in Kennet, vol. i. p. 455.
‡ Leland, Coll. vol. ii. p. 508.

could have been only with the hope that a chance arrow might pierce the brain or the heart of his rival.

Admitting, therefore, that grounds exist for suspecting King Edward of having rid himself of his unhappy prisoner by foul means, we have next to inquire into the nature of the evidence which charges Richard of Gloucester with having participated in or committed the crime. Certainly more than one writer, either contemporary or very nearly contemporary with him, have unhesitatingly charged him with the guilt. "He killed by others," says the chronicler Rous, "or, as many believe, with his own hand, that most sacred man King Henry VI."[*] Again, Philip de Commines writes, "Immediately after this battle, the Duke of Gloucester either killed with his own hand, or caused to be murdered in his presence, in some spot apart, this good man King Henry."[†] These passages are doubtless remarkable. Let us turn, however, on the other hand, to less prejudiced contemporary authority, and we shall either find no mention of Gloucester's name as connected with the foul transaction, or else his presumed participation

---

[*] Rous's words are: "Et quod in Dei et omnium Anglicorum, immo omnium nationum ad quorum notitiam pervenit, detestabilissimum erat, ipsum sanctissimum virum regem Henricum Sextum per alios, vel multis credentibus manu potius propria, interfecit."—*Joannis Rossi Historia Regum Angliæ*, p. 215.

[†] De Commines, tome i. p. 261.

in it is merely introduced as one of the rumours of the time. "Of the death of this prince," says Fabyan, "diverse tales were told, but *the most common fame went* that he was stykked with a dagger by the hands of the Duke of Gloucester."* Even Polydore Virgil confines himself to the remark that common report attributed the crime to Gloucester. "Henry VI.," he says "being not long before deprived of his diadem, was put to death in the Tower of London. The *continual report* is that Richard Duke of Gloucester killed him with a sword, whereby his brother might be delivered from all fear of hostility."† "He slew," says Sir Thomas More, "with his own hand, *as men constantly say*, King Henry VI., being prisoner in the Tower."‡ On the other hand, the trustworthy continuator of Croyland, though he entertains no doubt of King Henry having been murdered in the Tower, omits all mention of the name of Gloucester in connection with that mysterious event.§ The

* Fabyan's Chronicle, p. 662.

† Polydore Virgil, "Ut fama constans est," lib. xxiv. p. 674; and Camd. Soc. Trans. p. 156.

‡ Sir T. More's Richard III. p. 9.

§ The writer seems, by implication, to lay the crime at Edward's door: "I would pass over in silence the fact that at this period King Henry was found dead in the Tower of London; may God spare and grant time for repentance to the person, whoever he was, who thus dared to lay sacrilegious hands upon the Lord's anointed! Hence it is that he who perpetrated this has justly earned the title of tyrant, while he who thus suffered has gained that of a glorious martyr."—*Croyl. Chron. Cont.* p. 468.

Fleetwood and Warkworth chronicles are equally silent. Some weight indeed has been attached to the following passage in the latter chronicle, as indirectly tending to implicate Richard :—" The same night that King Edward came to London, King Harry, being in ward in prison in the Tower of London, was put to death the 21st day of May, on a Tuesday night, betwixt eleven and twelve of the clock; being then at the Tower the Duke of Gloucester, brother to King Edward, and many others."* But supposing it to be the case that Richard passed that eventful night in the Tower, the fact adds no additional weight to the scanty evidence which has been brought forward against him. The Tower of London, it must be remembered, was at this period, and had long been, a royal residence. Here the queen of Edward II. was delivered of her eldest daughter, "Jane of the Tower."†

With Edward III. it seems to have been a favorite place of abode, and here, in 1342, his queen presented him with a princess.‡ It had witnessed the bridal pleasures of the unfortunate Richard II. in 1396,§ and hither Edward IV. had conducted his beautiful queen after their romantic marriage was announced to the world. Their daughter, the queen of Henry VII., afterwards lay-in there of her last

* Warkworth Chronicle, p. 21.
† Bayley's Tower of London, p. 22.
‡ Ibid. p. 26.
§ Ibid. p. 35.

child.   Moreover, at this very time, the queen, with "my lord prince, and my ladies his daughters," were residing at the Tower.*   Thither, then, the king, as a matter of course, proceeded to embrace and to receive the congratulations of his wife and children.   Thither also his brother Richard doubtless accompanied him.   Unmarried, and apparently having at this time no fixed London residence of his own, what could be more natural than that the young prince should have passed, under the same roof with his royal relatives, the single night which the troubled state of his kingdom permitted the two brothers to pass in London?

Such is the principal evidence on which Richard of Gloucester has been accused of having committed one of the most atrocious crimes on record. But is it likely, is it even conceivable, that he was the cold-blooded assassin such as he is described by Shakspeare and the later chroniclers?   He was only in the nineteenth year of his age.   No man living shrank from incurring the censure of mankind with greater sensitiveness.   No man living took greater pleasure in listening to the shouts and applause of his fellow-men.   As Habington observes,—"I cannot believe that a man so cunning in declining envy, and winning honour to his name, would have undertaken such a business."†   More-

* Fleetwood Chronicle, pp. 34, 37.
† Habington in Kennet, vol i, p. 455.

over, on the single day which the royal brothers
passed in London,* Gloucester would seem to have
been present with the king in all the bustling and
exciting scenes consequent on the latter's triumphant return to his capital.† He was present at the
knighting of the lord-mayor, the recorder, and the
aldermen, who had so recently and so bravely de-
fended the city for their sovereign against the
Lancastrian forces commanded by the Bastard Falconbridge. He was present at the reception of the
nobles who came to congratulate the king on his
recent triumphs; at the banquet which was held in
celebration of these triumphs; and lastly at the
councils which met to advise with the king as to
the best means of securing stability to his throne
and future tranquillity to the commonwealth. A
more busy and eventful day it would be difficult to
imagine. And yet we are called upon to believe
that a valiant youth of eighteen could secretly steal
away from scenes of excitement so congenial to his
nature, in order to stab or stifle in his bed an old
and feeble man, in whose death or in whose existence he could scarcely have any personal interest
whatever.

It may be argued, indeed, that Richard had an
object in getting rid of King Henry, in order to

* "The king, incontinent after his coming to London, tarried but
one day, and went with his whole army after his said traitors into
Kent."—*Fleetwood Chronicle*, p. 38.

† S. Turner's Middle Ages, vol. iii. p. 320.

place himself nearer in succession to the throne. But, unless by a series of accidents altogether beyond the range of human probability, or unless by a series of wholesale premeditated crimes which the imagination shudders in contemplating, the probability of Richard of Gloucester ascending the throne of the Plantagenets was slender in the extreme. His brother Edward was not only in the prime of youth, but was already the father of several children. His brother Clarence had recently married a beautiful girl, who, in all probability, would increase the number of princes of the house of York. Lastly, presuming that it was in the nature of Richard of Gloucester to commit so dastardly a crime, he was to all appearance deprived of the means. The apartments of so important a prisoner of state as Henry VI. must have been sentinelled by no inconsiderable military guard. We have evidence that two esquires, Robert Ratcliffe and William Sayer, with no fewer than ten or eleven other persons, were appointed to attend upon the unhappy monarch.* Richard, moreover, held no military command within the walls of the Tower; and, lastly, Anthony Earl Rivers, who at this period was lieutenant of this palatial fortress, was not only on bad terms with Richard, but was also one of the most unlikely men living to lend himself to the commission of a cold-blooded

* Rymer's Fœdera, vol. xi. p. 712.

murder. Again, one contemporary writer, at least, has attributed the death of Henry to mere natural causes. According to his statement, such was the effect produced on the mind of the imbecile king by his personal misfortunes and the utter ruin of his friends, that "of pure displeasure and melancholy he died."* And after all, considering the maze of confusion and prejudice through which we are forced to grope our way to the light, this may possibly be the true version of a story which for centuries has been invested by the poet and the historian with so much mystery and horror.

It would be no less interesting than curious were we enabled to trace under what circumstances and at what particular period Richard and the Lady Anne first met after the battle of Tewkesbury. It suited the genius of Shakspeare to represent their meeting as having taken place at night in the streets of London, some twenty days after the battle. It was on that sad occasion, according to the immortal dramatist, when the corpse of King Henry VI. was carried, "without singing or saying," from St. Paul's to Blackfriars, at which latter place it was subsequently embarked in "a kind of barge solemnly prepared and provided with lighted torches,"† for the purpose of being conveyed by water to Chertsey. Anne, as chief mourner, is de-

* Fleetwood Chronicle, p. 38.
† Croyl. Chron. Cont. p. 468.

scribed as ordering the bearers to "set down their honourable load," and then, after a pathetic address to the corpse, uttering the most terrible imprecations against the assumed murderer of her husband and of her father-in-law,—

> "Be it lawful that I invocate thy ghost,
> To hear the lamentations of poor Anne,
> Wife to thy Edward, to thy slaughtered son,
> Stabbed by the self-same hand that made these wounds!
> Lo! in these windows that let forth thy life,
> I pour the helpless balm of my poor eyes:
> O, cursed be the hand that made these holes!
> Cursed the heart that had the heart to do it!
> Cursed the blood that let this blood from hence!
> More direful hap betide that hated wretch,
> That makes us wretched by the death of thee,
> Than I can wish to adders, spiders, toads,
> Or any creeping venomed thing that lives!
> If ever he have child, abortive be it,
> Prodigious, and untimely brought to light,
> Whose ugly and unnatural aspect
> May fright the hopeful mother at the view;
> And that be heir to his unhappiness!
> If ever he have wife, let her be made
> More miserable by the death of him
> Than I am made by my young lord and thee!—
> Come now, toward Chertsey with your holy load."*

Richard is then represented as appearing on the stage as if by accident, when there takes place that striking scene, in which Richard of Gloucester woos, flatters, and wins the Lady Anne.

> "Your beauty, that did haunt me in my sleep,
> To undertake the death of all the world,
> So I might live one hour in your sweet bosom."†

---

* King Richard III. Act i. Scene 2.   † Ibid.

That such a scene of intemperate recrimination should have taken place between a royal youth of eighteen and a high-born young lady of seventeen, at such a spot, too, and under such circumstances, is, to say the least, extremely unlikely. But not only is it improbable, but we have evidence that no such interview could by any possibility have taken place. At the time when the corpse of Henry VI. was on its way to Chertsey, Richard was marching with his brother, King Edward, against the Bastard Falconbridge; while Anne, who had fallen into the hands of Edward after the battle of Tewkesbury,* was in all probability in close custody with her mother-in-law, Queen Margaret, in the Tower.

From the Tower, Anne Neville would seem to have been transferred by the king to the charge and keeping of her sister, the Duchess of Clarence. We might have presumed, therefore, that from this period Gloucester was afforded every favourable opportunity of conversing with, and paying court to, his fair cousin. We have evidence, however, that such was far from having been the case. Clarence, indeed, had good reasons for wishing to keep his brother and sister-in-law apart. In right of his wife, the eldest daughter of the Earl of Warwick, he claimed to be the sole possessor of the princely domains of the Kingmaker; whereas, in the event of Gloucester marrying the younger sister, there

* Leland's Collect. vol. ii. p. 506.

could be little doubt but that he would endeavor to obtain a share of the inheritance. Clarence therefore resolved to oppose their union by every means within his power.

Under these circumstances, Gloucester not only found himself denied all opportunity of preferring his suit, but Anne suddenly and mysteriously disappeared from the halls of Clarence. Powerful as Gloucester's position was in the State, high too as he stood in favour with his brother Edward, the probability seems to be that the king was on the point of adopting stringent measures to secure him the hand of Anne Neville, when Clarence, in order to counteract their intentions, "caused the damsel to be concealed."* It would be interesting to be able to follow Richard in the search which he instituted to discover the lady of his love. Only the romantic fact, however, has been handed down to us, that when at length he traced her to her place of concealment, he found the heiress of the Nevilles and of the Beauchamps, the affianced of a Prince of Wales, and the cousin of the reigning sovereign, in an obscure street in London, disguised in the garb of a kitchen-maid. By those who have been taught to regard Richard of Gloucester as the deformed monster and cold-blooded miscreant which history has usually painted him, it might naturally be imagined that in assuming the garb and submitting

* Croyl. Chron. Cont. p. 469.

to the drudgery of a serving-woman, the object of
Anne Neville was to escape from the hateful impor-
tunities of a man whom she believed to have been
her husband's assassin. On the contrary, she
seems to have placed herself, without any hesitation, under the protection of Richard, who, in the
first instance, removed her to the sanctuary of St.
Martin's-le-Grand, from whence she was afterwards
transferred to the guardianship of her uncle, George
Neville, Archbishop of York. In the mean time
Gloucester made successful suit to the king for her
hand. The date of his marriage to the Lady Anne
is uncertain, but as she bore him a child in 1473,*
the probability is that they were united in the
course of the preceding year, possibly as soon as
her year of mourning for young Edward had expired.

Such appears to have been the commencement of
the famous quarrel between the Dukes of Clarence
and Gloucester. When the latter subsequently
laid claim to a moiety of the Kingmaker's estates,
Clarence, highly incensed, insisted on his own ex-
clusive right to the lands of the Nevilles. "He
may well have my lady sister-in-law," said Clarence, "but we will part no livelihood."† So
great was his exasperation, that a hostile encoun-

* Speed's Hist. of Great Britain, p. 726; Sandford's Geneal. Hist.
book v. p. 410.

† Paston Letters, by Fenn, vol. ii. p. 92.

ter between the two brothers was considered at the time as not improbable. "As for other tidings," writes Sir John Paston, "I trust to God that the two Dukes of Clarence and Gloucester shall be set at one by the award of the king." * Subsequently both brothers made an appeal to the king, who decided that they should plead their several causes before him in council. Great ability is said to have been displayed on both sides. "So many arguments," writes a contemporary, "were, with the greatest acuteness, put forward on either side, in the king's presence, who sat in judgment in the council-chamber, that all present, and the lawyers even, were quite surprised that these princes should find arguments in such abundance by means of which to support their respective causes." † Subsequently an act of parliament was passed (1474) which divided the inheritance of the two sisters between them, giving to each brother a life-interest in his wife's estates, in the event of his surviving her.‡ Among other lands of the Beauchamps and Nevilles, Richard became possessed of another princely residence in the north, Barnard Castle, in the county of Durham.§ The only sufferer by the transaction was the illustrious widow of the King-

* Paston Letters, by Fenn, vol. v. p. 60.

† Croy. Chron. Cont. p. 470.

‡ S. Turner's Middle Ages, vol. iii. p. 324.

§ Surtees' Hist. of Durham, vol. iv. p. 66.

maker,—the sole heiress and mistress of the magnificent estates of the Beauchamps, Earls of Warwick,—who was thus left dependent and almost penniless.*

And when Richard of Gloucester played the lover, was he in reality the deformed, crooked, repulsive being, such as he is described in the prejudiced pages of the Lancastrian chroniclers and in the immortal dramas of Shakspeare? According to Sir Thomas More, he was "little of stature, ill-featured of limbs, crook-backed, his left shoulder much higher than his right, and hard-featured of visage." †   Hall and Speed draw an exactly similar picture of Richard.‡   Holinshed also describes him as "small and little of stature," his body "greatly deformed," his "countenance cruel," and "savouring of malice, fraud, and deceit." §   His very birth is described as having been a monstrous and unnatural one. According to one writer, his mother, the Duchess of York, was two years pregnant of him; and when at length she gave birth to him, she suffered intolerable anguish.‖   Hall tells us that he came into the world "feet forward."   "At his nativity," says the chronicler Rous, "the scorpion was in the ascendant; he came into the

* Croy. Chron. Cont. p. 470.
† Sir T. More's King Richard III. p. 8.
‡ Hall's Chronicle, p. 342; Speed, p. 694.
§ Holinshed's Chronicle, vol. iii. p. 447.
‖ Rossi Hist. Reg. Ang. p. 215; More, ut supra, p. 8.

world with teeth, and with a head of hair reaching
to his shoulders." *

> "For I have often heard my mother say
> I came into the world with my legs forward :
> Had I not reason, think ye, to make haste
> And seek their ruin that usurped our right ?
> The midwife wondered ; and the women cried,
> 'O Jesus bless us, he is born with teeth !'
> And so I was, which plainly signified
> That I should snarl, and bite, and play the dog." †

According to Camden, "his monstrous birth fore-
showed his monstrous proceedings, for he was born
with all his teeth, and hair to his shoulders."‡
Sir Thomas More also tells us that he came into the
world "with his feet forward," and also "not un-
toothed." § To sum up, in fact, his assumed im-
perfections in a single sentence,—"Of body he
was but low, crooked-backed, hook-shouldered,
splay-footed, and goggle-eyed; his face little and
round, his complexion swarthy, his left arm from
his birth dry and withered; born a monster in
nature, with all his teeth, with hair on his head,
and nails on his fingers and toes: and just such
were the qualities of his mind." ‖

Such are the deformities of body and mind which
ignorance and prejudice formerly delighted to at-

* Rossi Hist. p. 215.

† King Henry VI. Part III. Act v. Sc. 6.

‡ Camden's Remains, p. 353.

§ Sir T. More's Richard III. p. 8.

‖ Baker's Chronicles of the Kings of England, p. 234.

tribute to Richard of Gloucester. Let us turn, however, to the pages of contemporary writers, more than one of whom were not only familiar with the person of Richard, but had actually conversed with him, and we shall discover no evidence whatever to corroborate the distorted and ridiculous pictures drawn of him by the chroniclers who wrote under the Tudor dynasty. Neither the continuator of the chronicle of Croyland, nor William of Wyrcester, nor Abbot Whethamstede, nor the author of the Fleetwood chronicle makes allusion to any deformity in the person of Richard of Gloucester. Rous, another contemporary, bitterly prejudiced as he is against Richard, contents himself with averring that he was small of stature, having a short face and uneven shoulders, the left being lower than the right. But even Rous seems to admit that his countenance was not disagreeable.* His face is said to have borne a resemblance to that of his late father the Duke of York, a circumstance which was afterwards alluded to by Dr. Shaw from the pulpit at Paul's Cross before a large concourse of people, when Richard was himself present. According to the reverend doctor, Richard stood before them " the special pattern of knightly prowess, as well in all princely behaviour as in the lineaments and favour of his visage, representing

* Rous's expression is, " ut scorpio vultu blandiens, cauda pungens, sic et ipse cunctis se ostendit."—*Hist. Reg. Ang.* p. 215.

the very face of the noble duke his father." *
Had Richard been the " hard-visaged," " goggle-
eyed," " cruel-countenanced " being he has been described, the crowd would have replied to the idle
flattery with a shout of derision. Philip de Commines, who must have often seen Richard in company with his brother Edward, twice speaks of the
latter as the most beautiful prince he had ever seen.†
Surely, therefore, if there had existed any remarkable contrast in the personal appearance of the two
brothers, it would have been pointed out by the
gossiping and free-spoken historian. Again, Stow,
who was inquisitive and curious in regard to the
habits and persons of princes, though he seems to
have made diligent inquiries among " ancient
men," who had seen and remembered Richard of
Gloucester, could arrive at no other conclusion
than that he was " of bodily shape comely enough,
only of low stature." ‡ Lastly, the " old Countess of
Desmond," who had danced with Richard, declared
to more than one of her contemporaries that he
was the handsomest man in the room, except his

----

* Holinshed, vol. iii. p. 389 ; Buck in Kennet, vol. i. p. 548.

† Mémoires, vol. i. pp. 239, 374.

‡ Survey of London Life prefixed to vol. i. p. xviii. ; and Buck in
Kennet, vol. i. p. 548. "This prince," says Hume, "was of a small
stature, hump-backed, and had a harsh, disagreeable countenance."—
Hist. of Engl. vol. iii. p. 288. According to a more diligent inquirer
than Hume, "his face was handsome."—Sharon Turner's Middle Ages,
vol. iii. p. 443.

brother Edward, and very well made.* Our own impression is, that though his stature was low he was not misshapen; that though his figure was slight it was compact and muscular; and that, though not exactly handsome, his countenance was far from being unprepossessing.†

It seems to have been shortly after his marriage with Anne Neville that Richard quitted the voluptuous court of his brother Edward, for the purpose of discharging his important duties as chief seneschal of the duchy of Lancaster, and superintending his princely estates in the north of England. Some notion may be formed of the vastness of his territorial possessions in the north, when we mention that, in addition to the castle and domain of Sheriff-Hutton, he now held the castle and manor of Middleham, another magnificent abode of the great Earl of Warwick, as well as the noble castle, manor, and demesnes of Skipton, in the deanery of Craven, which had been seized by the crown on the death of John Lord Clifford at the battle of Towton. Of these Middleham appears to have been his

* See Appendix A.

† Lord Orford is of opinion that what Rous tells us of Richard having had unequal shoulders is the truth, but that, with this exception, the king had no personal deformity. "The truth I take to have been this. Richard, who was slender and not tall, had one shoulder a little higher than the other; a defect, by the magnifying glasses of party, by distance of time, and by the amplification of tradition, easily swelled into shocking deformity."—*Historic Doubts*, Lord Orford's Works, vol. ii. p. 166.

favourite residence.   Here, in his boyhood, he had first gazed upon the fair face of Anne Neville, and here, in 1473, she presented him with the only child which she is known to have borne him, Edward, afterwards Prince of Wales.   It was, however, at Pomfret or Pontefract Castle, at that time one of the most magnificent baronial residences in England, that Richard principally held his court. Here, invested with almost regal powers, and living in almost regal splendour, he continued for the next few years to discharge with justice and vigour the high duties intrusted to him; winning for himself the golden opinions of men by his charities, his condescension and inflexible probity, and at the same time firmly attaching the people of the north to the government of his brother Edward.   Thus high stood the character, and thus unimpeachable was the conduct, of Richard Duke of Gloucester, at the age of twenty-two.

It was in the month of June 1475 that Edward IV., carrying with him, besides a large force of infantry, fifteen thousand mounted archers, and attended by the flower of his nobility, sailed from Sandwich for the purpose of claiming the crown of France.   De Commines tells us that no king of England had ever invaded France at the head of so splendid an army.*   Richard of Gloucester followed the banner of his chivalrous brother, and landed at

* Mémoires, tome i. p. 336.

Calais by his side. The story of that unsatisfactory
expedition, and of the disgraceful treaty by which
it was followed, may be related in a few words.
The challenge, which Edward sent to Louis XI. to
resign the crown of France, was answered by civil-
ities; his threats were responded to by bribes.
Eventually the two monarchs met personally, and
exchanged courtesies, on a bridge over the Somme
at Picquigny, between Calais and Amiens. Across
the bridge was erected a rail or trellis of woodwork,
in which interstices were contrived of sufficient size
only to admit of one monarch taking the hand of
the other. Close to the bridge were posted twenty-
two English lancemen, who kept guard so long as
their master remained in conference with the French
king. "During this time," writes Monstrelet, "a
very heavy fall of rain came on, to the great vexa-
tion of the French lords, who had dressed themselves and their horses in their richest habiliments,
in honour to King Edward."* The conference
terminated by the English monarch guaranteeing to
withdraw his splendid army from France, on condition of receiving an earnest of 75,000 crowns and
an annual tribute of 50,000 crowns. The ministers
and favourites of King Edward also came in for
their share of French gold. Lord Howard, besides
a pension, received 24,000 crowns in money and
plate; Lord Hastings was awarded 1000 marks in

* Monstrelet's Chronicles, vol. iv. p. 351.

plate, and a pension of 2000 crowns a year.   Even the Lord Chancellor and the Master of the Rolls made no scruple of receiving French gold.   "The king," writes Monstrelet, "made very liberal presents to all the courtiers of Edward, and to the heralds and trumpets, who made great rejoicings for the same, crying out,—'*Largesse au très noble et puissant roi de France! Largesse, largesse!*'"* In the time of Philip de Commines, the receipts given by the English nobles for their pensions and bribes were still to be seen in the chamber of accounts.   Hastings alone refused to give any written acknowledgment for what he had received.   "If you wish me to take it," he said, "you may put it into my sleeve."†

Thus was concluded the treaty of Picquigny, a treaty most disgraceful to both monarchs. Richard of Gloucester, alone, of all the generals and ministers of Edward, refused to barter the honour of his country for gold.   He even refused to be present at the meeting of the two kings at Picquigny.‡ After defiance sent, and a crown challenged, "what," he said, "would the world think of the wisdom and courage of England, that could cross the seas with so noble and expensive an expedition, and then return without drawing a sword?"§ Even Lord

* Monstrelet's Chronicles, pp. 352, 353.
† De Commines, tome ii. pp. 167, 169.
‡ Ibid. tome i. p. 377.
§ Habington in Kennet, vol. i. p. 465.

Bacon, prejudiced as he is against Richard of Gloucester, has done justice to his patriotism and disinterestedness. "As upon all other occasions," he writes, "Richard, then Duke of Gloucester, stood upon the side of honour, raising his own reputation to the disadvantage of the king his brother, and drawing the eyes of all, especially of the nobles and soldiers, upon himself."*

The next events of importance connected with the story of the Duke of Gloucester, were the trial and execution of his fickle and intriguing brother, the Duke of Clarence. Delighting to implicate the young prince in almost every crime and every tragical event which occurred during his eventful career, the Tudor historians, as usual, overlook the cruel and vindictive character of Edward IV., and confidently attribute his having signed the death-warrant of his brother to the intrigues and persuasions of Gloucester. No man, according to Lord Bacon, "thought any ignominy or contumely unworthy of him who had been the executioner of King Henry VI. with his own hands, and the contriver of the death of the Duke of Clarence, his brother."† Sir Thomas More, another of his accusers, aggravates his presumed offence by taxing him with the grossest hypocrisy. "Some wise men," he writes, "ween that his drift, covertly

* Bacon's Life of Henry VII. in Kennet, vol. i. p. 578.
† Ibid.

conveyed, lacked not in helping forth his brother of Clarence to his death; which he resisted openly."* "After Clarence," writes a later historian, "had offered his mass-penny in the Tower of London, he was drowned in a butt of malmsey; his brother, the Duke of Gloucester, assisting thereat with his own proper hands."† Lastly, Shakspeare not only charges him with fratricide, but represents him as carrying the death-warrant to the Tower, and urging the murderers to despatch :—

> "—— Sirs, be sudden in the execution,
> Withal obdurate; do not hear him plead;
> For Clarence is well spoken, and, perhaps,
> May move your hearts to pity if you mark him."‡

Before arraigning a suspected person of crime, we should in the first instance look for the motive. It may be argued, in the present case, that Gloucester's motives for getting rid of an elder brother were sufficiently strong and apparent : viz. that he was unscrupulously bent on obtaining possession of the crown; that Clarence not only stood individually in the way of his ambition, but that, had he lived, he would probably have begot numerous heirs to the crown; and, lastly, that, as Clarence's only son, the infant Earl of Warwick, was included in the attainder of his father, Richard, by one

* Sir T. More's Richard III. p. 10.
† Sandford's Geneal. Hist. book v. p. 438.
‡ King Richard III. Act i. Sc. 3.

stroke of cruel policy, hoped to effect the removal
of two persons who opposed themselves to the realization of his ambitious hopes.

But of what use is it to imagine a motive, unless
the guilt be also substantiated by evidence? In the
present case, not only does no such evidence seem
to be forthcoming, but such evidence as exists appears to be in favour of Richard's innocence. For
instance, two of the most bigoted of the Tudor
chroniclers, Hall and Holinshed, not only are silent
on the charge of his having been the instigator of
his brother's death, but admit that he impugned
the rigour of the sentence passed upon Clarence.
Again, had that unhappy prince been sent to execution by the individual fiat of his brother Edward,
it might, with some shadow of argument, be
reasoned that Gloucester was the king's secret
adviser on the occasion. So far, however, from
Clarence having been sent to his last account by
this summary process, it is an historical fact that
he was not only publicly tried and condemned by
the highest tribunal in the realm, the House of
Lords, but, moreover, in so heinous a light were his
treasonable practices regarded, that the House of
Commons, with the Speaker at their head, appeared
at the bar of the Lords and pressed for his execution.* Certainly, had Richard availed himself of
his privilege as a peer, and sat and voted at

* Croyl. Chron. Cont. p. 480.

Clarence's trial, presumptive evidence would have been afforded that he desired his brother's death. But not only is there no evidence of his having sat at that tribunal, but, on the contrary, there is much more reason for arriving at the conclusion that, at the time of Clarence's trial and execution, Richard was quietly discharging the duties of his government in the north of England.*

It has been asserted, that it was with much unwillingness that Edward signed the death-warrant of Clarence; and, chiefly on this ground, it has been assumed that Richard must have taken upon himself the diabolical office of arresting the hand of mercy. But, supposing that King Edward really displayed such scruples, and that those scruples were sincere, were there not other persons, who were interested quite as much as Gloucester, in endeavoring to stifle them? By the queen and her ambitious and grasping kindred, Clarence had been long held in fear and detestation. Rivers, more especially, envied him his princely estates, the greater portion of which were actually conferred upon him by the king after the death of Clarence. The latter, moreover, had been the rival of Rivers for the hand of the heiress of Burgundy.+ But, of all men, the king himself was the most

* Halsted's Life of Richard III. vol. i. p. 331.

+ Polydore Virgil, lib. xxiv. p. 681; Speed, p. 689; Hall, p. 326; Rymer's Foedera, vol. xii. p. 95.

interested in getting rid of Clarence. Not only was Clarence obnoxious to him on account of his former and successful rebellion, but the king had still every reason to dread him as a popular idol, a turbulent subject, and an irreclaimable traitor. Accordingly, we not only find Edward standing personally forward as his brother's accuser, but actually pleading against him in the House of Lords. In that "sad strife," writes the Croyland continuator, "not a single person uttered a word against the duke except the king; not one individual made answer to the king except the duke." *
But Clarence had been guilty of two other offences, neither of which Edward was likely to forgive. In the first place, Clarence had openly disputed his brother's legitimacy, on the ground of their mother's incontinency; † and, in the next place, the act of parliament which had declared Edward to be a usurper, and had settled the crown on Clarence and his descendants after the demise of Edward, son of Henry VI., was still unrepealed. Considering, therefore, how unpardonable were these offences, and how jealous and vindictive was the king's disposition, we may perhaps not be very uncharitable in assuming that it required no extraordinary persuasions, from any person whatever, to induce Edward to consent to his brother's death.‡

* Croyl. Chron. Cont. p. 479.

† Rot. Parl. vol. vi. p. 194.

‡ It may be mentioned that one of the first steps taken by Edward

after his brother's execution was to obtain a repeal of the obnoxious
acts of parliament which had been passed during Warwick's usurpation; viz. "the pretensed 49th year of the reign of King Henry VI."
Up to the date of their repeal, the young Earl of Warwick, as heir to
the late Duke of Clarence, was *de jure* King of England.   Rot. Parl.
vol. vi. p. 191.

CHAPTER III.

A S keeper of the Northern Marches, the Duke of
Gloucester held for some years the most important military command in England. It was not,
however, till the year 1482, when war broke out
between Edward of England and James III. of
Scotland, that Richard was again afforded an opportunity of displaying that military ability of which,
in his boyhood, he had given such high promise at
Barnet and Tewkesbury. Having resolved on the
invasion of Scotland, Edward intrusted the entire
command of his army, consisting of 25,000 men, to
his brother Gloucester. Henry Earl of Northumberland led the van; Thomas Lord Stanley commanded the rear. The expedition appears to have
been conducted with great ability, and proved to
be eminently successful. Gloucester's first attempt
was upon Berwick, which city he entered without
opposition. The castle, however, proved to be
strong enough to maintain a protracted siege, and
accordingly, leaving Lord Stanley to besiege it with
a force of 4000 men, Richard pushed forward into
the heart of Scotland with the remainder of his

army.   In the mean time, unprepared for so rapid
an advance as that of Gloucester, King James had
shut himself up in Edinburgh Castle.   His only
hope was in his warlike barons, who, disgusted
with the conduct of their unworthy sovereign, withdrew their aid from him in his hour of need.
Gloucester was thus enabled to enter Edinburgh in
triumph.   At the earnest entreaty of the Duke of
Albany, who accompanied him on his march, he
saved the town and inhabitants from fire and sword.
"His entry," says Habington, "was only a specta-
cle of glory, the people applauding the mercy of
an enemy who presented them with a triumph, not
a battle."*   At the same time he displayed a determination which completely overawed the Scottish
people; causing it to be proclaimed by sound of
trumpet, in the different quarters of the city, that,
unless the demands of the King of England were
complied with before the month of September, he
would lay waste the whole kingdom with fire and
sword.   This threat produced the desired effect.
Trembling at the prospect of the disasters which
threatened their country, the Scottish nobles sent
to him to entreat a suspension of arms.   Subsequently a treaty was executed, by one of the articles of which Berwick Castle was delivered up to
the English.   Having thus achieved the objects of
his expedition, the young duke returned to his own

* Habington in Kennet, vol. i p. 476.

country, to receive the thanks of parliament and the applause of his fellow-countrymen.

On the 9th of April 1483, in the forty-second year of his age, died the victor of nine pitched battles, King Edward IV. Valiant almost to rashness, beautiful in person,* majestic in stature, and dangerously fascinating in his manners and address, he united with his outward accomplishments qualities of a higher order, which ought to have rendered his name illustrious. Unfortunately, however, the only atmosphere which he loved was that of pleasure; the only deity which he worshipped was female beauty. "His thoughts," says De Commines, "were always occupied with the ladies, with hunting, and with dress. When he hunted, his custom was to have several tents set up for the ladies, whom he entertained in a magnificent manner."† The enervating delights of the banquet, the pursuit of a new mistress, or the invention of some fashion in dress more graceful or more magnificent than the last, constituted the daily and nightly occupations of the English Sardanapalus. The fascination which he exercised over women may be exemplified by an amusing anecdote related by Holinshed. At a time when his pecuniary

* Philip de Commines, who had more than once conversed with Edward, speaks of him on one occasion as the handsomest prince, and on another occasion as the handsomest man, whom he had ever seen. Mémoires de Commines, vol. i. pp. 239, 374.

† De Commines, tome i. p. 246, tome ii. p. 281.

difficulties compelled him to exact money from his subjects under the name of benevolence, he sent, among other persons, for a wealthy widow, of whom he inquired, with a smile, how much she would subscribe towards the prosecution of the war. Charmed by his· grace and beauty,—" For thy sweet face," said the old lady, "thou shalt have twenty pounds."   As this was double the amount which the young king had expected to obtain from her, he accompanied his thanks by a kiss.   This act of royal condescension was irresistible.   Instead of twenty pounds, the delighted matron promised him forty.*

Vigorous as was Edward's constitution, it gradually yielded to the inroads occasioned by his exceeding indulgence in the pleasures of the table, and the frequency of his amours.   The personal beauty, for which he had been so conspicuous, passed away, and, though not "seized by any known kind of malady,"† it became evident for some time before his death that he was gradually sinking into his grave.   Had his days been providentially prolonged till his son, the Prince of Wales, had attained his majority, his subjects, perhaps, would have had little reason to regret the royal voluptuary.   But at that turbulent period of our history, when the rule of a woman or of a minor almost inevitably

* Holinshed's Chronicles, vol. iii. p. 330.
† Croyl. Chron. Cont. p. 483.

induced a violent struggle for the possession of the sovereign authority, the premature death of King Edward could scarcely fail to be productive of renewed misfortunes and bloodshed to his country, as well as of peril to his children. Eighty years later we find the celebrated John Knox propounding from the pulpit at Edinburgh, in the very presence of the husband of his queen, that God occasionally sets boys and women over a nation to punish it for its crimes. The dangers and inconveniences to be apprehended from the rule of women and minors was the excuse which the Duke of Buckingham subsequently made when he preferred Richard of Gloucester to be his king instead of his legitimate sovereign Edward V. It was perhaps the best excuse which could be made for Richard when he deposed his nephew; perhaps the only excuse for the bishops and mitred abbots who abetted and sanctioned his usurpation.

Fortunately for Edward, he had the satisfaction, at the close of his days, of flattering himself that he had reconciled hatred and envy to one another, and the conviction, vain as it was, soothed him at the last. His death became him better than his life. The closing days of his existence were spent in tender endeavours to secure the future happiness and welfare of his children, in devising means for repairing the injuries which he had inflicted on his subjects, and in humble and penitent attempts to render himself less unworthy of appearing in the presence of his Creator.

The death of his brother Edward naturally effected an extraordinary revolution in the position and fortunes of Richard of Gloucester. It at once opened to him a career in which, by his masterly talents, he was well qualified to play a prominent part, whether for good or for evil. To every reflecting and well-informed person in England, a civil war at this period must have appeared almost inevitable. One individual only there was who, from his exalted rank,—his high reputation as a statesman and a soldier,—his independence of faction,—the friendly terms on which he had ever associated with men of all parties,—his profound knowledge of human character and of the motives of human action, as well as his singular power of concealing his own thoughts and feelings from the scrutiny of others,—was capable of grappling with every emergency, and of thus preserving his country from the horrors of civil war. That man was Richard Duke of Gloucester.

At the time when King Edward breathed his last, the two great opposing parties in the State consisted, on the one hand, of the Woodville faction, supported by the authority and influence of the queen, and, on the other, of the ancient nobility, at the head of whom was a prince of the house of Lancaster, Henry Stafford, Duke of Buckingham.

The queen, during the lifetime of her husband, had pursued a policy, the wisdom of which was now about to be put to the test. Eager to maintain her influence over him so long as he lived, and, in the event of his death, to rule in the name of her son, she had warmly and successfully advocated the principle of curbing the dangerous power of the old nobility by the creation of a new aristocracy. Men had been advanced to the peerage who had little pretension to the honour; the ancient nobility may be said to have been banished from court. The queen more especially delighted to surround herself with her own friends and her own kindred.

This invidious and short-sighted policy naturally threatened to be productive of future evil. So long, indeed, as Edward continued in the fulness and splendour of his power, he had found little difficulty in preventing open contentions between the queen's faction and the irritated barons. But, as his end approached, the fatal consequences, which might result from the undue partiality which he had displayed, began to fill his mind with painful apprehensions. His children, he felt, might be sacrificed to the rage of faction; his first-born might be robbed of his inheritance. It was to the credit of Edward that he had not only ever shown himself a most affectionate father, but, even in his worst days of indolence and sensuality, he had manifested a deep interest in the spiritual as well

as temporal welfare of his offspring.* No time
was now to be lost in remedying the imprudence
of the past; and accordingly, having summoned to
his sick-chamber the leaders of the rival factions,
the dying monarch in the most solemn manner exhorted them, for the sake of the love which they
bore him, and the loyalty which they owed to his
son, to forget their mutual animosities, and to
unite in one endeavour to secure the tranquillity
and well-being of the State. "And therewithal,"
writes Sir Thomas More, "the king, no longer
enduring to sit up, laid him down on his right side,
his face toward them; and none was there present
that could refrain from weeping."†

Thus solemnly appealed to, the rival leaders were
induced to embrace each other, and an ostensible
reconciliation took place. But the ancient families
of England had far too much cause to be offended
and disgusted with the upstart Woodvilles to admit
of its being a lasting one. The grasping and inordinate ambition of the queen's kindred, their
rapid and provoking rise from the position of
simple esquires and gentlewomen to the possession

---

* Sharon Turner has published, from a MS. in the British Museum,
a code of instructions drawn up by King Edward for the guidance of
his son's studies and devotions; a document, scarcely more interesting
as evincing the interest which the king took in his son's welfare, than
as affording a curious picture of the habits and customs of the age.
Hist. of the Middle Ages, vol. iii. p. 342.

† Sir T. More's Richard III. p. 17.

of the proudest honours of the peerage, as well as
the greediness which they had manifested in seeking to monopolize the highest offices in the State
and the wealthiest heiresses in the land, were
offences in the eyes of the old feudal nobility which
could be expiated only by their degradation or
their blood. Through the queen's influence with
her husband, her brother, Anthony Woodville, had
married Elizabeth, the wealthy heiress of Thomas
Lord Scales. Her younger brother John had married the dowager Duchess of Norfolk,—the union
of a youth of nineteen to a woman in her eightieth
year. Thomas Grey, the queen's son by her former
husband, had married the king's niece Anne,
daughter and heiress of Henry Duke of Exeter.
Of the queen's six sisters, five were severally married to the Duke of Buckingham, to the Earls of
Arundel, Essex, Huntingdon, and Lord Strange
of Knokyn. The rapacity of the queen's kindred
had already fomented a formidable rebellion in
England, in which her father, recently created
Earl Rivers, and her brother John, lost their
heads.*   Instead, however, of taking warning

* The insurrection, headed by Robin of Redesdale, in 1469. The
substance of the grievances of which the insurgents complained, was,
" that the king had been too lavish of gifts to the queen's relations and
some others; that through them he had spent church monies, without
repayment; that they had caused him to diminish his household and
charge the commons with great impositions; that they would not suffer
the king's laws to be executed but through them; and that .they had
caused him to estrange the true lords of his blood from his secret coun-

from the past, they persisted in provoking an hostility which effected the change of a dynasty and involved the ruin of their house.

Of the queen's obnoxious relatives, the two highest in power and place, at this period, were Thomas Grey, Marquis of Dorset, the queen's son by her first husband, Sir John Grey; and her splendid and accomplished brother, Anthony Woodville, Earl Rivers. For many reasons the latter was the object of the greatest jealousy and dislike. Preferring him above the proudest barons of the realm, King Edward had sought to obtain for him the hand of Margaret, sister of the King of Scotland, and on another occasion had sanctioned his coming forward as the rival of the king's brother, the Duke of Clarence, for the hand of the heiress of Burgundy. These were unpardonable offences in the eyes of the old nobility. But the barons had not only reason to be jealous of, but also to fear, the power of the Woodvilles. To obtain the guardianship of the young king,—to establish a complete ascendency over his mind,—and by this means to carry out their project of completely crushing the ancient nobility, and obtaining for themselves a monopoly over the highest honours and offices of the State,—were only too obviously the policy and the intention of the queen and her kindred.

cil."—*Harl. MS.* No. 543, quoted in S. Turner's Middle Ages, vol. iii. p. 254.

We have already mentioned that the queen was the main stay of the Woodville faction; the Duke of Buckingham the head of the rival party. But there were two other influential persons, who may be said to have belonged to neither party, who, from their high rank, their integrity, their ability, and experience in the affairs of state, were naturally looked up to and courted by both of the opposing factions. Those persons were the celebrated William Lord Hastings, and Thomas Lord Stanley. The former, uniting the brilliant qualities of the warrior with the wisdom of the statesman and the accomplishments of the courtier, had for many years been the chosen and beloved companion of the late king. He had fought by the side of his royal master on many a field of battle; had cheerfully accompanied him when he was compelled to fly to the Low Countries; and, no less fascinating at the banquet than renowned on the field of battle, was alike his adviser in the closet, the sharer of his pleasures, and the confidant of his amours. The character of Lord Stanley was more reserved, and his nature more cold than that of Hastings. Nevertheless, though Edward apparently loved him less than he loved Hastings, he seems to have been no less trusted and esteemed by the late king. Both of these powerful noblemen were strongly prejudiced against the queen and her kindred, and were therefore likely to join in any constitutional opposition which might be formed for depriving them of the management of affairs. But, on the other hand, they had been personally and devotedly attached to Edward; they had solemnly sworn to him to maintain the rights and interests of his heir; and, accordingly, not only were they likely to prove formidable antagonists in the event of any attempt made to put aside the youthful heir of the house of York, but there can be little doubt that, had the alternative been forced upon them, they would have preferred perishing on the scaffold rather than have failed in their loyalty to the living and their promises to the dead.

At such a crisis it was natural that the thoughts, not only of the two rival factions, but of all moderate men, should turn with anxiety to Richard of Gloucester. His character for wisdom and valour was established beyond all question. No man living was more interested in averting the horrors of civil war. As governor of the Northern Marches he was in command of the largest military force in England. Hitherto, with his usual prudence, Gloucester had abstained from identifying himself with either party; both sides, therefore, were sanguine of obtaining his countenance and support. As for Richard individually, all his prejudices were naturally on the side of the barons. Aware doubtless of this fact, Buckingham, shortly after the death of the king, secretly despatched an express to him, intimating his want of confidence in the government of the queen, and expressing his conviction that he was the proper person to rule the realm during the minority of his nephew. That such was not only the conscientious opinion of Buckingham and Hastings, but the general conviction of the people of England, there seems to be little doubt. Richard, in fact, as the only prince of the house of Plantagenet who had attained the age of manhood, and as the paternal uncle of the youthful monarch, was doubtless, according to precedent, the proper person to be invested with the regency. King Edward, moreover, in his last moments, had shown how great was the sense which he entertained of his brother's integrity, by nominating him the guardian of his sons.*

And what, may be asked, was at this period the true character of Richard of Gloucester? Are we to regard him in the light in which the Tudor chroniclers have painted him,—as not only the convicted perpetrator of past murders, but as the deliberate and cold-blooded projector of future and and still more atrocious crimes? Can it be true that from his boyhood he had been secretly the ambitious plotter,—that he was in reality the wily and unscrupulous villain such as history usually represents him? Can it be true that his virtues were but a name, and his good actions but cloaks for dis-

* Polydore Virgil, p. 171, Camd. Soc. Trans.

simulation and hypocrisy? In a word, are we to believe that he had been lying in wait but till the breath should have quitted the body of his brother Edward, in order to spring upon his remaining victims, and, by means of the most crooked and barbarous policy, seize the crown which was the birthright of another?

Certainly, there is much of this sweeping obloquy of which we are inclined to relieve the memory of this extraordinary prince. Had Richard, in fact, been even the suspected, much less the convicted, villain which our early historians represent him to have been, is it probable that he would have been trusted to the last by men who were not only personally and intimately acquainted with him, but who were also experienced and keen-sighted observers of human character? Is it likely that so shrewd a prince as Edward IV. would in his last moments have confided to him the guardianship of his beloved children,—those children whom Richard had only to put out of the way in order himself to mount the throne? Or, if Buckingham and Hastings had entertained any suspicion of his true character, would they have helped to invest him with an authority which subsequently enabled him to shed their blood on the scaffold, and to seize a crown which Hastings, at least, would have died to preserve for another?

That Richard was deeply impregnated with that

inordinate ambition which was the ruling passion and vice of the Plantagenets,—that he yielded to temptation so soon as the allurement became difficult to resist,—and, lastly, that he possessed himself of the sovereign power by unjustifiable and unpardonable means,—we are not prepared to deny. At present, however, this is not the point at issue. The question we would solve is, at what particular period of his life temptation grew too powerful to be resisted, and consequently diverted him from the path of virtue and honour to that of perfidy and crime. In our own opinion,—which, however, with deference we submit,—Richard, to the close of Edward's reign, had continued to be a loyal subject, a devoted brother, a useful citizen, and an upright man. Even when the death of Edward forced him into a more extended sphere of action, the probability, we think, is that he originally entertained no deeper design than that of obtaining the guardianship of the young king, and, during his minority, the protectorship of the realm. But as he advanced, step by step, towards the accomplishment of these legitimate ends, the complicated difficulties which encountered him, the plots laid by others against his government and person, and the dangerous possession of

"a power too great to keep or to resign,"—

added, no doubt, to his natural and insatiable ambition, and the dazzling temptation of a crown,—

had each their share in inducing him to consult his
own safety by the destruction of others, and to
grasp the glittering prize which was placed within
his reach. That, from the moment in which he
aspired to the protectorship, he brought into play
those powers of deception and dissimulation of
which he was so finished a master, there seems to
be no question. It was not, however, we conceive,
till a later period, that he devised and committed
those blacker acts of blood and treachery which,
after a lapse of two years, were avenged by his
tragical death on the field of Bosworth. To us
Richard figures, at two different periods of his life,
as a different and distinct person. As much as the
Diana of the Greeks differed from the Astarte of
the Carthaginians, and as the Satan of Milton
differs from the cloven-footed bugbear of the nursery, so great does the distinction appear to have
been between the youthful and upright prince who
dispensed even justice at Pontefract and spurned
the gold of King Louis at Picquigny, and the Richard who subsequently became the murderer of his
nephews and the guilty possesser of a crown.*

* Had Richard's designs upon the throne been entertained at so early
a period as has usually been imagined, surely he would have hastened
to London, either during his brother's last illness or else immediately
after his decease, for the purpose of counteracting the measures of his
opponents, courting the suffrages of the citizens of London, and otherwise advancing his ends. Edward, however, died on the 9th of April,
whereas Richard remained in the north till the end of the month, and
did not reach London till the 4th of May.

Of the ability of Richard of Gloucester there can be no more question than there is of the intensity of his ambition or of the profoundness of his dissimulation. His conduct, from the hour when greatness tempted him, till the hour in which he achieved greatness, displays a masterpiece of statecraft. True it is that his policy was tortuous and guilty; but it must be remembered that he had to deal with men as guilty and almost as wily as himself. Moreover, before judging him too severely, we should carefully consider the character of the age in which he lived. It was an age when men were inflamed against each other by feelings of the fiercest vindictiveness; when human life was held at a fearful discount, and when deception was regarded almost as an accomplishment. He lived in the middle ages, when belted knights deemed it a meritorious act to knock out the brains of a defenceless prelate at the altar; in an age, when an abbot went publicly forth with assassins to waylay and murder a brother abbot; and when a Duke of Burgundy suborned men of birth to assassinate a Duke of Orleans in his presence.* Richard, moreover, had lived through a war of extermination, unsur-

* Even at a considerably later period, we find the Cardinal of Lorraine confidently charged with having poisoned the Cardinal d'Armagnac; and, again, Henry III. of France causing the Duc de Guise to be massacred before his face. As Henry gazed on the lifeless but magnificent form which lay at his feet, "Mon Dieu," he calmly said, "*comme il est grand, étant mort !*"

passed perhaps in the annals of ferocious retaliation. From his childhood, he had been conversant with proscriptions, with bloodshed, and deceit. He had not only witnessed the cruelties perpetrated by his brother Edward, and by Margaret of Anjou, —the wholesale slaughter of thousands flying from the field of battle, and the deliberate butchery of the noblest and the bravest on the scaffold,—but he had been accustomed to regard these atrocities as part of a necessary policy. Moreover, it may be questioned whether his guilt in seizing a crown is so heinous as it appears at first sight. We must remember that the throne of England was virtually elective; that the accession of the young in years, or the feeble in mind, was almost certain to provoke a contention for the kingly power; that the king himself was but the head of the barons, and that, in troubled times, the most powerful of the barons looked upon the crown as a prize within the legitimate scope of his ambition.

Assuming it to be true, that, from the time of his brother's decease, Richard secretly aspired to invest himself with the kingly power, the obstacles against which he had to contend must, even to himself, have appeared almost insurmountable. The success which crowned his machinations was amazing. That he should have been able to overcome the powerful Woodville faction, strengthened as it was by the authority of the queen, and by having possession of the king's person.—that he should have been able to crush the scarcely less powerful party of which Hastings and Stanley were the chiefs,—that he should have found the means of duping the people, and intimidating parliament, into an approval of his usurpation; in a word, that, within the short space of eleven weeks after his brother's death, he should have sat on the kingly seat in Westminster Hall, and have accomplished this great object without occasioning a single popular tumult or shedding a drop of plebeian blood,—certainly impresses us with a high opinion of his fearlessness and talents, whatever judgment we may form of his motives and his conduct.

King Edward IV. was the father of two sons, the unfortunate Edward V., now in his thirteenth year, and Richard Duke of York, in his eleventh year.*   At the time of his father's death, the young king was residing at Ludlow Castle on the borders of Wales, under the especial guardianship of his gallant and accomplished uncle, Anthony Earl Rivers.   The Duke of York was residing at court with his mother.

At the first council held after the death of her husband, the widowed queen sat at the head of the table, listening with deep interest to the deliberations.   On one point, at least, all present appear to

* The former was born on the 1st of November 1470, the latter in 1472.

have been agreed. It was decided that no time should be lost in bringing the young king to London, and a day so early as the 4th of May was fixed upon for his coronation. But at this point their good understanding ceased. Rivers, having the government of South Wales, had under his command a considerable military force, at the head of which it was suggested by the queen that her son should be escorted to London. This project met with prompt and strong opposition from certain members of the council, and more especially from Hastings. Between him and Rivers there existed a deadly hostility. Rivers hated Hastings because the late king had preferred him to be governor of Calais and Guines; while Hastings had every reason to attribute to Rivers an imprisonment which he had formerly undergone in the Tower, and his narrow escape from the block. The queen, too, seems to have conceived an invincible aversion to Hastings; believing him to have been too "secretly familiar with her late husband in wanton company." Under these circumstances, the arrival of Rivers in the metropolis at the head of an army would probably have been the signal for sending Hastings to the scaffold. But Hastings had also ample public, as well as private motives, for his opposition. The anxiety of the Woodvilles to fill London with armed men was sufficiently indicative of their intention to maintain their power by force, and consequently could not fail to excite the alarm and jealousy of the accomplished statesman. Accordingly, he boldly denounced the precaution, not only as unnecessary, but as a signal for again lighting up civil war. He even threatened to depart for his government at Calais. Who, he inquired, were the king's foes, against whom it was considered necessary to defend him? Was it his Grace of Gloucester,—was it Lord Stanley,—was it himself? Eventually the arguments and opposition of Hastings and his friends prevailed. It was arranged, by way of compromise, that the young king should be escorted from Ludlow by no larger a force than two thousand followers.*

In the mean time, though still absent at his government in the north, the Duke of Gloucester had been kept duly informed by his partisans of every important event that had transpired at court. That, as yet, he entertained no guilty design of usurping the sovereign authority, we have already expressed our conviction. But, on the other hand, that he was secretly bent on obtaining possession of the king's person and the protectorship of the realm, and by these means crushing the powerful and aspiring Woodvilles, seems scarcely to admit of a doubt. Accordingly, no sooner had he concerted his plans, than he proceeded to carry them into execution with that astuteness and secresy,

* Croyl. Chron. Cont. p. 485.

which henceforth we shall find characterizing all
the actions of this extraordinary man. Every step
which he took was calculated to remove suspicion
from himself, and to acquire for him the confidence
of others. To the queen he addressed a letter of
condolence, consoling her with the assurance of his
speedy arrival in London, and promising "all duty,
fealty, and due obedience to his king and lord,
Edward V."* He even went so far as to write
"lovingly" to her detested kindred.† To the world
he gave out, that his absence from his government
was only temporary, and had no other object than
to enable him to do homage to his young nephew
at his coronation. When at length it suited him to
take his departure from the north, he was attended
only by a small though chosen cavalcade, consisting of six hundred knights and esquires. During
his progress towards the south, he manifested, in
the most amiable manner, his loyalty to the living
and his reverence for the dead. At the time, probably, he was sincere in both. The gentlemen of
Yorkshire were summoned to swear allegiance to
his nephew;—"himself," we are told, "being the
first to take that oath, which soon after he was the
first to violate."‡ In the large towns through

* Croyl. Chron. Cont. p. 486.

† Sir T. More's Richard III. p. 23.

‡ Polydore Virgil, lib. xxv. p. 685, and Camd. Soc. Trans. p. 173;
Croyl. Chron. Cont. p. 486.

which he passed, he caused requiems to be sung for the repose of the soul of the late king; and, at York especially, "performed a solemn funeral service, the same being accompanied with plenteous tears."* Every appearance of military display seems to have been sedulously avoided. His retinue of knights and esquires were arrayed in the garb of mourning. He himself wore that air of humility and grief, which was only too well calculated to deceive mankind.

In the mean time, after having waited at Ludlow to celebrate St. George's day with due solemnity, the young king set out, accompanied by his uncle, Earl Rivers, and his half-brother, Sir Richard Grey. Surrounded by those nearest allied to him in blood, and by faces endeared to him since infancy, a splendid future, to all appearance, lay before him. As he rode on to take possession of the throne of the Plantagenets, little could he have anticipated the bitter reverse which was to consign him to the gloom of the dungeon and to the grasp of the assassin! But already the black clouds were gathering over his head. The royal cavalcade had proceeded as far as Northampton, when information reached Rivers and Grey that the Duke of Gloucester was approaching with his retinue. Rivers took the precaution of sending forward the young king to Stony Stratford, a town thirteen miles nearer to

* Croyl. Chron. Cont. p. 486; Sir T. More's Richard III. p. 134.

the metropolis, while he himself remained behind with Grey at Northampton, with the ostensible object of paying their respects to Richard as first prince of the blood, and submitting to his "will and discretion" the ceremonials which they proposed to adopt on the occasion of the king's entry into his capital.

Disappointed as Gloucester must have been at not meeting with his nephew, he nevertheless received Rivers and Grey with the greatest courtesy and apparent kindness. He invited them to sup at his table, and the evening, we are told, passed "in very pleasant conversation."* While they were thus agreeably employed, an addition was unexpectedly made to the party by the arrival of a fourth person, Henry Duke of Buckingham, who, though he had married a sister of the queen, of all men most detested the Woodvilles. The duke reached Northampton at the head of three hundred horsemen, thus swelling the military train of Richard to a rather formidable number. The news which he brought to Gloucester from court was of the most serious importance. The queen and her kindred had thrown off the mask; her brother, the Marquis of Dorset, had seized the king's treasure, and, moreover, as admiral of England, had given orders for the equipment of a naval force. The news was in all probability far from

* Croyl. Chron. Cont. p. 486.

being unpalatable to Richard. It was clear that the Woodvilles must henceforth stand convicted of having been the first to break the laws, thus giving him an advantage of which he instantly perceived the importance. Indeed, but for this imprudent conduct on the part of the Woodvilles, he would have found it difficult to justify to the world the act of violence which, on that memorable night, he projected with Buckingham.

But whatever reflections the tidings brought by Buckingham may have given rise to in the mind of Gloucester, the remainder of the evening passed away in the greatest harmony. The fact is somewhat remarkable, that, of the four men who on that evening pledged each other in the wine-cup at Northampton, and endeavoured to cajole one another with professions of friendship, one and all were nearly allied to the reigning monarch. Gloucester and Rivers were his uncles; Buckingham was his uncle by marriage; Sir Richard Grey, as we have said, was his half-brother. Within little more than two years, all four perished by a violent death, either on the scaffold or on the field of battle.

But to return to our narrative. Rivers and Grey had no sooner retired to rest, than Gloucester and Buckingham shut themselves up in a private apartment, where they passed the greater part of the night in secret consultation. The recent acts of the Woodvilles,—the anxiety which they had betrayed to escort the young king to London at the head of a powerful military force,—the seizure of the royal treasure,—and, lastly, the conduct of Rivers in hurrying on the king to Stony Stratford, left not a doubt of the nature of their ambitious designs. Not a moment was to be lost in counteracting them. The bold measure of seizing the person of the king was finally resolved upon. Before day dawned the conspirators had decided on their plan of operation: their orders were promptly given, and as promptly obeyed. To prevent all communication between Rivers and the king was of course their first object. Accordingly, horsemen were sent out to patrol the roads between Northampton and Stony Stratford; the keys of the hostelry were brought to Gloucester; not a servant was allowed to quit the place.*

The consternation of Rivers and Grey, on discovering the fatal snare into which they had fallen, may be readily imagined. They did their best, however, to conceal their emotion, as together, and apparently in perfect amity, the four lords set off on horseback for Stony Stratford. It was not till that town appeared in sight that Gloucester threw off the mask. Suddenly Rivers and Grey were arrested by his orders and hurried off, under the charge of an escort, towards the north. Glouces-

* Sir T. More's Richard III. p. 24.

ter and Buckingham then rushed forward to the king's quarters. With the utmost promptitude, the king's chamberlain, Sir Thomas Vaughan, his preceptor, Dr. Alcock, Bishop of Worcester, and others of his trusted and confidential servants, were arrested and hurried into confinement. Almost before the young king had time to shed a tear for the misfortune which had befallen his nearest relatives and friends, Gloucester and Buckingham, with every outward mark of homage and affection, were kneeling at his feet. The separation from those he loved seems to have been bitterly felt by him. "At this dealing," says Sir Thomas More, "he wept, and was nothing content; but it booted not."*

In due time, attended respectfully by the two dukes, the young king made his public entry into London. His servants and retinue were clad in deep mourning. Edward alone appeared conspicuous in the cavalcade, habited in royal robes of purple velvet. By his side rode his uncle Gloucester, bareheaded. Near Hornsey they were met by the lord-mayor and aldermen in their scarlet robes, followed by five hundred citizens on horseback, in purple-coloured gowns. As the gallant procession wended its way through the streets of London, Gloucester repeatedly, and with great apparent enthusiasm, pointed out his royal nephew

* Sir T. More's Richard III. p. 27.

to the populace. "Behold," he said, "your prince and sovereign lord!"* The love and reverence which he displayed towards his nephew excited universal admiration. His recent violent seizure of the hateful Woodvilles had lost him none of his popularity. "He was on all hands," says Sir Thomas More, "accounted the best, as he was the first, subject in the kingdom."† Followed by the blessings and acclamations of his subjects, the young king was conducted in the first instance to the palace of the Bishop of London, near St. Paul's Cathedral, where he received the homage and congratulations of his nobles. Some days afterwards he was escorted to the royal apartments in the Tower.

The arrest of Rivers and Grey produced the effect desired by Richard. The queen and her kindred gave up the contest in despair; Elizabeth, with her second son and her fair daughters, flew affrighted to the sanctuary at Westminster, where she was subsequently joined by her son, the Marquis of Dorset. When, shortly before daybreak, the Lord Chancellor Rotheram, Archbishop of York, repaired to her with the great seal, he witnessed, we are told, a most painful scene of "heaviness, rumble, haste, and business." The royal servants were hurrying into the sanctuary, bearing

* Fabyan, p. 608; Hall, p. 351.

† Sir T. More's Life of Edward V. in Kennet, vol. i. p. 486.

chests, household-stuffs, and other valuable goods.* The queen herself "sat alow on the rushes, all desolate and dismayed."

When at length the day dawned, and the archbishop looked forth upon the Thames, he beheld the river covered with boats, full of the Duke of Gloucester's servants, "watching that no one should go to sanctuary."† Some intention there seems to have been, on the part of the queen's friends, of opposing force to force.‡ The vigilance of Hastings, however, and the great interest which he had contrived to establish with the citizens of London, effectually prevented any commotion.

Thus, within the space of a few days, had Richard of Gloucester raised himself to be the foremost person in the kingdom, the "observed of all observers." Society blessed him for having prevented the horrors of civil war; the commonalty admired him for the extraordinary zeal he professed for the interests of his nephew; while the ancient nobility, delighted at the fatal blow which he had struck at the power of the Woodvilles, flocked to him with offers of service and enthusiastic expressions of applause. "He was suddenly fallen into so great trust," writes Sir Thomas More, "that, at the council next assembled, he was made the only man

* Sir T. More's Life of Edward V. in Kennet, vol. i. p. 485.

† Sir T. More's Richard III. pp. 30, 31 ; Hall, p. 350.

‡ Croyl. Chron. Cont. p. 487.

chosen, and thought most meet to be protector of
the king and his realm."* So guarded had been
Richard's conduct, so warily and wisely had he
pursued his object, that his secret designs, whatever they may have been, continued to be unsus-
pected even by the most suspicious. The levees
which he held at his princely mansion, Crosby
Place, in Bishopsgate Street, were crowded by the
noblest and wisest of the land. The young king
was left "in a manner desolate."† The spiritual
lords seem to have vied with the temporal lords in
doing honour to Richard. The coveted protectorship may almost be said to have been forced upon
him. Following a precedent in the case of Humphrey Duke of Gloucester, who had been appointed
protector during the minority of Henry VI., the
council of state, "with the consent and good will
of all the lords,"‡ invested Richard with the dignity. No single individual seems to have objected
to the appointment; the popular feeling in his
favour appears to have been universal; so much so
that the concurrence of parliament seems to have
been considered not only as unessential, but, for the
time, to have been absolutely disregarded. Even
Hastings, affectionately as he watched over the interests of the young king, and deeply read as he

* Sir T. More's Richard III. p. 35.
† Ibid. p. 66.
‡ Croyl. Chron. Cont. p. 488.

was in human nature, could discover no grounds except for congratulation in the elevation of Richard of Gloucester.* Moreover, the active preparations which were apparently being made for his nephew's coronation had the effect of averting suspicion, and aiding to increase his popularity with the vulgar. Even at this late period, it seems questionable whether Richard entertained any serious thoughts of deposing his brother's son, much less of procuring his assassination.

On the 19th of May we find the young king addressing the assembled peers in parliament. The 22nd of June, the feast of the Nativity of St. John the Baptist, was the day fixed upon for the solemnization of the ceremony. The coronation-robes were prepared. The barons of England, who had been summoned from all parts of the realm, "came thick" to swear allegiance to their sovereign. The "pageants and subtleties were in making day and night." The viands for the great banquet in Westminster had been actually purchased from the purveyors.†

As the day, which had been fixed upon for the coronation, drew near, doubtless many perplexing thoughts passed through the mind of the protector. By the law of the land, the protectorship would

* Croyl. Chron. Cont. p. 489.

† Sir T. More's Richard III. pp. 69, 70; Harl. MS. (No. 433, Art. 1651), quoted in Halsted's Rich. III. vol. ii. p. 68.

cease so soon as that ceremony had been performed; young Edward would then, as anointed king, assume the sovereign power. No option therefore remained to Gloucester, but either to descend with a good grace into his former station as a subject, or else to stifle every compunction of conscience, and seize the crown which he had solemnly sworn to defend for another.

To a man of Richard's aspiring nature and boundless ambition, the prospect of exchanging almost sovereign power for the subordinate rank and honours of a mere prince of the blood, must have appeared intolerable. Moreover, putting the question of ambition altogether aside, his descent from power must necessarily entail imminent personal danger both on himself and his friends. Not only had he offended the Woodvilles beyond all hope of reconciliation, but his recent seizure of Edward's person at Stony Stratford, and the arrest and imprisonment of the king's dearest friends and nearest relatives, were acts which no sovereign was likely to forget or forgive. Let the crown once descend upon the brow of young Edward, and who could doubt but that the queen-mother and her kindred would bring all their influence into play to prejudice him against their arch-enemy, and that Richard's ruin, and perhaps his death on the scaffold, would be the result?

It may be argued that it was the interest, as well

as the duty of the protector, to establish his nephew firmly on the throne; to release Lord Rivers and Sir Richard Grey from imprisonment; to identify himself with the fortunes of the queen and her powerful kindred; and to render himself as trusted and beloved by Edward V. as he had formerly been by Edward IV. But such a step would have completely stultified the revolution which he had so recently effected. Moreover, it would have been the grossest act of treachery towards the nobles who had assisted him in destroying the power of the Woodvilles, and in all probability would have hurried Buckingham, Hastings, and others to the block. These misfortunes, indeed, might possibly have been prevented by an appeal to arms; but no greater disaster could have befallen England at this period than a renewal of the civil war, a catastrophe which the protector seems to have been resolved at all hazards to prevent.

But whatever may have been the motives which finally determined Richard of Gloucester to usurp the throne, no one can question the consummate cunning and ability with which he carried his plans into execution.

The persons, whose opposition he had the greatest reason to dread, were Buckingham and Hastings on the part of the old feudal aristocracy, and Rivers and Grey on the side of the queen and her kindred. Buckingham, a man of great ambition and avarice, the protector seems to have found little difficulty in corrupting. The duke, moreover, was too much detested by the Woodvilles, and had too much reason to dread their vengeance, not to enter heartily into any scheme which promised to strip them of power. Hastings, as we shall presently discover, proved incorruptible. As for Rivers and Grey, they were already in the toils of the protector, and he was resolved that they should never escape from them. As it was never the policy of the protector to shed blood unnecessarily, the probability seems to be that it was the discovery of plots for the release of these unhappy noblemen, and also, as Richard himself confidently asserted, the existence of a deep-laid conspiracy against his authority, which subsequently induced him to sacrifice their lives in order to secure his own.

Hastings, as we have seen, was resolved at all hazards to stand by the son of his dead master. He was, at this time, apparently reconciled to the queen and the Woodvilles, and deeply implicated in their conspiracies against the protector. From his boyhood Richard had been accustomed to regard Hastings with admiration, as the most accomplished courtier and soldier of his age. He is even said to have loved him more than any other living man; and certainly, of all living men, he would seem to have been the last whom Richard would wantonly have consigned to the scaffold. He resolved, therefore, in the first instance, to sound Hastings, and, if possible, to induce him to embrace his views. The person whom he employed on this delicate service was one Catesby, an able and designing lawyer, whom Hastings had admitted to his confidence. Catesby's propositions, carefully as they were worded, could not fail to startle Hastings. The times, Catesby said, were pregnant with danger, both to the throne and to the commonwealth; it was of vital importance that an "experienced person and brave commander" should take the helm of government; and who so fitted to be a pilot in stormy times, both from his position as first prince of the blood, and from his ability and firmness, as the Duke of Gloucester? Not, argued Catesby, that the protector and his friends had any intention of prejudicing the interests of the young monarch, much less of supplanting him on the throne. The simple proposition was that the protector should wear the crown till the young king had attained the age of twenty-five, at which time, it was presumed, he would be capable of governing the realm as "an able and efficient king." The veil with which Richard sought to disguise his intended usurpation, was too flimsy to conceal his real purpose. With a disinterestedness, which reflects the highest credit on his memory, Hastings not only refused to listen to the proposition, but replied to Catesby in such "terrible words," as could not fail to give deep offence to the protector.* Catesby carried back the reply to his employer, and from that moment, doubtless, the head of Hastings was doomed to fall upon the scaffold.

* Sir T. More's Richard III. p. 69; More's Life of Edward V. in Kennet, vol. i. p. 493.

CHAPTER IV.

ON Friday, the 13th of June 1483, there took place that memorable council in the Tower of London, which the pen of Sir Thomas More has so graphically described, and which the genius of Shakspeare has immortalized. At the council-table sat, among other lords, the Archbishop of York, Lord Hastings, Lord Stanley, and Dr. Morton, Bishop of Ely, afterwards cardinal and Archbishop of Canterbury. The three latter had been the personal friends of the late king; all three were devoted to the interests of his son.

It was nine o'clock in the morning when the protector entered the council-chamber and took his seat at the head of the table. He had played the sluggard, he said pleasantly; he hoped the lords would forgive him for being late. His countenance retained its usual imperturbable expression. Not a word nor gesture of uneasiness escaped him. He even appeared to be in the highest spirits possible; jesting with the Bishop of Ely on the excellence of his strawberries, for which the garden of his episcopal residence, Ely House in Holborn, was famous.

> "My lord of Ely, when I was last in Holborn,
>   I saw good strawberries in your garden there;
>   I do beseech you send for some of them."
>
> *King Richard III* Act. iii. Sc. 4.

The bishop accordingly despatched a servant for the fruit. In the mean time, having excused his absence to the members of the council, the protector retired awhile from the apartment, desiring the lords to proceed with their deliberations. When, in about an hour, he returned, his manner and appearance had undergone a complete and painful change. On his countenance rage, hatred, and vengeance are said to have been forcibly and terribly depicted. A brief but awful pause ensued, during which the protector sat at the council-table, contracting his brows and biting his lips. At length he started up. Closely allied as he was, he said, to the king, and intrusted with the administration of government, what punishment did those persons deserve who compassed and imagined his destruction? The lords of the council, completely confounded, remained silent. At length, Hastings, emboldened perhaps by their long friendship, and the affection which the protector was believed to entertain for him, ventured to reply to the infuriated prince. " Surely, my lord," he said, " they deserve to be punished as heinous traitors, whoever they be." At these words the rage of the protector seemed to increase. "Those traitors," he exclaimed, boldly accusing the queen, "are the sorceress, my brother's wife, and his mistress, Jane Shore: see how by their sorcery and witchcraft they have miserably destroyed my body!" And therewith, writes Sir Thomas More, "he plucked up his doublet-sleeve to his elbow upon his left arm; where he showed a werish withered arm and small."* The lords of the council looked at each other in terror and amazement. Again Hastings was the first to attempt to pacify him. "Certainly, my lord," he said, "*if* they have indeed done any such thing, they deserve to be both severely punished." "And do you answer me," thundered the protector, "with *ifs* and *ands?* I tell thee, traitor, they have done it, and thou hast joined with them in this villany; I swear by St. Paul I will not dine before your head be brought to me!"†

At this instant the protector struck the table furiously with his clenched hand, on which the guard, crying "Treason! treason!" rushed violently into the apartment. A scene of indescribable confusion

---

* This is, apparently, another of those imaginary personal deformities which vulgar report or political malignancy formerly delighted to attribute to Richard of Gloucester. If, as has been asserted, his left shoulder was somewhat lower than the right, it may not improbably have given rise to this additional calumny. See ante, pp. 75—78.

† Sir. T. More's Richard III. pp. 70—73; More's Life of Edward V. in Kennet, vol. i. pp. 493—4.

followed. Lord Stanley, the Archbishop of York, the Bishop of Ely, and other lords of the council, were immediately arrested and carried off to different prison-rooms. In the *mêlée* Stanley received a violent blow on the head from a pole-axe, which sent the blood streaming down his ears. But it was in Hastings that all the rage of the protector is said to have centred. " I arrest thee, traitor," he repeated, " and by St. Paul I will not dine till thy head be off!" Hastings accordingly was seized and dragged to the green in front of the Tower chapel; a priest was hurriedly obtained to receive his confession; a log of wood, provided for the repair of the chapel, served as a block. Thus perished the wise, the brilliant and fascinating Hastings! A more honourable fate awaited his remains. His head and body were conveyed to Windsor, where, in the royal chapel of St. George, they were placed by the side of the great king whom he had formerly so loyally and affectionately served, and the rights of whose son he had died in his endeavours to defend.*

---

*Sir T. More's Richard III. pp. 73, 74 ; More's Life of Edward V. in Kennet, vol. i. p. 494. It appears by Hastings' will, dated 27th June 1481, that the late king, Edward IV., had formerly expressed an affectionate wish that Hastings should be buried near him at Windsor. "And forasmuch as the king, of his abundant grace, for the true service that I have done, and at the least intended to have done to his grace, hath willed and offered me to be buried in the church or chapel of St. George at Windsor, in a place by his grace assigned, in which college his grace is disposed to be buried, I therefore bequeath my

In the mean time, the queen-dowager, much to the annoyance of the protector, had persisted in detaining her younger son, the Duke of York, in the sanctuary at Westminster. As Richard unquestionably displayed great anxiety to withdraw him from thence, the detractors of the protector are not to be blamed, if, from this circumstance, they draw a not unreasonable inference that he already contemplated, not only the dethronement of one brother, but the murder of both. But, on the one hand, the charge, thus preferred, rests upon mere assumption; whereas, on the other hand, Richard had not only excellent state reasons for wishing to withdraw his nephew from the influence of his mother and her kindred, but those reasons had been solemnly deliberated at the council-table, and pronounced to be unanswerable. The public had declared the Woodvilles to be the enemies of the State, and therefore improper parties to have the

simple body to be buried in the said chapel and college in the said place, &c."—*Testamenta Vetusta*, vol. i. pp. 368-9. " I bequeath my body," runs the last will of Queen Elizabeth Woodville, " to be buried with the body of my lord, at Windsor, according to the will of my said lord and mine, without pompous interring or costly expenses."—*Ibid.* vol. i. p. 25. There is something not only touchingly striking, but tending to redeem the character of King Edward in our eyes, that the friend who was most intimately acquainted with his failings, and the wife who had forgiven him so many infidelities, should have recorded their solemn wish that, in accordance with the express desire of the late king, their dust might mingle with his. A copy of King Edward's own will, the existence of which was formerly questioned, will be found in the Excerpta Historica, p. 366.

charge of the person and education of the heir presumptive to the throne.   It was argued at the council-table, and with sober reason, that the young king had not only a kingly, but a natural right, to insist on enjoying the companionship of his own brother,—that the queen's detention of the Duke of York in sanctuary was a tacit libel on the government of the protector,—that it was calculated to excite a popular apprehension that the king's life was in danger,—that it tended to occasion scandal at foreign courts,—that, should the young king happen to die, his successor on the throne would be left in most improper hands,—and lastly, it was insisted how great would be the increase of scandal, both at home and abroad, should the king walk at his coronation unsupported by the presence of his only brother.*

Richard, it is said, but for the opposition which he encountered from the Archbishops of Canterbury and York, would have taken his nephew out of sanctuary by force.   Five hundred years, they said, had passed, since St. Peter, attended by multitudes of angels, had descended from heaven in the night, and had consecrated the ground on which were built the church and sanctuary of Westminster.†

---

* More's Edward V. in Kennet, vol. i. pp. 486–7.

† It would appear that a cope, said to have been worn by St. Peter on the occasion, was at this time preserved in Westminster Abbey, as a "proof" of the saint's visitation.   More's Hist. of Richard III. p. 40.

Since then, they added, no king of England had dared to violate that sanctuary, and such an act of desecration would doubtless draw down the just vengeance of heaven on the whole kingdom. Eventually it was decided, that Cardinal Bourchier, Archbishop of Canterbury, should proceed with some of the temporal peers to the sanctuary, and endeavour to reason the queen into a compliance with the wishes of the council. For a considerable time the unhappy mother remained obdurate. Being assured, however, that force would be resorted to if necessary, she was at length induced to bring forth the royal boy and to present him to the members of the council. "My lord," she said to the archbishop, "and all my lords now present, I will not be so suspicious as to mistrust your truths."* Nevertheless, at the moment of parting, a presentiment of the dark fate which awaited her beloved child appears to have flashed across her mind. "Farewell," she said, "mine own sweet son; God send you good keeping; let me kiss you once ere yet you go, for God knoweth when we shall kiss together again." And therewith she kissed him, and blessed him, turned her back and wept, and went her way, leaving the child weeping as fast.† The boy, it appears, was delivered by the queen to the archbishop, the lord-chancellor, and "many

* Sir T. More's Edward V. in Kennet, vol. i. p. 491.
† More's Hist. of Richard III. p. 62.

other lords temporal," by whom he was conducted to the centre of Westminster Hall, where he was received by the Duke of Buckingham. At the door of the Star Chamber he was met by the protector, who, running towards him with open arms, kissed him with great apparent affection. "Now welcome," he said, "my lord, with all my heart." And thereupon, writes Sir Thomas More, "forthwith they brought him to the king, his brother, into the bishop's palace at St. Paul's, and from thence, through the city, honourably into the Tower, out of which, after that day, they never came abroad."*

The protector, by this time, held in durance all the most influential persons from whom he had reason to anticipate opposition in carrying out his ambitious views. Supposing him, indeed, to have been bent on usurping the sovereign authority, his nephews continued to be formidable obstacles in his way, but they were entirely in his power. In order to found a dynasty, it was of course expedient to extirpate the male heirs of his late brother, Edward IV. But, even though Richard were the bloodthirsty and unscrupulous monster which history usually represents him to have been, it was manifestly not his policy, at this time, to call to his aid

* Sir T. More's Rich. III. p. 62; More's Edward V. in Kennet, vol. i. p. 491. Letter, dated London, 21st June 1483, addressed to Sir William Stoner, knight, by Simon Stallworthe. Excerpta Historica, pp. 12, et seq. See post, p. 126, note.

the services of the midnight assassin. Whatever may have been his scruples in other respects, his authority as yet rested on too insecure a basis to permit his name to be associated with the crime of murder. Accordingly, he seems to have eagerly embraced an expedient, which, at the same time that it relieved him from the commission of a fearful crime, promised to lend a colour of justice to his usurpation.

At the time when Edward IV. breathed his last, there were interposed, between the Duke of Gloucester and the succession, the two sons and the five daughters of the late king, and the son and daughter of the late Duke of Clarence. But, in those turbulent times, when the interests of society rendered absolutely necessary the rule of an energetic monarch in order to avert the horrors of anarchy, there was perhaps not a baron in England so romantic as to have raised his banner for the purpose of exalting a female to the throne. A people, who, little more than eighty years previously, had tacitly declared the monarchy of England to be an elective one, by preferring Henry of Lancaster to their legitimate sovereign, Richard II., could scarcely be expected to uphold, in times of almost unprecedented difficulty, the claims of a girl and a minor. Virtually, therefore, the only individuals who stood in the way of Richard were the two sons of his brother Edward, and the young Earl of

Warwick, the son of his brother Clarence. But Warwick had already been set aside by the act of parliament which had included him in the attainder of his father, and accordingly, as far as the succession in the male line was in question, Edward V. and his brother were the only obstacles to the protector, in the ambitious course which he was now evidently pursuing.

It was in this, his hour of difficulty and need, that there arrayed himself on the side of the protector, a man whose high position in the church, whose long experience in state affairs, and whose profound knowledge of the law, rendered him a most valuable auxiliary. This person was Robert Stillington, Bishop of Bath and Wells, whose industry and eminent talents had, in the late reign, raised him from the plebeian ranks to the episcopal bench, and to the lord-chancellorship of England. He had quitted the university with a high reputation for learning. The applause with which he took his degree of Doctor of Laws has been especially recorded. To King Edward IV. he had lain under the deepest obligations. By that monarch he had been successively advanced to the archdeaconry of Taunton, the bishopric of Bath and Wells, the keepership of the Privy Seal, and the lord-chancellorship. The latter appointment he held from the 8th of June 1467, to the 8th of June 1473, when ill health is said to have com-

pelled him to resign the seals. That, while out
of office, he was not also out of favour, may be
presumed by King Edward selecting him, two
years afterwards, to preside over a secret and not
very dignified mission to the court of Brittany.
When, in pursuance of his ruthless purpose of ex-
tirpating the house of Lancaster, Edward sought to
entrap the young Earl of Richmond, afterwards
Henry VII., into his power, Bishop Stillington was
chosen as the person best qualified to induce the
Duke of Brittany, either by cajolery or bribes, to
deliver up the exile to his arch-enemy. Whether
the ill-success, which the ex-chancellor encountered
on this occasion, prejudiced him in the eyes of his
sovereign, or whether, as seems not impossible, he
had implicated himself in the treason of Warwick
and Clarence, certain it is that he was subjected to
persecution and disgrace. He was charged with
having broken his oath of allegiance;* and,
although the fact exists on official record that a
solemn tribunal, composed of the lords spiritual
and temporal, eventually acquitted him of the
charge, he is said to have not only suffered imprisonment, but to have been forced to pay a considerable sum as the price of his release.† According to De Commines, a well-informed contemporary,

* "Post et contra juramentum fidelitatis suæ."—*Rymer's Fœdera*, vol.
xii. p. 66.

† De Commines, tome ii. p. 156.

the treatment which the bishop met with on this
occasion so rankled in his mind, that, years afterwards, he visited on the innocent children of his
royal benefactor, the injustice which he imagined
he had encountered at the hands of their parent.*

From the time of Stillington's disgrace, till
Richard was in the midst of his designs on the
protectorship, if not on the throne, we lose sight
of the discontented prelate. Then it was, however, that he not only reappeared on the stage as
the zealous supporter of the protector, but divulged,
or pretended to divulge, a secret of such vital importance, that, if its truth could be established, it
would certainly go far to justify Richard in his
designs on the throne. According to the account
promulgated at the time, the gravity of which rests
entirely upon the testimony of the bishop, the late
king, previously to his romantic marriage with
Elizabeth Woodville, had fallen in love with the
Lady Eleanor Boteler,† daughter of the Earl of

* De Commines, tome ii. p. 244.

† This lady is said to have been the widow of Thomas Boteler, Lord
Sudley, and daughter of John Talbot, Earl of Shrewsbury, by Catherine, daughter of Humphrey Stafford, Duke of Buckingham.   Buck
in Kennet, vol. i. p. 562; Hist. Doubts, Walpole's Works, vol.
ii. p. 248.   The identity, however, has never been proved.   One
of our historians even goes so far as to question whether such a person
ever existed.   See Lingard's Hist. of England, vol. iv. p. 235, note, ed.
1849.   The curious in such matters may also perhaps find researches
assisted by referring to Dugdale's Baronage, vol. i. pp. 331-2 & 596, and
vol. ii. p. 235; Rot. Parl. vol. vi. p. 441; Croyl. Chron. p. 489; and
Sir E. Brydges' Peerage, vol. iii. p. 19.   There is one great difficulty

Shrewsbury. Failing in his attempt to corrupt her virtue, Edward, it was said, secretly made her his wife. According to the bishop, he himself performed the ceremony, and was the sole witness present on the occasion.*

Whether such a marriage was ever really solemnized, it is now impossible to determine. Certainly there are many circumstances which render it in the highest degree improbable. That an event of such importance should have been kept a profound secret for twenty years, is of itself extremely unlikely. And yet, that no suspicion of it had hitherto got abroad, there can be little question. Had the contrary been the case, the sovereigns of Europe would never have consented to contract their children in marriage with those of Edward; neither can we doubt but that Clarence and Warwick, when they rebelled against his authority, would have availed themselves of their knowledge of so important a fact, which, inasmuch as it bastardized the children of his elder brother, would have left Clarence the nearest heir to the throne. Moreover, there are other circumstances,—such as no witnesses having apparently been examined, and no

opposed to the view which Buck and Walpole take in regard to the lady's identity; viz. that the name of the daughter of John Earl of Shrewsbury, who married Thomas Boteler, Lord Sudley, was not Eleanor, but Anne. She was left a widow till 1473, nine years after Edward had married Elizabeth Woodville.

* De Commines, tome ii. p. 157.

evidence produced, as well as the suspicious fact of the alleged marriage having been kept a secret till those who might have disproved it, were in their graves,—which tend to throw discredit on the bishop's statement. True it is, that parliament subsequently pronounced the marriage, or pre-contract, between the late king and the Lady Eleanor Boteler to have been proved, and, in consequence, bastardized his children.* But the document on which the act of parliament was founded, is known to have been drawn up by the unfriendly Stillington; † and, moreover, the attestation which one parliament declared to be valid, another parliament, in the succeeding reign, declared to be false and worthless. The judges even went so far as to pronounce the former act to be a scandalous cal-

---

* Rot. Parl. vol. vi. p. 241. The reader must on no account confound, as Sir Thomas More would seem to have done, the Lady Eleanor Boteler with a once famous mistress of Edward IV., Elizabeth Lucy, by whom he is said to have had an illegitimate son, Arthur Plantagenet, Viscount l'Isle. The Lady Eleanor is, in fact, the only person with whom we have to concern ourselves as regards the abstract question of King Edward's former marriage. The act of parliament, which subsequently bastardized the children of the late king, expressly defines, that at the time of his "pretended marriage" with Elizabeth Woodville, "and before and long time after, the said King Edward was, and stood married and troth plight to one Dame Eleanor Boteler, *daughter of the old Earl of Shrewsbury.*"—*Rot. Parl.* ut supra. Elizabeth Lucy, on the other hand, is said to have been the daughter of one Wyat of Southampton, "a mean gentleman, if he were one," and the wife of one Lucy, "as mean a man as Wyat."—*Buck in Kennet,* vol. i. p. 565.

† Lingard's Hist. of Eng. p. 573, Appendix.

umny, and, by the adoption of an unprecedented departure from parliamentary usage, prevented its being perpetuated on the statute-book. It was further proposed to summon Stillington to the bar of parliament. By some means, however, he contrived to obtain a pardon from his sovereign, and escaped the threatened inquiry into his conduct.*

Whether Stillington, presuming him to have been guilty, was stimulated by the thirst for revenge which has been attributed to him; whether, by earning the gratitude of Richard, he hoped to recover his former high position in the State; or whether, as is possible, he may have considered that by putting aside the young king and his brother, he was averting great disasters from his country, must of course be a matter of mere conjecture. According to De Commines, a desire to elevate, to a far higher position than his birth entitled him to, an illegitimate son to whom he was much attached, was the principal motive of the bishop. The youth is said to have aspired to the hand of the most illustrious maiden in the land, the Princess Elizabeth, afterwards Queen of England. The bishop abetted the aspirations of his son, and, as a reward for aiding Richard in his designs on the throne, is said to have obtained a promise from him, that so soon as the law should have reduced the daughters of the late king to the position of

* Lingard's Hist. of Eng. p. 575, Appendix.

private gentlewomen, his son should marry the
princess. In the mean time, the protector took the
young man into favour, and sent him on a mission
beyond sea. A different fortune, however, awaited
him from that which he had anticipated. The ship
in which he sailed was captured off the coast of
Normandy, and the youth was sent a prisoner to
the French capital. Whatever may have been the
offence with which he was charged, he was examined before the parliament at Paris, and thrown
into the prison of the *Petit Châtelet.* Here, it is
said, he died of want and neglect. Not impossibly,
however, some zealous English exile, eager to avert
the indignity which threatened the house of Plantagenet, may have found means to induce the func-
tionaries of the prison to shorten, by a more summary process, the existence of the aspiring youth.*

The subsequent story of Bishop Stillington, no
less than that of his past career, tends to the conviction that he was little better than the restless
and ambitious priest, such as he is represented in
the pages of De Commines. Nearly thirty years
after he had sat on the woolsack as lord-chancellor,
we find the veteran priest supporting the flimsy
pretensions of Lambert Simnel, and consequently
compelled to fly the sanctuary in the University of
Oxford. The university consented to deliver him
up to Henry VII., on condition that his life should

* De Commines, tome ii. p. 245.

be spared.　He died in durance in Windsor Castle, in the month of June 1491.*

In the mean time, the execution of Hastings, and the imprisonment of Lord Stanley and the two prelates, instead of creating alarm, would seem to have increased the confidence of the public in the government of the protector.　There were many causes which tended to this result.　Not only had the report of the previous marriage of the late king been sedulously and successfully promulgated by the partisans of Richard,† but they had even gone so far as to insist that Edward IV. himself had been of spurious birth, and consequently that his children were excluded, by a double bar of illegitimacy, from all title to the throne.　Although the venerable Duchess of York was still living, it was pretended that in the lifetime of her husband, she had been lavish in her favours to other men, one of whom was the father of King Edward and of the Duke of Clarence.　Difficult as it is to imagine that a son could be found base enough to prefer charges of adultery against his own mother, it had nevertheless formerly suited Clarence, when he disputed the title of his brother Edward to the throne, to countenance, if he did not originate, this shameful scandal.‡　As regards the conduct of the pro-

* Lord Campbell's Lives of the Chancellors, vol. i p. 391.

† Sir T. More's Richard III. pp. 96–97, 99.

‡ Rot. Parl. vol. vi. p. 194

tector, however, not only would he seem to have been innocent of all share in reviving the slander, but subsequently, when one of his over-zealous partisans descanted on it from the pulpit, he is said to have been extremely displeased.

There were many other circumstances which favoured Richard in his ambitious designs. The young king was only in his thirteenth year, and, as we have seen, the rule of a minor was anticipated with the greatest apprehension. Richard, on the contrary, was in the prime of life; he had shown himself one of the wisest princes of the age in the cabinet, and one of the most valiant on the field of battle. The barons looked up to him as the principal bulwark against the return of the hateful Woodvilles to power; while the clergy were inclined to uphold him on account of the respect which he had ever manifested for the church, as a founder of public charities, a restorer of churches, and a warm advocate and promoter of the cause of private morality and virtue. It was obviously, we think, to obtain popularity with the clergy, that he compelled the frail, but charitable and warm-hearted Jane Shore, to do penance in the streets of London. Moreover, there were probably many persons who sincerely believed in the asserted illegitimacy of the young king and his brother, as well as in the validity of the attainder which excluded the Earl of Warwick from the succession. Lastly, the selfish interests of mankind were ranged on the side of the protector. The rule of a wise, an experienced, and a vigorous prince was calculated to insure peace and prosperity to the realm ; while, on the other hand, should the sceptre be transferred to the young king, puppet as he was likely to prove in the hands of the queen and her kindred, there would in all probability ensue a renewal of those cruel civil contests, which for years had wasted the blood and treasure of the country.

We have now accompanied the protector in his career to the 21st of June, the day previous to that which had been fixed upon for the coronation of the young king. On that day London is described, in a remarkble contemporary letter written on the spot, as being in a most agitated state. The writer, who, in a former letter, had urged his correspondent to attend the coronation, where he "would know all the world," now congratulates him on being absent from the metropolis at so alarming a crisis.* From what quarter,—whether from the ambition of the protector, or from the intrigues of the queen and her still powerful faction,—the threatened danger was expected to arrive, no intimation or hint unfortunately escapes the writer.

* Letters from Simon Stallworthe to Sir William Stoner, knight, dated severally from London, 9th and 21st June 1483. Stallworthe is presumed to have been an officer in the household, and in the confidence, of John Russell, Bishop of Lincoln, at this time lord-chancellor. Excerpta Historica, pp. 13, 16.

The quarter, however, from which it was least to be apprehended, seems to have been from Richard himself. Certainly, a few days previously, Richard—styling himself " protector, defender, great chamberlain, constable, and admiral of England " —had addressed an urgent appeal to the mayor and citizens of York, intimating that " the queen, her bloody adherents and affinity, intended, and daily did intend, to destroy him, our cousin the Duke of Buckingham, and the *old royal blood of the realm*," and urging his old friends in the north to send to his aid and assistance as many armed men as they could " defensively array."* But, so far from this appeal having been made with any attempt at concealment, there is evidence that the arrival of an armed force in the metropolis, at the invitation of the protector, was, daily almost, expected by the citizens. Had Richard, then, been as much dreaded and suspected by his fellow-countrymen as the Tudor chroniclers would lead us to believe, surely a contemporary, in communicating to his correspondent a proceeding apparently so singular and fraught with danger, would have coupled it with some expression of apprehension or alarm. But even the well-informed confidential servant of the lord-chancellor can see nothing but what is laudable in the policy of the protector. " It is thought," he writes, " there shall

* Drake's Eboracum, p. 111.

be 20,000 of my lord protector and my lord of Buckingham's men in London this week; to what intent I know not, but to keep the peace."* The dismay, then, which pervaded London on the 21st, may reasonably be attributed, not to any apprehension of the protector, but to the expectation of an approaching outbreak on the part of the queen and "her bloody adherents and affinity." That such a plot really existed, we have not only the uncontradicted assertion of Richard himself, but the fact seems to account for, and perhaps to justify, the summary trial and execution of Rivers, and of two others of the queen's relations, Sir Richard Grey and Sir Thomas Vaughan,† who were beheaded, in the sight of the people, only a day or two afterwards at Pomfret.‡ On the other hand, the cause of the protector seems to have been regarded, by the majority of his countrymen, as the cause of

* Excerp. Hist. p. 17.

† Sir Thomas Vaughan was nearly related to the Woodvilles, a significant circumstance which Miss Halsted has pointed out in her Life of Richard III. vol. ii. p. 55, note.

‡ Rous, Hist. Reg. Ang. pp. 213–4; Croyl. Chron. Cont. p. 489. Rivers' will is dated at the castle of Sheriff-Hutton, 23rd June, and it seems to have been immediately afterwards that he was arraigned and tried before Henry Earl of Northumberland and forthwith sent to execution. That a brave and respectable nobleman like Northumberland, one, moreover, who was bound by all the ties of gratitude and loyalty to maintain the rights of the young king, should have consented to preside at the mock trial and cruel murder of the uncle of his sovereign, is of itself a very improbable circumstance. But great doubt even seems to exist whether the treatment which Rivers met with was

conservatism and order, and consequently the expected arrival of an armed force in London, at the summons of the chief magistrate, would naturally be regarded by the citizens as a subject for congratulation rather than alarm.

With the exception of the asserted murder of his nephews, there are no two acts of Richard's life which have drawn down upon him a greater amount of obloquy than the execution of Hastings, and the arbitrary seizure of Rivers and Grey. At the time, probably, public opinion was divided as to his conduct. Many, perhaps, taxed him with being merciless if not cruel; while many more, doubtless, acquitted him on the score of his having been impelled by a stern and necessary policy. But, in whatever light his conduct on these occasions may have been regarded by his contemporaries, it may

considered to be undeserved even by himself. For instance, considering the share which Sir William Catesby, as "a great instrument of Richard's crimes" (Hume, vol. iii. p. 287), may be presumed to have had in sending Rivers to the block, we are not a little startled at finding the earl actually selecting him to be one of the executors of his last will. Again, not less curious is the confidence with which Rivers seems to look forward that the protector will see justice done to him after his death. His will proceeds,—"I beseech humbly my lord of Gloucester, in the worship of Christ's passion, and for the merit and weal of his soul, to comfort, help and assist, as supervisor (for very trust) of this testament, that mine executors may with his pleasure fulfil this my last will."—*Will of Anthony, Earl Rvyers*, Excerp. Hist. p. 248. Surely these are neither the acts nor the language which might be expected from an injured man towards the persons who he had every reason to believe were bent on consigning him to a cruel death.

at least be presumed that in the breasts of the queen's relations, and of the followers of the gallant and idolized Hastings, no other feelings could have existed towards him than those of revenge and indignation. Yet, on the contrary, strange as it may appear, the contents of the valuable letter, to which we are so much indebted, induce us to arrive at an almost opposite conclusion. Not only are we informed that Lord Lisle, brother to the queen's first husband, Sir John Grey, has "come to my lord protector and waits upon him,"* but also that the followers of Hastings had actually entered the service of the protector's chief ally and abettor, the Duke of Buckingham.†

That, by this time, Richard had secretly sounded the views of many of the most influential of the lords spiritual and temporal, and had obtained their approval of his aspiring to the crown, there cannot, we think, exist a doubt. But he had yet to obtain the sanction and concurrence of that once important and formidable body of men, the magistrates and citizens of London. To obtain their suffrages, therefore,—to accustom them to that formal assertion of his rights which he was on the eve of submitting to parliament,—to propound to them the defective title of his nephew on the ground of illegitimacy, as well as the evils which the rule of a minor was certain to entail on the

* Excerp. Hist. p. 17. † Ibid.

commonwealth,—were now the policy of the protector.

In order clearly to understand the relative position of Richard and the citizens of London, it becomes necessary, in the first place, to divest ourselves of the prejudices of the age in which we live. For instance, the worthy alderman of the present day has no more in common with the alderman of the middle ages, than the easy peer who, in the nineteenth century, wears the garter at a drawing-room at St. James's, has in common with the stalwart warriors who, at Cressy and Agincourt, won the proudest military order in Christendom. In the middle ages, a London alderman not only ranked with the barons of England, but at his decease the same military honours were assigned to both.* The banner and the shield were carried before the corpse; the helmet was laid on the coffin; and the war-horse, with its martial trappings, followed its master to the grave. The prototypes of the aldermen of London of old may be discovered in such men as Sir William Walworth, who felled Wat Tyler to the earth at Smithfield; in Sir John Crosby, who, as a warrior, grasped the hand of the fourth Edward on his landing at Ravenspur, and, as a civilian, played the part of the polished ambassador at the courts of Burgundy and Brittany; and, lastly, in Sir Thomas Sutton, whom

* Stow's Survey of London, book v. p. 81.

we discover encouraging the advancement of letters
and superintending the progress of his magnificent
foundation, the Charter House, with the same zeal
that he had formerly directed the firing of the
"great guns" at the siege of Edinburgh.

In the age of which we are writing, not only were
the citizens trained to arms, but it required no very
great provocation, nor any very imminent danger,
to induce the apprentice to fly to seize his club, and
the citizen his halberd. "Furious assaults and
slaughters" were of no very unfrequent occurrence.* The seizure of the Tower, and the decapi-
tation of the Archbishop of Canterbury, in 1381;
the sanguinary encounter between the rival com-
panies of the Skinners and Fishmongers in 1399,
and the fight between the citizens and the sanctu-
ary-men of St. Martin's-le-Grand in 1454, may be
mentioned as passing evidences of the martial spirit
which pervaded the age. At the great meeting of
the barons in London, in 1458, the lord-mayor, as
we have seen, was enabled to patrol the streets,
night and day, with a guard of five thousand armed
citizens.† Moreover, since then, the civil war had
drained the resources and lessened the military
power of the barons, while the strength and importance of the towns had increased instead of having
diminished. Considering its extent, and the martial spirit which distinguished its inhabitants, at no

* Stow's Survey of London, vol. ii., Appendix, p. 7.　† See ante, p. 41.

time during the civil wars would a military occupation of London have been practicable. Neither Edward IV. nor Queen Margaret, in the days of their respective triumphs, had dared to oppose the citizens by force of arms. When the latter, after the second battle of St. Albans, approached the metropolis at the head of a victorious army, a simple intimation from the lord-mayor that the citizens were unfriendly to her cause, was sufficient to check her progress. Again, when Edward entered London in 1471, it was not at the head of the army, which a few days afterwards he led to victory at Barnet, but, by the favour of the principal citizens, through a postern-gate. The Bastard Falconbridge alone had dared to attempt to take the capital by assault, and, after a fierce and bloody contest, found himself signally defeated at every point.

Such, then, being the military strength of London, and such the martial ardour of the citizens, surely the protector, unsupported as he was by any considerable armed force, would never have contemplated the bold step which he was about to take, unless he had previously satisfied himself that the commonalty was in his favour. The fact, too, of his throwing off the mask before the expected arrival of his reinforcements from York; the circumstance, moreover, of his doing so at a time when London was in a state of panic, which it was clearly his policy not to augment, but to allay;

and, lastly, his selecting the very day on which the disappointed citizens had expected to regale themselves with the sight of a coronation,—seem to afford convincing evidence how persuaded Richard was, if not of the justice, at least of the popularity of his cause. At a time, when there was "much trouble, each man doubting the other,"* surely Richard would never have dared to publish his designs on the crown, unless the public had apprehended danger from some other quarter than Crosby Place, or unless the majority of the influential citizens had looked up to him as, in every sense of the word, their protector.

The means which Richard adopted to give publicity to his intended usurpation, were characteristic of the age and of the man. According to previous invitation, a numerous meeting of the citizens took place on Sunday, the 22nd of June, in the large open space in front of St. Paul's Cathedral. The orator selected to harangue them was an eminent popular preacher of the day, Dr. Raaf Shaw, brother of Sir Edmund Shaw, lord-mayor of London. The spot from which he addressed the people was the celebrated Paul's Cross. Choosing for his text the words, "Bastard slips shall not take deep root,"† he not only insisted on the ille-

---

* Excerp. Hist. p. 16.

† "But the multiplying brood of the ungodly shall not thrive, nor take deep rooting from bastard slips, nor lay any fast foundation."— *Book of Wisdom*, iv. 3.

gitimacy of the young king and his brother, but is said to have had the boldness to descant upon the assumed frailty of the illustrious lady of whom Richard was the eleventh child. The late king and the late Duke of Clarence he affirmed to be bastards: Richard alone he declared to be the true heir of the late Duke of York. The lord protector, he said, represented in his lineaments "the very face" of the noble duke his father; he was "the same undoubted image, the express likeness, of that noble duke." According to Sir Thomas More, it had been preconcerted between the protector and the preacher, that, at this moment, the former should present himself, as if by accident, to the people, when it was hoped that "the multitude, taking the doctor's words as proceeding from divine inspiration, would have been induced to cry out *God save King Richard!*"* If this clap-trap device was really projected by Richard and his partisans, it signally failed: the protector, according to Sir Thomas More, not making his appearance at the happy moment, and the preacher being put to such utter confusion, that he shortly afterwards died of grief and remorse. Our own conviction, however, is that the story is altogether apocryphal. Not only was so paltry an artifice incompatible with the protector's admitted sagacity and strong sense,

* Sir T. More's Edward V. in Kennet, vol. i. p. 497; More's Hist. of Richard III. p. 101.

but we search in vain for any corroboration of it by contemporary writers. The fact is a significant one, that Fabyan—who, as a citizen of London, was not unlikely to have listened to Dr. Shaw's sermon—should, on the one hand, substantiate the important circumstance of the preacher having impugned the legitimacy of the children of Edward IV., and yet should make no allusion to any slur having been thrown on the reputation of the Duchess of York.*

On the 24th of June, two days after Dr. Shaw had advocated the protector's claims at St. Paul's, a still more important meeting took place in the Guildhall of the city of London. The principal orator on this occasion was the Duke of Buckingham, who brought into play, in favour of the protector, all the influence which he possessed as a prince of the blood, as well as the powerful eloquence for which his contemporaries have given him credit. "Many a wise man that day," writes Fabyan, "marvelled and commended him for the good ordering of his words, but not for the intent and purpose, the which thereupon ensued."† Even Sir Thomas More admits that Buckingham delivered himself with "such grace and eloquence,

* Fabyan's Chronicles, p. 669. This writer informs us that Shaw was a man famous in his day, "both of his learning and also of natural wit."—*Ibid.*

† Fabyan's Chronicles, p. 669.

that never so ill a subject was handled with so much oratory."*

If the further account of the illustrious lord-chancellor is to be credited, the eloquence of Buckingham, powerful as it was, fell flat upon the assembled citizens; only "some of the protector's and the duke's servants—some of the city apprentices and the rabble that had crowded into the hall—crying, *King Richard! King Richard!* and throwing up their hats in token of joy." According to the same authority, the proposition to put the young king aside, in favour of his uncle, was received by the multitude with positive lamentations. "The assembly," he writes, "broke up; the most part of them with weeping eyes and aching hearts, though they were forced to hide their tears and their sorrows as much as possible, for fear of giving offence, which had been dangerous."†

But, whatever may have been the feelings with which the citizens listened to the arguments of Buckingham, nothing can be more certain than that the first persons in the realm regarded it as sufficiently satisfactory to justify them in making the protector a formal offer of the crown. "The barons and commons," says Buck, "with one general dislike of, and an universal negative voice, refused the sons of King Edward; not for any ill-

* Sir T. More's Edward V. in Kennet, vol. i. p. 499.
† Ibid.

will or malice, but for their disabilities and incapacities. The opinions of those times, too, held them not legitimate, and the Queen Elizabeth Grey, or Woodville, no lawful wife, nor yet a woman worthy to be the king's wife, by reason of her extreme unequal quality. For these and other causes, the barons and prelates unanimously cast their election upon the protector, as the most worthiest and nearest, by the experience of his own deservings and the strength of his alliance."*

Accordingly, on the very day after the meeting at Guildhall, the Duke of Buckingham, "accompanied by many of the chief lords and other grave and learned persons," was admitted to an audience with the protector in the "great chamber" of Baynard's Castle, then the residence of his venerable mother, the Duchess of York.† In the court-yard of the castle were assembled the aldermen of London and a large body of the citizens, whom the

* Buck's Life of Richard III. in Kennet, vol. i. p. 523.

† The fact of Richard having received the deputation under his mother's roof, instead of at his own residence, Crosby Place, appears to us as doubly curious. In the first place, it tends to the supposition that the duchess preferred the claims of her youngest son, Richard, to those of her grandsons; and, in the next place, it goes far to give the lie to the cruel charge, which has been brought against the protector, that he sanctioned the foul aspersions which the preacher Shaw had cast on the fair fame of his mother. "Is it, can it be credible," writes Lord Orford, "that Richard actuated a venal preacher to declare to the people from the pulpit of St. Paul's that his mother had been an adulteress, and that her two eldest sons, Edward IV. and the Duke of Clarence, were spurious, and that the good lady had not given

lord-mayor, Sir Edmund Shaw,* one of the protector's most devoted partisans, had convened to do him honour. According to Sir Thomas More, it was not till after much importunity, and not without great apparent reluctance, that the protector was prevailed upon to receive the deputation, and to listen to their arguments and persuasions. The statement is probably correct. No one could be more aware than the protector of the fickleness and uncertainty of popular favour. He knew that the day would probably arrive in which his conduct to his nephews would be charged against him as a crime. What could be more natural, then, than that he should have shrunk from being the only traitor? In the day when he might be called upon for his defence, he would be enabled to plead that his advisers and abettors had been the noblest and the wisest in the land; that when he accepted

a legitimate child to her husband but the protector, and, I suppose, the Duchess of Suffolk?"—*Hist. Doubts*, Lord Orford's Works, vol. ii. pp. 131, 200.

 * This munificent and respectable citizen was a member of the Goldsmiths' Company. Besides rebuilding "the old gate called Cripplegate, at his own expense" (*Stow*, book i. p. 18), he founded and endowed a free school at Stockport, in Cheshire (Ibid. book v. p 60). Six months after Richard's elevation to the throne, we find him selling to Shaw, whom he calls his merchant, a considerable portion of his plate, viz. 275 lbs. 4 oz. of troy weight. The amount received by Richard was 550*l*. 13*s*. 4*d*., which was paid, on the 23rd December 1483, to Mr. Edmund Chatterton, treasurer of the king's chamber. A list of the articles sold may be found in Stow's "Survey." Ibid. book v. p. 124.

a crown, it was contrary to his own wishes and better judgment, and solely in deference to the solicitations of the "lords spiritual and temporal," and "for the public weal and tranquillity of the land."*

> *Glouc.* Cousin of Buckingham, and sage grave men,
> Since you will buckle fortune on my back,
> To bear her burthen, whether I will or no,
> I must have patience to endure the load :
> But if black scandal, or foul-faced reproach,
> Attend the sequel of your imposition,
> Your mere enforcement shall acquittance me
> From all the impure blots and stains thereof:
> For God doth know, and you may partly see,
> How far I am from the desire of this.
>
> *King Richard III.* Act. iii. Sc. 7.

Thus the protector coquetted, so long as it was safe and decent, with his proffered greatness. At length, being assured by Buckingham that the barons and commons of England would on no ac-

---

* Previously to his coronation, a roll containing certain articles was presented to him on behalf of the three estates of the realm, "by many and divers lords, spiritual and temporal," and other nobles and commons, to which he, "for the public weal and tranquillity of the land, benignly assented."—*Rot. Parl.* vol vi. p. 240. "It was set forth," writes the Croyland continuator, "by way of prayer, in a certain roll of parchment, that the sons of King Edward were bastards, on the ground that he had contracted a marriage with one Lady Eleanor Boteler before his marriage to Queen Elizabeth ; added to which, the blood of his other brother, George Duke of Clarence, had been attainted ; so that, at the present time, no certain and uncorrupted lineal blood could be found of Richard Duke of York, except in the person of the said Richard Duke of Gloucester. For which reason he was *entreated*, at the end of the said roll, *on part of the lords and commons of the realm*, to assume his lawful rights."—*Croyl. Chron. Cont.* p. 489.

count consent to be ruled over by the sons of Edward IV., and, furthermore, that, if he persisted in refusing the crown, they would be compelled to look out for some other "worthy person" to be their sovereign, the heart of the protector is said to have gradually relented, and in a short speech, distinguished by humility and piety, he consented to wield the sceptre of the Plantagenets. "With this," says Sir Thomas More, "there was a great shout, saying, *King Richard! King Richard!* And then the lords went up to the king, and the people departed, talking diversely of the matter, every man as his fantasy gave him." *

The following day the protector was proclaimed in the cities of London and Westminster by the title of King Richard III. The same day, having the Duke of Norfolk on his right hand, and the Duke of Suffolk on his left, he ascended the marble seat in Westminster Hall, and from thence delivered a gracious speech to his assembled subjects. Having ordered the judges to be summoned into his presence, he exhorted them to administer the laws with diligence and justice; he pronounced a free pardon for all offences committed against himself, and ordered a general amnesty to be proclaimed throughout the land. He even sent for one Fogg, who, having given him grievous offence, had sought refuge in sanctuary, and, taking him gra-

* Sir T. More's Richard III. p. 123.

ciously by the hand in the face of the multitude,
assured him of his forgiveness.* From the great
hall he proceeded to the abbey, at the door of
which he was met by the abbot of Westminster,
who presented to him the sceptre of King Edward.
He then ascended, and offered at, the shrine of St.
Edward; after which—accompanied by the principal ecclesiastics in procession, with the monks
singing *Te Deum*—he quitted the abbey to take
possession of the neighbouring palace of the Confessor.

Thus, at the age of thirty years and eight months,
and after the lapse of only two months and seventeen days from the date of his brother Edward's
death, was Richard of Gloucester advanced to the
supreme power. If he obtained his ends by means
of dissimulation and crime, he had at least the
excuse that he had in all probability averted the
horrors of civil war, and that his usurpation had
been encouraged and abetted, not only by the lords
spiritual and temporal, but by the commons of
England. Usurpation is usually accompanied by
military violence; but it was the suffrage, not the
sword, which elevated Richard to the throne.
True it is, that, at his earnest request, the citizens
of York had despatched an armed force to his
assistance; but as it was not till after the 25th of
June, two days after which Rivers was beheaded,

* Sir T. More's Richard III. p. 125.

that they marched from Pomfret,* they could not
have arrived in London till after the 26th, the day on
which Richard had been solemnly and peacefully invested with the sovereign power. Moreover, as we
have already suggested, this force, in all probability, was intended, not to overawe, but to co-operate
with, the citizens of London, in the event of a rising
on the part of the Woodvilles and their friends.
A city, which was able to protect itself, daily and
nightly, with a military patrol of 5000 men, had
little to apprehend from men, who, as the chronicler informs us, were so "evil apparelled and worse
harnessed," that, when they assembled at muster
in Finsbury Fields,† the citizens of London used to
laugh them to scorn. Thus, not only on the part
of the lay and spiritual lords, but on the part of
the commonalty, we search in vain for evidence
that the usurpation of Richard provoked the dis-
approbation much less the indignation, of his
countrymen.

If further proof were wanted that his usurpation
was sanctioned by his subjects, we may point to the
great concourse of holy and high-born men who
flocked to do honour to him at his coronation.
Never had a more splendid or more solemn pageant
been witnessed on a similar occasion. When, on
the day previous to the ceremony,—preceded by
heralds, and trumpets and clarions,—he rode forth

* Croyl. Chron. Cont. p. 489.   † Hall, p. 375.

from under the gloomy portal of the Tower of London, there followed in his train three dukes, nine earls, and twenty-two barons, in addition to a countless array of knights and esquires. The sanction which the city of London gave to his usurpation was manifested by the lord-mayor, and the aldermen in their scarlet robes, riding in the procession. That the Church, also, looked upon him as the anointed of the Lord, is proved by the array of mitres and croziers which swelled his triumph on reaching Westminster. The exact number of prelates who were present we know not. Certain, however, it is, that, in addition to the Cardinal Archbishop of Canterbury,—himself a Plantagenet on the mother's side, and great-grandson of Edward III.*—the Bishops of Rochester, Bath, Durham, Exeter, and Norwich, forgot the oaths of allegiance which they had so recently taken to Edward V., and scrupled not to sanction and grace the pageant by their presence.

On the following day, a far more gorgeous procession passed from the great hall at Westminster to the neighbouring abbey. First issued forth the trumpets and clarions, the sergeants-at-arms, and the heralds and pursuivants carrying the king's

---

* The archbishop was the son of William de Bourchier, created by Henry V. Earl of Ewe in Normandy, by the Lady Anne Plantagenet, daughter of Thomas of Woodstock, Duke of Gloucester, fifth son to King Edward III.

armorial insignia.   Then came the bishops with
the mitres on their heads, and the abbots with their
croziers in their hands; Audley, Bishop of Rochester, bearing the cross before Cardinal Bourchier,
Archbishop of Canterbury.   Next followed the
Earl of Northumberland carrying the pointless
sword of mercy; Lord Stanley bearing the mass;
the Duke of Suffolk with the sceptre; the Earl of
Lincoln with the cross and globe, and the Earls of
Kent and Surrey, and Lord Lovel, carrying other
swords of state.   Before the king walked the Earl
Marshal of England, the Duke of Norfolk, bearing
the crown, and immediately after him followed
Richard himself, gorgeously arrayed in robes of
purple velvet, furred with ermine, with a coat and
surcoat of crimson satin.   Over his head was borne
a rich canopy supported by the barons of the Cinque
Ports.   On one side of him walked Stillington,
Bishop of Bath, and on the other, Dudley, Bishop
of Durham: the Duke of Buckingham held up his
train.   The procession was closed by a long train
of earls and barons.

After the procession of the king followed that of
his queen, Anne Neville.   The Earl of Huntingdon
bore her sceptre; the Viscount Lisle the rod and
dove; and the Earl of Wiltshire her crown.   Then
came the queen herself, habited in robes of purple
velvet furred with ermine, having "on her head a
circlet of gold with many precious stones set there-

in." Over her head was borne a "cloth of estate." On one side of her walked Courtenay, Bishop of Exeter; on the other, Goldwell, Bishop of Norwich. A princess of the blood, the celebrated Margaret Countess of Richmond, mother of Henry VII., supported her train. After the queen walked the king's sister, Elizabeth Duchess of Suffolk, having "on her head a circlet of gold;" and, after her, followed the Duchess of Norfolk and a train of high-born ladies, succeeded by another train of knights and esquires.*

Entering the abbey at the great west door, the king and queen "took their seats of state, staying till divers holy hymns were sung," when they ascended to the high altar, where the ceremony of anointment took place. Then "the king and queen put off their robes, and there stood all naked from the middle upwards, and anon the bishops anointed both the king and queen." This ceremony having been performed, they exchanged their mantles of purple velvet for robes of cloth of gold, and were solemnly crowned by the Archbishop of Canterbury, assisted by the other bishops. The archbishop subsequently performed high mass, and administered the holy communion to the king and

* MS. in the Harleian collection, quoted in Brayley and Britton's History of the Palace of Westminster, pp. 332–3; Excerpta Historica, p. 380, &c.; Buck's Richard III. in Kennet, vol. i. p. 526; Hall, pp. 375, 376.

queen; after which they offered at St. Edward's shrine, where the king laid down King Edward's crown and put on another, and so returned to Westminster Hall in the same state they came.*

The banquet, which took place at four o'clock in the great hall, is described as having been magnificent in the extreme. The king and queen were served on dishes of gold and silver; Lord Audley performed the office of state-carver; Thomas Lord Scrope of Upsal, that of cup-bearer; Lord Lovel, during the entertainment, stood before the king, "two esquires lying under the board at the king's feet." On each side of the queen stood a countess with a plaisance, or napkin, for her use. Over the head of each was held a canopy supported by peers and peeresses. The guests consisted of the cardinal archbishop, the lord-chancellor, the prelates, the judges and nobles of the land, and the lord-mayor and principal citizens of London.† The ladies sat

* Buck in Kennet, vol. i. p. 526 ; Excerpta Hist. pp. 381-2.

† The lord-mayor, according to ancient usage, served the king and queen with wine at the banquet, as chief butler of England. " And the same mayor, after dinner ended, offered to the said lord the king, wine in a gold cup, with a golden vial [cum fiolâ aureâ] full of water to temper the wine. And after the wine was taken by the lord king, the mayor retained the said cup and vial of gold to his own proper use. In like manner, the mayor offered to the queen, after the feast ended, wine in a golden cup, with a gold vial full of water. And after wine taken by the said queen, she gave the cup with the vial to the mayor, according to the privileges, liberties, and customs of the city of London, in such cases used."—*Stow's Survey of London*, book v. pp. 153-4.

by themselves on the side of a long table in the middle of the hall. As soon as the second course was put on the table, the king's champion, Sir Robert Dymoke, rode into the hall; "his horse being trapped with white silk and red, and himself in white harness; the heralds of arms standing upon a stage among all the company. Then the king's champion rode up before the king, asking, before all the people, if there was any man would say against King Richard III. why he should not pretend to the crown. And when he had so said, all the hall cried *King Richard!* all with one voice. And when this was done, anon one of the lords brought unto the champion a covered cup full of red wine, and so he took the cup and uncovered it, and drank thereof. And when he had done, anon he cast out the wine, and covered the cup again; and making his obeysance to the king, turned his horse about, and rode through the hall, with his cup in his right hand, and that he had for his labour." Then Garter king-at-arms, supported by eighteen other heralds, advanced before the king, and solemnly proclaimed his style and titles. No single untoward accident seems to have marred the harmony or splendour of the day. When at length it began to close, the hall was illuminated by a "great light of wax torches and torchets," apparently the signal for the king and queen to retire. Accordingly, wafers and hippocras having

been previously served, Richard and his consort
rose up and departed to their private apartments in
the palace.*

* Harl. MS. ut supra ; Excerpta Hist. pp. 382–3.

CHAPTER V.

THE GREATNESS AND THE SIN OF RICHARD OF GLOUCESTER.

THE conduct of Richard III. on ascending the throne of the Plantagenets, was such as to hold out every promise to his subjects of a just, happy, and prosperous reign. Addressing himself to the barons, after his coronation, he enjoined them to insure good government in their several counties, and to see that none of his subjects were wronged.* He himself occasionally presided in person in the courts of law. He won the hearts of his subjects by mingling familiarly with them, and addressing them in kind and encouraging language. He performed a highly popular act by disforesting a large tract of land at Witchwood, which his brother Edward had enclosed as a deer-forest.† Again, when London, and certain counties, offered him a benevolence, he refused it, saying, " I would rather have your hearts than your money." ‡

He had not only released from imprisonment and

---

* Sir T. More's Edward V. in Kennet, vol. i. p. 501.

† Rous, Hist. Ang. Reg. p. 216; Sandford, Gen. Hist. book v. p. 434.

‡ Rous, ut supra, p. 216 · Camden's Remains, p. 353.

pardoned Lord Stanley, but he appointed him
Lord High Steward of his household. He released
the title and estates of the late Lord Hastings from
attainder and forfeiture; securing the possession
of them to his widow, the sister of the great Earl
of Warwick, whom he engaged to protect and defend as her good and gracious sovereign lord, and
" to suffer none to do her wrong." * He listened
complacently to a petition from the university of
Cambridge, in favour of their chancellor, the Archbishop of York, whom, at their solicitation, he released from confinement. He even liberated from
the Tower one of the most active and powerful of
his enemies, Morton, Bishop of Ely; contenting
himself with committing him to the safe keeping
of the Duke of Buckingham, by whom the bishop
was honourably entertained at his castle of Brecknock. Of his former friends, and of those who
had served him faithfully, not one, it is said, was
left unrewarded, much less forgotten. John Lord
Howard was created Duke of Norfolk, and appointed earl marshal and admiral of England and
Ireland. His son, Sir Thomas Howard, was created
Earl of Surrey and invested with the Garter. The
Duke of Buckingham, who of all men had been
chiefly instrumental in elevating Richard to the
throne, was awarded the princely lordships and

* Harl. MSS. 433, p. 108, quoted in S. Turner's Middle Ages, vol.
iv. p. 27.

lands of the De Bohuns, Earls of Hereford, and the lucrative stewardship of many of the crown manors. He was also appointed constable of England and governor of the royal castles in Wales. William Viscount Berkeley was created Earl of Nottingham, and Francis Lord Lovel appointed chamberlain of the household, constable of the castle of Wallingford, and chief butler of England.

On the 23rd July, King Richard set forth from Windsor on a magnificent progress through the middle and northern counties of England. That, only seventeen days after his coronation, he should have considered it safe to leave the capital unawed by his presence, evinces the confidence which he must have felt in the goodwill, if not in the affections, of his subjects. Moreover, he had previously sent back his northern army with presents to their homes, thus leaving behind him no military force to support his authority in the event of danger.

In the north, his former good government had been fully appreciated, and his person regarded with affection.* Scarcely three months had elapsed since he bade farewell to his friends as Duke of Gloucester, and a mere subject like themselves. It was not unnatural, therefore, that he should avail himself of the earliest opportunity of display-

* Surtees' Hist. of Durham, vol. iv. p. 66; Drake's Eboracum, pp. 118, 120.

ing to them "the high and kingly station" which in the mean time he had acquired.*

At Oxford the new king was received with that reverence and enthusiasm which this loyal university has ever been accustomed to display towards the sovereign of the hour. At the entrance to the city he was met by the chancellor and the heads of the colleges. The Bishops of Durham, Worcester, St. Asaph, and St. David's, the Earls of Lincoln and Surrey, Lord Lovel, Lord Stanley, Lord Audley, Lord Beauchamp, and other nobles, swelled his train. Waynflete, Bishop of Winchester, conducted him to the royal apartments in Magdalen College, of which that eminent prelate was the founder.† At Gloucester, the city from which he had derived his ducal title, he was received with the heartiest welcome. Thus far he had been attended by the princely and the ambitious Buckingham; and here, in "most loving and trusty manner," they took leave of each other.‡ At Tewkesbury, Richard again stood on the memorable battle-field which had witnessed the chivalry of his boyhood, and where he had established his military reputation. At Warwick he was joined by his gentle queen, and here in the halls of the dead

* Croyl. Chron. Cont. p. 490.

† Wood's Hist. of Oxford, by Gutch, vol. i. p. 639; Chalmers' Hist. of Oxford, p. 210.

‡ Sir T. More's Richard III. p. 137.

Kingmaker, under the roof of which she was born, he received the ambassador of Isabella of Castile, as well as the envoys of the King of France and the Duke of Burgundy, who came to congratulate him on his accession. On the 15th of August we find him at Coventry, on the 17th at Leicester, and on the 22nd at Nottingham.

But it was reserved for the city of York to witness his crowning triumph. His visit to the ancient city was celebrated by the inhabitants with banquets, pageants, and every description of rejoicing and festivity.* The clergy and the nobles seem to have vied with each other who could do him the greatest honour. Here, whether from a desire to gratify his northern friends,—whether from a yearning for popularity, or perhaps from some sounder motive of policy,—he caused himself to be a second time crowned. The ceremony was performed in the noble cathedral by Rotheram, Arch-

* Richard would seem to have been extremely anxious to meet with a hearty and princely reception from the city of York. Accordingly, on the 23rd of August, we find his secretary, John Kendale, writing to the lord-mayor and aldermen of that important city: "This I advise you, as laudably as your wisdom can imagine, to receive him and the queen at his coming, as well with pageants and with such good speeches as can goodly, this short warning considered, be devised; and under such form as Master Lancaster, of the king's council, this bringer shall somewhat advertise you of my mind in that behalf; as in hanging the streets, through which the king's grace shall come, with cloths of arras, tapestry-work and other, for there come many southern lords and men of worship with them, which will mark greatly your receiving their graces."—*Drake's Ebor.* p. 116.

bishop of York, with scarcely less pomp and magnificence, than when Cardinal Bourchier had placed
the crown on his head in the abbey of Westminster.*   Richard may possibly have been not only
the unprincipled usurper, but the atrocious crimi-
nal, which he has been represented. But, on the
other hand, when, on these solemn occasions, we
not only find the Archbishops of Canterbury and
York countenancing his usurpation by their presence, but receiving and sanctifying his coronation-
oath, administering to him the Holy Sacrament,
and granting him absolution for his sins, surely it
is more reasonable and more agreeable to believe
that these reverend prelates regarded his recent
acts as justified by circumstances or by necessity,
than that in their hearts they should have held
him an abandoned murderer and oppressor, and
therefore, by abetting his crimes and invoking
the blessing of Heaven on his reign, have
rendered themselves as culpable as he was himself.

Not the least interesting figure that walked in
procession at the second coronation of Richard III.,
was his only legitimate offspring, a child ten years
of age, Edward Earl of Salisbury. In his hand the
boy held a rod of gold; his brows supported a
demi-crown, the appointed head-dress on such

* Hall's Chron. p. 380; Buck in Kennet, vol. i. p. 527; Drake's
Eboracum, p. 117.

state occasions for the heir to the throne of England. The queen, his mother, walked by his side, holding him by her left hand. In this promising child were centred all the hopes and fears of his ambitious sire. Through his means he trusted to bequeath a sceptre which would descend to generations of kings. He loved him as he seems to have loved no other being on earth. For that child he had watched and toiled and intrigued till he found the sceptre within his grasp: and, lastly, it was for his aggrandizement, apparently, that he was subsequently induced to commit that fearful and memorable crime which has handed down his name, branded with the crime of murder, to succeeding generations. How inscrutable are the dispensations of Providence! On the day of his second coronation, the fond father, surrounded by the most powerful and the wisest in the land, had solemnly created his son Prince of Wales and Earl of Chester. And yet, less than seven months from that day of triumph, the innocent object of aspirations so high, and of greatness so ill-gotten, was numbered with the dead.

Hitherto Richard's conduct from the time of his accession had been not only blameless, but laudable. His progress had everywhere been marked by popular and beneficent acts. The anxiety which he showed to redress the wrongs of his subjects, and to insure an impartial administration of the laws, has been especially recorded. "Thanked be Jesu," writes the secretary Kendale, "the king's grace is in good health, as is likewise the queen's grace: and in all their progress have been worshipfully received with pageants and other, &c., &c.; and his lords and judges, in every place, sitting determining the complaints of poor folks, with due punition of offenders against his laws." *

Hitherto also his progress, like his reign, had been prosperous and tranquil. On his arrival at Lincoln, however, rumours appear to have reached him which occasioned him the deepest anxiety. Although the nobles and prelates of England, whether from fear or from motives of political expediency, had preferred Richard of Gloucester to be their sovereign, there must necessarily have been many among them who were indebted either for their coronets or their mitres to the great king whom they had so recently followed to the tomb, and to whom therefore the welfare of his unoffending offspring must have been a matter of interest. Men, in that turbulent age, may have set little value on human life. They may have been fierce in their revenge, and unscrupulous in seizing the property of their adversaries; but, on the other hand, they were not, necessarily, either ungenerous or ungrateful. Fallen greatness, more especially when associated with innocence and youth,

* Drake's Ebor. p. 116.

can scarcely fail, even among the fiercest and most selfish, to attract commiseration. Of the peers and prelates who had preferred and exalted Richard of Gloucester to be their sovereign, not one probably had anticipated that the young prince whom they deposed would be exposed to personal danger and discomfort; and still less that he should be doomed to that miserable and mysterious fate which has since aroused the curiosity and the pity of centuries. Up to the day of his deposition Edward V. had been attended with all the respect and ceremony due to the heir of the Plantagenets. But from that time no tidings of him had transpired beyond his dark prison-house in the Tower. Of the peers and prelates who, on the 4th of May, had knelt and paid homage to him, not one probably could have told how fared it with the unoffending children of their late master,—whether they were immured in the dungeons of the Tower, or whether even a darker fate might have befallen them.

Nor was it only in the halls of the great that the mysterious fate of the young princes was a subject of interest and curiosity, but by degrees it excited general anxiety. Gradually rumours got abroad, which attributed to the darkest motives the king's seclusion of his nephews from the light of heaven. Since the day of Richard's coronation, the young princes had been beheld by no human eye but those of their keepers and attendants. Accordingly, in many places, and especially in the southern and western counties, secret meetings were held with the object of effecting their release from imprisonment, and, if possible, of restoring young Edward to the throne of his ancestors. Among other suggestions, it was proposed that one or more of the daughters of the late king should be conveyed in disguise out of the sanctuary at Westminster, and transported into foreign parts. Thus should any "fatal mishap" have befallen the young princes, the crown might yet be transmitted in the direct line to the heirs of the house of York.*

By degrees these meetings in favour of the young princes began to be more openly held and much more numerously attended. Of course, so jealous and vigilant a monarch as Richard could not long be kept in ignorance of their existence. Accordingly, he no sooner discovered the storm which was gathering than he prepared to encounter it with the energy and resolution which characterized him in every emergency. From the extraordinary precautions which he took to prevent the escape of the young princesses from the sanctuary at Westminster, we are inclined to think either that the male heirs of King Edward's body had already been put to death, or else that their immediate destruction had been resolved upon. According to a contem-

* Croyl. Chron. Cont. p. 491.

porary writer,—"The noble church of the monks at Westminster, and all the neighbouring parts, assumed the appearance of a castle and fortress; while men of the greatest austerity were appointed by Richard to act as keepers thereof. The captain and head of these was John Nesfield, esquire, who set a watch upon all the inlets and outlets of the monastery, so that not one of the persons there shut up could go forth, and no one could enter, without his permission."*

The usurper was probably congratulating himself, that, by his vigorous precautions, he had averted the perils which beset his throne, when, to his exceeding astonishment, he received intelligence that the Duke of Buckingham had entered into a secret alliance with his enemies. That Buckingham,—his accomplice, his chief adviser, his friend and confidant,—he who of all others had been most instrumental in placing the crown on his head, and on whom in return he had lavished wealth and honour,—should league himself with his deadliest foes, and, to use the king's own expressive words, prove the "most untrue creature living,"† appears to have wounded and disturbed the usurper more than any other event of his life. Hollow, indeed, did it prove the ground to be on

* Croyl. Chron. Cont. p. 491.

† Letter from the king to the Lord Chancellor Russell, Bishop of Lincoln, dated Lincoln, 12th October.—*Kennet's Complete Hist.* vol. i. p. 532, note.

which he stood. If Buckingham could desert him, who, of all the others who had sworn fidelity to him on his coronation day, were likely to prove more grateful or more true? Henceforth it was evident that safety and success must depend upon his own watchful sagacity, his indomitable courage and masterly talents.

Buckingham's apostasy has been attributed to different motives. According to some accounts he was dissatisfied with the manner in which his services had been rewarded; according to others, he aimed at the deposition of Richard and gaining the crown for himself. Little more than three months had elapsed since he had cheerfully carried the white staff at the coronation of Richard; little more than two months since, apparently on the most loving terms, they had bidden farewell to each other at Gloucester. Assuredly this was a very short period to revolutionize the principles and policy even of the most mercurial of statesmen and the falsest of friends. The probability we consider to be—and the supposition accords with the state of reaction in the public mind in favour of the young princes,—that the principal, if not the sole, cause of Buckingham's defalcation, was that which he himself assigned to Morton, Bishop of Ely, at Brecknock. "When," he said, "I was credibly informed of the death of the two young innocents, his (Richard's) own natural nephews, contrary to his faith and promise,—to the which, God be my judge, I never agreed nor condescended,—how my body trembled, and how my heart inwardly grudged! Insomuch that I so abhorred the sight, and much more the company of him, that I could no longer abide in his court, except I should be openly revenged. The end whereof was doubtful, and so I feigned a cause to depart; and with a merry countenance and a despiteful heart, I took my leave humbly of him; he thinking nothing less than that I was displeased, and so returned to Brecknock."* As Buckingham was uncle by marriage to the young princes, and as, at this time, he was by far the most powerful subject in the realm, his secession from the cause of the usurper was naturally of the utmost importance to the conspirators. The time, however, for open insurrection had yet to arrive.

Very different from what we might have anticipated was the conduct of Richard, when apprized that his subjects suspected him of foul play towards his nephews and more than murmured their indignation. Presuming the young king and his brother to have been still in existence, surely the true policy of Richard was to have led them forth into the open light of heaven; or, at all events, to have satisfied his subjects, by the testimony of unprejudiced eye-witnesses, that they were

* Grafton's Cont. of More, vol. ii. p. 127.

still living and in safe and honourable keeping. For instance, when, only a few years later, the world whispered that Henry VII. had secretly put to death the last male heir of the Plantagenets, Edward Earl of Warwick, Henry at once silenced the scandal by causing him to be brought, on a Sunday, "throughout the principal streets of London, to be seen by the people."* Richard, on the contrary, not only took no steps to give the lie to popular clamour, but at once set the opinion of the world at defiance, by acknowledging that his unhappy nephews had passed away from the earth.† Certainly, if he sought to silence the clamour and stifle the plots of the partisans of the young princes, by demonstrating to them how idle it was to struggle any longer for rights which the grave had swallowed up, the policy of Richard is rendered intelligible. But, on the other hand, it was scarcely less certain that the announcement of the premature deaths of two young and unoffending children, would not only lend weight to the suspicions of foul play which were already prevalent, but would call up a storm of indignation against which no monarch, however despotic, or insensible to the opinion of his subjects, could expect long to contend.

Such, in fact, proved to be the result. The in-

* Lord Bacon in Kennet, vol. i. p. 585.
† Grafton, vol. ii. p. 119; Polydore Virgil, lib. xxv. p. 694.

creasing conviction in men's minds, that the innocent princes had met with a cruel and untimely end, excited deep and almost universal commiseration. According to the chronicler Grafton, " When the fame of this detestable act was revealed and demulged through the whole realm, there fell generally such a dolour and inward sorrow into the hearts of all the people, that, all fear of his cruelty set aside, they in every town, street, and place, openly wept and piteously sobbed."* Moreover, notwithstanding her former unpopularity, men's minds could scarcely fail to sympathize with the sorrow-stricken widow of Edward IV., who only a few months previously had watched over the death-bed of a beloved husband, had mourned the tragical fate of a brother and a son, and who was now called upon to bewail the deaths of two other children, her pride, her comfort, and her hope. When the sad tidings were conveyed to her in the sanctuary, so grievously, we are told, was she " amazed with the greatness of the cruelty," that she fell on the ground in a swoon, and was apparently in the agonies of death. On recovering herself, Elizabeth, in the most pitiable manner, called upon her children by name; bitterly reproaching herself for having been induced to deliver up her youngest son into the hands of his enemies, and wildly invoking the vengeance of heaven on the

* Grafton's Chronicle, vol. ii. p. 119.

heads of the murderers of her beloved ones. When, a few months afterwards, Richard was bowed to the earth by the death of his only and beloved child, men, in that superstitious age, naturally traced his great affliction to the execrations of that agonized mother.

The earliest writer, who professes to furnish any details relating to the fate of the young princes, is Jean Molinet, a contemporary, who died in 1507. With few exceptions, the accounts which foreigners give of events which have occurred in England must be received with caution, if not with mistrust. Molinet, however, as librarian to Margaret of Austria and historiographer to the house of Burgundy, may be presumed to have been in a position to collect tolerably accurate information of what was transpiring at the court of Richard. According to his account, the young king, impressed with a conviction of the murderous intentions of his uncle, sank into a state of deep melancholy. The younger prince, on the contrary, is described as not only cheerful and gay, but as enlivening their prison-room with the sports and gambols of childhood, and endeavouring to raise the spirits of his elder brother by his innocent hilarity. Attracted apparently by the bright insignia of the order of the Garter, which the young king was still allowed to wear, the child, during his capers about the apartment, is said to have inquired of his brother why he did not learn to dance. "It were better," replied the elder brother, "that we should learn to die, for I fear that our days in this world will not be long." *

The brief details related by Molinet are, moreover, curiously corroborative of the more recent, but more celebrated, narrative of Sir Thomas More.†‡ Both writers agree in their accounts of the state of dejection into which the elder prince had sunk; both agree in regard to a more important, and much disputed point, the exact date at which the murders were committed. According to Sir Thomas More, the young princes, from the time of their uncle's usurpation, had been stripped of all

---

* Chroniques de Jean Molinet, in Buchon's Chron. Nat. Franc. tom. xliv. p. 402. In a contemporary letter, dated 21st June 1483, the younger prince is described as being, "blessed be Jesu, merry." Excerp. Hist. p. 17.

† That Sir Thomas More's History of King Richard III. is highly tinged by party prejudice, and that many errors and inaccuracies are to be found in it, it would be useless to deny. Nevertheless, the work must always be held of great authority and importance, not only from the circumstance of Sir Thomas having lived so near to the times of which he wrote, and from the excellent means which he had of acquiring the truest information, but because it is impossible to believe that the great and upright lord-chancellor—he who suffered martyrdom for the sake of religion—would knowingly and willingly falsify historical truth. More, as is well known, was in his youth in the household of Bishop (afterwards Cardinal) Morton; and from this and other circumstances, it has sometimes been supposed that the cardinal, in fact, was the author of the work, and More merely the transcriber. After all, however, this is little more than conjecture. See Buck in Kennet, vol. i. pp. 546–7; Sir Henry Ellis's Preface to Hardyng's Chronicle; Notes and Queries, vol. i. p. 105, 2nd Series.

the appurtenances of royalty. From that day till the "traitorous deed" was accomplished, the young king anticipated the worst. "Alas!" he is said to have exclaimed, "would that mine uncle would let me have my life, though I lose my kingdom?" Immured together in close confinement, deprived of the familiar faces of their former attendants, guarded by common gaolers, and with only one grim attendant, William Slaughter, or "Black Will," as he was styled, to wait upon them,*—the misery of two youths so highly born and so delicately nurtured may be more readily imagined than described. According to tradition, the stronghold in which the young princes were immured, after their removal from the state apartments in the Tower of London, is that which is so familiarly known as the Bloody Tower, the same which, six years previously, had witnessed the death-scene of the unhappy Clarence.

> *P. Edward.*   Yet before we go,
> One question more with you, master lieutenant.
> We like you well; and, but we do perceive
> More comfort in your looks than in these walls,
> For all our uncle Gloster's friendly speech
> Our hearts would be as heavy still as lead.
> I pray you tell me at which door or gate
> Was it my uncle Clarence did go in,
> When he was sent a prisoner to this place?
> *Brakenbury.*   At this, my liege! Why sighs your majesty?

---

* Sir T. More, Hist. of Richard III. p. 130.

P. Edward. He went in here that ne'er came back again !
But as God hath decreed, so let it be !
Come, brother, shall we go ?
    P. Richard. Yes, brother, anywhere with you.
          Heywood's King Edward IV. Part II. Act iii. Sc. 2.

Immured in this gloomy prison-house, the two brothers are described as clinging together in the vain hope of finding comfort in each other's embraces; as neglecting their dress, and anticipating with childhood's horror the dark doom which awaited them. "The prince," says Sir Thomas More, "never tied his points nor aught wrought of himself; but with that young babe, his brother, lingered in thought and heaviness, till a traitorous death delivered them of that wretchedness."[*]

    P. Richard. How does your lordship?
    P. Edward.   Well, good brother Richard:
How does yourself?   You told me your head ached.
    P. Richard. Indeed it does, my lord! feel with your hands
How hot it is!
    P. Edward. Indeed you have caught cold,
With sitting yesternight to hear me read;
I pray thee go to bed, sweet Dick ! poor little heart!
    P. Richard. You'll give me leave to wait upon your lordship?
    P. Edward. I had more need, brother, to wait on you ;
For you are sick, and so am not I.
    P. Richard. Oh, lord! methinks this going to our bed,
How like it is going to our grave.
    P. Edward. I pray thee do not speak of graves, sweet heart;
Indeed thou frightest me.
    P. Richard. Why, my lord brother, did not our tutor teach us,
That when at night we went unto our bed,
We still should think we went unto our grave?

---

[*] Sir T. More, Hist. of Richard III. p. 130.

P. Edward. Yes, that is true,
If we should do as every Christian ought
To be prepared to die at every hour.
But I am heavy.
    P. Richard.   Indeed so am I.
    P. Edward. Then let us to our prayers and go to bed.
        Heywood's King Edward IV. Part II. Act iii. Sc. 5.

Presuming that due confidence is to be placed in the confession said to have been made by Sir James Tyrrell in the following reign. Richard was on his northern progress, and was approaching the neighbourhood of Gloucester, when, for the first time, he allowed his cruel intentions, in regard to his nephews, to transpire. At this time the constable of the Tower was his former friend and devoted adherent, Sir Robert Brakenbury. To Brakenbury, accordingly, the king despatched one of his creatures, John Green, furnishing him with written orders to the constable to put the two princes to death; the which John Green, we are told, "did his errand unto Brakenbury, kneeling before our Lady in the Tower." In the mean time the king had advanced as far as Warwick, where he was subsequently rejoined by his emissary Green.* The

* Sir T. More, Hist. of Richard III. pp. 127–8. There seems to be no difficulty in fixing the date of Green's mission as the beginning of August. The king reached Reading shortly after the 23rd of July; made a short stay at Oxford; proceeded from thence to Gloucester, and eventually reached Tewkesbury on the 4th of August. Before the 8th of August he was at Warwick. Green, though Lord Bacon speaks of him as a "page," was probably a gentleman of good family, holding not the menial appointment of a page of the chamber, but that of an esquire

answer which the latter brought him from Brakenbury occasioned him great displeasure. The constable, it seems had more gentleness in his nature
than to commit so foul a crime, and, accordingly,
had peremptorily, though doubtless respectfully,
refused to obey the orders of his king.

That night, as the king paced his apartment in
the noble castle of Warwick, he was unable to conceal the perturbation of his mind from the favourite
page who was in attendance on him. Some queru-
lous remarks which escaped him, intimating how
little trust he could place even in those on whom he
had heaped the greatest favours, induced the page

of the body, which would place him in immediate attendance on the
person of his sovereign. For instance, in the ordinances for the government of the household of Edward IV., we find esquires of the body
denoted as "noble of condition, whereof always two be attendant upon
the king's person to array and unarray him," &c.—*Royal Household
Ordinances,* p. 36. Again, in the reign of Henry VII.: "The esquires
of the body ought to array the king, and unarray him, and no man else
to set hand on the king; and if it please the king to have a pallet without his traverse, there must be two esquires for the body, or else a
knight for the body, to lie there, or else in the next chamber."—*Ibid.* p.
118. The duties of the page, on the contrary, appear to have been
those of the commonest menial. "Pages of the chamber [temp.
Edward IV.], besides the both wardrobes, to wait upon and to keep
clean the king's chamber, and most honest from faults of hounds, as of
other; and to help truss, and clean harness, cloth, sacks, and other
things necessary, as they be commanded by such as are above them,"
&c.—*Ibid.* p. 41. That a person, whose province it was to discharge
these mean offices, should not only have been admitted by Richard to
familiar intercourse with him, but that he should have been selected to
be the confidant of his terrible intentions, appears to be in the highest
degree improbable.

to address himself to his royal master.   He knew a
man, he said, who was lying on a pallet in the
outer chamber, who at all hazards would execute
his grace's pleasure.   The individual to whom he
alluded was Sir James Tyrrell, a man who had
achieved a high reputation for personal courage,
but whose estimate of the value of human life, and
of the importance of virtuous actions, was clearly
of the lowest stamp.   Like Sir Richard Ratcliffe
and Catesby, he had been a follower and a friend of
the usurper in former days.   To his extreme mortification he had seen those persons preferred to higher
favours or higher posts than had fallen to his own
share; and, accordingly, jealousy of the success of
others, as well as an innate craving for wealth and
distinction, predisposed him to become a ready tool
in the hands of his sovereign.*   Well pleased with
his attendant's suggestion, Richard forthwith proceeded to the outer apartment, where lay Sir James
and his brother Sir Thomas.   "What, sirs," he
said merrily, "be ye in bed so soon?"   He then
ordered Sir James to follow him into his own chamber, where he imparted to him the terrible purpose
for which he required his services.   The commission
is said to have been accepted without the slightest
hesitation.   Accordingly, on the following day
Tyrrell set out for London, carrying with him a
written order from the king to Sir Robert Braken-

* Sir T. More's Richard III. pp. 128–9.

bury to deliver up the keys of the Tower to Tyrrell for a single night.*

Having made the necessary communication to Brakenbury, Tyrrell fixed upon "the night next ensuing" as the fittest time for carrying out his terrible purpose. The shedding of blood might obviously have led to the detection of his projected guilt, and it was probably for this reason that he decided on the safer method of suffocating the young princes in their sleep. In the mean time, Tyrrell had contrived to secure the services of two ferocious adepts in villany, one John Dighton, his own horsekeeper, a "big, broad, square, and strong knave," and one Miles Forrest, a "fellow beforetime fleshed in murder." In the dead of the night, these two miscreants stole into the apartment in which the two young princes lay together in the same bed. The younger prince is said to have been awake at the time. Guessing the horrible purpose of the intruders, he roused his brother, exclaiming, "Wake, brother, for they are here who come to kill thee!" Then turning to the executioners,— "Why do you not kill me?" said the child: "kill me, and let him live!"† The appeal was made in vain. In an instant, the innocent heirs of the proudest house which ever held sway in England were wrapped and entangled in the bedclothes.

* Sir T. More's Richard III. pp. 129–30.
† Chroniques de Molinet, ut supra, p. 402.

Then came the painful climax described by Sir
Thomas More,—the assassins pressing the feather-
bed and pillows over the mouths of their victims,
till, smothered and stifled and their breath failing,
they gave up to God their innocent souls unto the
joys of heaven, leaving to their tormentors their
bodies dead in the bed."[*] The murderers then
called in their employer, in order that he might
satisfy himself that the work of death was complete.
Tyrrell waited only to give orders respecting the
interment of the princes, and then rode in all haste
to his royal master at York.[†]

> " *Tyrrell.*　The tyrannous and bloody act is done;
> The most arch deed of piteous massacre
> That ever yet this land was guilty of.
> Dighton and Forrest, whom I did suborn
> To do this piece of ruthless butchery,
> Albeit they were fleshed villains, bloody dogs,
> Melting with tenderness and mild compassion,
> Wept like to children, in their death's sad story.
> 'O thus,' quoth Dighton, 'lay the gentle babes;'—
> 'Thus, thus,' quoth Forrest, 'girdling one another
> Within their alabaster innocent arms;
> Their lips were four red roses on a stalk,
> And, in their summer beauty, kissed each other.

---

[*] Sir T. More's Richard III. pp. 130–1.

[†] From the statement of Sir Thomas More, as well as from a compari-
son of dates, the crime would seem to have been committed about the
middle of August.　Rous (Hist. Reg. Ang. p. 215) intimates that it took
place somewhat more than three months after Richard had waited on
the young king at Stony Stratford (viz. the 30th of April), and Molinet
at five weeks from the time that the young princes were treated as
prisoners.　Chroniques, p. 402.　The dates, therefore, assigned by these
three writers, very nearly agree.

> A book of prayers on their pillow lay;
> Which once,' quoth Forrest, 'almost changed my mind;
> But, O, the devil!'—there the villain stopped;
> When Dighton thus told on: 'We smothered
> The most replenished sweet work of nature,
> That, from the prime creation, e'er she framed.'
> Hence both are gone with conscience and remorse
> They could not speak; and so I left them both,
> To bear this tidings to the bloody king."
>
> *King Richard III.* Act iv. Sc. 3.

In accordance with the orders issued by Sir James Tyrrell to Dighton and Forrest, the young princes are said to have been interred "at the stair-foot, metely deep in the ground, under a great heap of stones." * One might have imagined that, so long as their graves disclosed no secrets, Richard would have troubled himself but little in regard either to the mode or the place of his nephews' burial. On the contrary, however, he is said to have exhibited a strange displeasure at no greater respect having been shown to their remains, and to have even given orders for their being disinterred and placed in consecrated ground. "Whereupon," says Sir Thomas More, "they say a priest of Sir Robert Brakenbury's took up the bodies again and secretly interred them in such place as, by the occasion of his death which only knew it, could never since come to light." † More than two centuries passed away from the date of their death, when, in the reign of Charles II., in "taking away

* Sir T. More, Hist. of Richard III. p. 131.
† Ibid. p. 132.

the stairs which led *from the royal lodgings to the chapel of the White Tower*," * there were discovered, about ten feet in the ground, on the south side of the White Tower, the remains of two human beings, corresponding in sex and age with what might be presumed to be those of the murdered princes.† Either, then, the king's orders were for some reason disobeyed, and consequently the spot in which the remains were found was the original "stair-foot" in which Dighton and Forrest deposited them; or else, which is more probable, the persons, who were intrusted with the second interment of the unfortunate princes, considered the staircase leading to the chapel royal as no less consecrated ground than the chapel itself, and thus in spirit carried out the king's injunctions, by burying them beneath it.

The further fact of the bodies having been discovered at the foot of the staircase leading from the royal apartments to the chapel royal, is not without its significance. Tradition, as we have already mentioned, points out the Bloody Tower as having witnessed the death-scene of the innocent princes.

---

* Wren's Parentalia, p. 283.

† Sandford's Geneal. Hist. book v. pp. 427–9. Sandford received his account of the disinterment from an eye-witness who was engaged in the investigation. The discovery took place in 1674. In Wren's Parentalia (p. 283) will be found the warrant from Charles II. to Sir Christopher Wren, then surveyor of the works, to reinter the bones, in "a white marble coffin," in Westminster Abbey.

From their high rank, however, we are more inclined to think that they perished in one of the
royal apartments of the Tower or in some chamber
close adjoining them, than in the miserable dungeon which is still pointed out as having been their
prison-house, and at the "stair-foot" of which gossip still idly indicates that their remains were eventually discovered.*   But to whomsoever those relics
of humanity may have belonged, it seems evident
they were those of no ordinary persons, and, moreover, that they were the remains of persons who
had met with a violent end.   In those days, it may
be mentioned, there was a direct communication
between the royal apartments at the southeast
angle of the fortress, and the state apartments, and
the chapel in the White Tower.   It was apparently,
then, at the foot of the very stairs,—which, when
the sovereign held his court in the Tower, he was
daily in the habit of ascending for the purpose of
offering up his devotions in the chapel royal—that

---

* On the ground floor of the White Tower, immediately below the
chapel, are three apartments, on the walls of which may still be seen
more than one interesting inscription, engraved by the unhappy prisoners who formerly tenanted them.   These apartments, from their having
almost adjoined the palatial chambers of the fortress, and also from
their close vicinity to the spot in which the bodies were discovered,
were not impossibly those in which the princes were imprisoned and
murdered.   Certainly, it was not till the latter end of the reign of
Elizabeth, that the Bloody Tower received its present name.   It had
previously been styled the Garden Tower.   Bayley's Tower of London.
p. 257.   See Appendix B.

the remains were discovered. That such a spot should have been selected for the interment of the dead,—unless for the purpose of preserving a weighty secret and concealing a fearful crime,—it would be difficult, we think, to imagine. To what other conclusion, then, can we reasonably arrive, but that the bones, which were discovered and exhumed in the seventeenth century, were no other than those of the murdered sons of King Edward IV.? It may be mentioned that Charles II. caused them to be collected and placed in a sarcophagus of white marble, which may be seen in the south aisle of Henry VII.'s chapel at Westminster.

CHAPTER VI.

MANY ingenious attempts have been made to relieve the character of Richard III. from so atrocious a crime as the murder of his nephews. Of the arguments which have been adduced in his favour, the most important are those which tend to support the presumption that at least one, if not both, of the two princes escaped from the Tower, and that the individual who afterwards figured so conspicuously, under the name of Perkin Warbeck, was in reality Richard Duke of York.

Unquestionably, the story of that mysterious adventurer, if adventurer he were, merits inquiry and consideration. That an obscure youth should have found means to shake one of the most powerful thrones in Europe; that the kings of France and of Scotland should not only have acknowledged him to be the heir to the throne of England, but should have caressed and entertained him at their courts with all the honors due to sovereign heads; that the Scottish monarch should have been so satisfied that his guest was the real Duke of York, that he gave

him in marriage his beautiful and near kinswoman,
the Lady Katherine Douglas, and invaded England
with an army for the purpose of placing him on
the throne of the Plantagenets; that the putative
son of a Belgian Jew should not only have been
gifted with a dignity of mien and a refinement of
manner which were admitted and admired even by
the most fastidious, but that his features should
have borne a remarkable resemblance to the beautiful prince whom he claimed to have been his father;
that he should have won the favour of the people
of Ireland, and that the nobles of England should
have raised their standards in his cause; that the
lord-chamberlain, Sir William Stanley, the
wealthiest subject in England and connected by
marriage with Henry VII., should not only have
embarked in it, but have suffered death in consequence on the scaffold; and, lastly, that the
Duchess of Burgundy, the sister of the late king,
should not only have received Warbeck with all
honour at her court, but have acknowledged him
as her nephew in the face of Europe,—are facts
which not only continue to excite curiosity and investigation in our own time, but seem, at one
period, to have raised doubts, if not apprehensions,
even in the mind of Henry himself.*

* See Carte's Hist. of Engl. vol. ii. p. 854, &c.; Historic Doubts,
Lord Orford's Works, vol. ii. p. 155, &c.; Laing's Dissertation in
Henry's Hist. of England, vol. xii. p. 431, App.; Bayley's Hist. of the
Tower of London, p. 335, &c.

But curious as these arguments undoubtedly are, they may be met by others equally weighty. If Charles of France acknowledged Warbeck to be the rightful heir to the throne of England, let it be remembered that it was at a time when it was clearly his object to distress and embarrass Henry, and further that, when that motive ceased to exist, he at once repudiated the adventurer. Neither is it clear that the conduct of James of Scotland was altogether disinterested.* Certain at least it is, that Warbeck secretly covenanted to deliver up to him the important city of Berwick, and to pay him fifty thousand marks in two years, in the event of his succeeding in dethroning Henry.† Moreover, the favour shown him by the Anglo-Irish can hardly be taken into serious account. A people who, a short time previously, had crowned Lam-

---

* Ellis's Orig. Letters, First Series, vol. i. p. 26; Pinkerton's Hist. of Scotl. vol. ii. pp. 2, 26. Tytler seems to be of opinion that James was accessory to Warbeck's imposition at a much earlier period than has been usually supposed, and although at the time he believed him to be an adventurer, yet he was afterwards induced to change his opinion. Hist. of Scotl. vol. iii. p. 474. A contemporary writer, moreover, whose authority is of value, tends to confirm the supposition that James, at one period at least, believed Warbeck to be the genuine Duke of York. "Rex errore deceptus, ut plerique alii, etiam prudentissimi." —*B. Andreas, Vita Hen. VII.* p. 70.

† And yet, in the declaration which Warbeck published on entering Northumberland with a Scottish army, we find him having the confidence solemnly to call the Almighty to witness that "his dearest cousin the King of Scotland's aiding him in person in this his righteous quarrel, was without any pact or promise, or so much as a demand of anything prejudicial to his crown or subjects."—*Carte,* vol. ii. p. 849.

bert Simnel in Christchurch Cathedral, Dublin, with a diadem taken from an image of the Virgin, were doubtless predisposed to hail with enthusiasm a far more plausible and fascinating pretender. Again, the fact of the Duchess of Burgundy having acknowledged Warbeck as her nephew, is not a little shorn of its importance by her having formerly supported the imposture of Simnel.* Her aversion to the new rule in England inclined her to adopt any expedient that might weaken the government of Henry VII. The duchess, as we find Henry himself complaining in a letter to Sir Gilbert Talbot, had formerly shown her malice " by sending hither one feigned boy," and now, " eftsoons," she must needs send over " another feigned lad, called Perkin Warbeck."†

Warbeck, in fact, would seem to have been merely one of a series of impostors, whom, from time to time, the secret machinations of a powerful and well-organized faction in England called into political existence, for the purpose of crippling and, if possible, uprooting the Tudor dynasty. The individual, in whom their hopes and fears were really centred, and whom they would willingly have placed on the throne in lieu of Henry, appears to have been the Earl of Warwick, who, after the death of his uncle, King Richard, had become the

* Lord Bacon's Henry VII. in Kennet, vol. i. pp. 585–6.
† Ellis's Orig. Letters, First Series, vol. i. pp. 19, 20.

last male heir of the great house of Plantagenet.* If the pretensions of Warwick had formerly been regarded in so formidable a light, both by Edward IV. and Richard III., that they kept him either closely watched or else in durance, how much greater apprehension were they calculated to inspire in the mind of a monarch who owed his crown neither to blood nor to election, but to the hateful pretext of conquest, and to a marriage which he had offensively postponed from time to time!

At the period when Warbeck appeared on the stage, the government of Henry VII. had become extremely unpopular among the aristocratic and commercial classes in England, and still more unpopular with the clergy. By the former, Henry's defective title to the throne, his spurious descent from John of Gaunt and Catherine Swynford, the questionable legitimacy of his queen, and the blood of the obscure and obnoxious Woodvilles which flowed in her veins, seem to have been regarded as unpardonable offences. In the eyes of the highborn partisans of the house of York, Henry's only title to the crown was derived from his queen, and, moreover, in the opinion of many persons, that title

* Lord Bacon, speaking of Lambert Simnel, observes: "And for the person of the counterfeit, it was agreed that, if all things succeeded well, he should be put down, and the true Plantagenet received."— *Life of Henry VII. in Kennet*, vol. i. p. 586. Doubtless it was intended to pursue the same course towards Perkin Warbeck, in the event of his enterprise proving successful.

was a very obnoxious one.   On the other hand, the
Earl of Warwick could boast an irreproachable
descent in the male line, from a long and illustrious race of kings.   In him were centred the
pure blood of the Plantagenets, the Beauchamps,
and the Nevilles.   But Warwick was unhappily a
prisoner in the hands of Henry, and, consequently,
any public declaration of his rights, or any insurrection in his favour, would doubtless have been the
signal for sending him to the scaffold.   With the
double object, then, of harassing the government
of Henry, and, at the same time, screening Warwick, were called into political existence, such convenient scapegoats as Lambert Simnel, Perkin
Warbeck, and Ralph Wilford.   Should they fail,
their miscarriage would in no way have jeopardized
the life of Warwick, whereas, had any one of them
succeeded in his enterprise, it would have been
easy enough to have set the impostor aside, and to
have conducted the true Plantagenet from a prison
to the throne.*

As regards Warbeck personally, many arguments
might be adduced tending to the conviction that
he was an impostor.   No evidence of his having
been the son of Edward IV. was ever produced by

* "This at least is certain," writes Lingard, "that as long as Warwick lived, pretenders to the crown rapidly succeeded each other:
after his execution, Henry was permitted to reign without molestation."
—*Hist. of Engl.* vol. iv. p. 584, App.

him. Of those persons, who, according to his own romantic account, either assisted him to escape from the Tower, or afterwards supported him in a foreign land, not one came forward either to substantiate his tale, or to claim the reward which they had earned by having rendered so important a service to the heir of England. There is reason, moreover, for believing that Warbeck had his lesson less accurately by heart than has usually been supposed ;* and, lastly,—unless his confession, printed by command of Henry, is to be regarded as an impudent fabrication,—Warbeck himself unhesitatingly admitted that he was an impostor.† It has been argued, that Henry's remissness in collecting and pub-

* In a letter from Warbeck to Queen Isabella of Castile, in which correctness was of the utmost importance to him, he shows himself so indifferently acquainted with the age of the individual whom he was personifying, as to represent himself as having been nearly nine, instead of eleven, years of age at the time when he insisted that he had escaped from the Tower. For this interesting letter and important fact we are indebted to the valuable researches of Sir Frederick Madden. See Archæologia, vol. xxvii. pp. 156, 161. The Duke of York was born on the 17th of August 1472. The date of his presumed assassination we have ventured to place in the middle of August 1483. See ante, p. 216, note.

† The genuineness of Perkin Warbeck's confession has occasionally been disputed. The remarkable fact, however, pointed out by Sir Frederick Madden in the Archæologia, on the authority of Bernard Andreas, that the confession was actually printed at the time, of course by the authority and license of Henry, proves it to be a state document of the highest importance. "Rex imprimi demandavit."—*B. Andreas, Vit. Hen. VII.* p. 14; Arch. vol. xxvii. p. 164. For Warbeck's confession, see Hall, pp. 448, 449; Grafton, vol. ii. p. 218; and Henry's Hist. of England, vol. xii. p. 392, Appendix.

lishing proofs of Warbeck's imposition, furnishes
presumptive evidence either that the English monarch had no case at all, or else that it was so weak
a one that he was afraid to submit it to the judgment of his subjects. But if Henry, after all his
inquiries, really believed that Warbeck was the true
Duke of York, would so merciless a monarch, as
he is usually represented to have been, have spared
the life of his foe, when on two different occasions
he held him in his power? If Henry had scrupled
not to send his friend and benefactor, Sir William
Stanley, to the block for abetting the pretensions of
Warbeck, is it likely that he would have shown
greater mercy to Warbeck himself? If he believed
in the truth of Warbeck's story, would he have exposed him to the curious and pitying gaze of the
citizens of London? Would he twice have exhibited in the public stocks the handsome youth
whom many living persons must have beheld in his
boyhood, the son of the magnificent monarch whose
affability and good nature still endeared him to
their hearts? Would Henry have allowed him to
wander about for months within the precincts of
the palace, liable at any moment to be recognized,
and greeted as their brother, by the queen and her
younger sisters? Lastly, if Warbeck had been the
important personage which he represented himself
to be, is it possible to believe that so stern and
jealous a monarch as Henry would have suffered

him to be so insufficiently guarded, or so carelessly watched, that the pretender was enabled to slip into a sanctuary when it suited his purpose?

The real fact appears to have been that, however threatening at its outset was Warbeck's conspiracy, it was confined, in England and Ireland at least, within much narrower limits than has usually been supposed. When once apprized of the real extent, or rather of the insignificance of the danger, we find Henry treating the pretensions of Warbeck— the *garçon*, as he twice styles him in his communications with the court of France—with the utmost unconcern and contempt.*   To this contempt,— added perhaps to a wise disinclination on the part of the king to convert an impostor into a martyr, as well as to the singular interest which both Henry and his queen seem to have taken in Warbeck's beautiful wife, the Lady Catherine,—the pretender was probably indebted for the clemency, which, as a notorious and convicted rebel, he had little reason to anticipate. It was not till Henry had ascertained that Warbeck was carrying on a secret correspondence with the Earl of Warwick, the only person whose pretensions to the crown he had reason to dread; not till he discovered the experienced and accomplished adventurer plotting with the last male heir of the house of Plantagenet to effect their escape from the Tower and to subvert his

* Archæologia, vol. xxvii. pp. 165, 167.

government,—that the sternest of the Tudors handed over his rival to the executioner. Then, indeed, he sent Warwick to suffer an honourable death by the axe on Tower Hill, leaving Warbeck to perish on the common gibbet at Tyburn.

But even allowing Perkin Warbeck to have been the real Duke of York, such an admission, instead of relieving the memory of Richard from the crime of murder, tends, on the other hand, we conceive, more directly to establish his guilt. For instance, if Warbeck had been a true Plantagenet, surely, instead of blackening the memory of his uncle, by charging him with the foulest of crimes, he would have done his utmost to vindicate the honour of the illustrious line of which he claimed to be the representative. But what was the story which he related to the King of Scotland? From the nursery, he said, he had been carried to a sanctuary, from a sanctuary to a prison, and from a prison he had been delivered over to the hands of the "tormentor." Thirsting for the crown of his elder brother, their "unnatural uncle," proceeded Warbeck, employed an assassin to murder them in the Tower. But the projected crime was only half completed. The young king, he said, was "cruelly slain;" but the assassin, either sated with blood, or actuated by some more amiable motive, not only spared the life of the younger brother, but assisted

him to escape beyond the sea.* The genuineness
of this reputed conversation appears to be borne
out by two very remarkable documents, which
emanated directly from Warbeck himself.
"Whereas," says Warbeck in his proclamation
to the English people, "we, in our tender years,
escaped, by God's great might, out of the Tower of
London, and were secretly conveyed over the sea to
other divers countries."† And again he writes to
Isabella of Castile,—"Whereas, the Prince of
Wales, eldest son of Edward, formerly king of
England, of pious memory, my dearest lord and
brother *was miserably put to death*, and I myself,
then nearly nine years of age, was also delivered to
a certain lord to be killed: [but] it pleased the
divine clemency, that that lord, having compassion
on my innocence, preserved me alive and in
safety."‡ Admitting, then, the truthfulness of
Warbeck's statement, to what other conclusion can
we arrive than that Richard contemplated the
murder of both his nephews, although he was
virtually the murderer only of one? The blood of
only one may have been actually on his head, but,
according to every principle human and divine, the

* Lord Bacon's Life of Henry VII. in Kennet, vol. i. p. 614; Hall,
p. 473; Archæologia, vol. xxvii. p. 154.

† Henry's Hist. of Engl. vol. xii. p. 387, where Warbeck's confession
is printed at length from the Birch MS. 4160, 5, collated with Harl.
MS. 482, fol. 128.

‡ Archæologia, vol. xxvii. p. 156.

crime was not the less heinous because by accident
it was only partially completed.

The remaining arguments, which tend to substantiate the guilt of Richard, admit of being more
concisely investigated and more hastily dismissed.
If, it may be inquired, Richard was really innocent,
what was the actual fate of the two brothers?
That they were alive, and inmates of the Tower, at
the time of his accession, not a doubt can exist.
What, then, became of them?   Richard alone had
the charge and custody of their persons.   As their
nearest male relation, as their uncle, as their guardian, as the chief of the State and the fountain of
justice, it was his bounden duty not only to protect
them from wrong, but to produce their persons if
required; or, at all events, satisfactorily to account
for their disappearance from the eye of man and
from the light of heaven.   No living being, except
by his express injunctions, would have dared to lift
a finger against them.   No living being, apparently,
had any interest in destroying them but himself.
Moreover, the tongues of men, not only at home,
but at foreign courts, charged him with the crime
of murder, yet he took no steps to prove his innocence.   Had his nephews died a natural death,
surely he would have been only too eager to dem-
onstrate so important a fact to the world.   Again,
there were periods in his career when it was his interest to prove that they were still in the land of the

living. If, then, he failed to produce them, to what other conclusion can we arrive, but that his victims had ceased to exist?

Many other circumstances might be adduced highly unfavorable to the presumption of King Richard's innocence. In the first place, indisputable evidence has been discovered, showing that the different persons, whose names are associated with the murder, received ample rewards from Richard. Brakenbury, who, though not a principal in the crime, was unquestionably in the secret, received numerous manors and other royal pecuniary grants. Green, the messenger who was sent to him by the king from Gloucestershire, was appointed receiver of the lordship of the Isle of Wight, and of the castle and lordship of Porchester. Sir James Tyrrell was enriched by a variety of appointments and royal grants. John Dighton, one of the actual assassins, was awarded the bailiffship of Aiton, in Staffordshire; and lastly, the other ruffian, Miles Forrest, " the fellow fleshed in murder," was not only appointed keeper of the wardrobe in one of the royal residences, Baenard Castle, but at his death, which occurred shortly after the assassination of the young princes, his widow was awarded a pension.*　Again, it has been asked, why was Richard so eager to obtain possession of the person

* Harleian MSS. var. quoted in S. Turner's Middle Ages, vol. iv. pp. 459, 460.

of the young Duke of York, unless he intended
to sacrifice him to his ambition? Why did the
sanctuary at Westminster remain unwatched so
long as the young princes were known to be alive;
and, why, at the very time when it was publicly
rumoured that the young princes were no more, was
it suddenly placed in a state of siege?* A simple
answer suggests itself,—that, by the death of her
brothers, the princess had become the rightful possessor of the throne; that her escape to the continent, and her marriage with the Earl of Richmond,
might have proved fatal to Richard's power; and
consequently that it was of the utmost importance
to him to secure her person, or, at all events, to
prevent her flight.

Moreover, unlike the majority of the fearful
crimes which have been attributed to Richard III.,
the story of the murder of the young princes is
clearly no invention of those later chroniclers who
wrote to flatter the prejudices of the Tudor kings.
Not only do contemporary writers record how
general was the suspicion that they had met with
an untimely end, but, as we have already seen,
dangerous conspiracies were the consequence. " A
rumour was spread," says the Croyland Chronicle,
" that the sons of King Edward before named had
died a violent death, but it was uncertain how."†
According to another contemporary, Rous, " it

<hr>

*See ante, p. 203.   † Croyl. Chron. Cont. p. 491.

was afterwards known to very few by what death they suffered martyrdom."* Philip de Commines informs us, that so convinced was Louis XI. that Richard had murdered his two nephews, that he "looked upon him as a cruel and wicked person, and would neither answer his letters, nor give audience to his ambassador."† Fabyan, who flourished as an alderman of London when London aldermen were of higher dignity and repute than they are in our time, informs us that "the common fame went that King Richard had within the Tower put into secret death the two sons of his brother, Edward IV."‡ Lastly, the evidence of Polydore Virgil and of Bernard Andreas, who may be almost considered as contemporaries, must be regarded as of some importance. The former, indeed, admits, that by "what kind of death these sely children were executed is yet not certainly known;" but, on the other hand, he substantiates the somewhat later authority of Sir Thomas More, that the Tower was the scene of their death, and, moreover, mentions Sir James Tyrrell as the chief agent of Richard in carrying out his atrocious project.§ Andreas, on the other hand, distinctly affirms that Richard caused his nephews to be put to death with the sword.‖ It may be argued and objected that these

---

* Hist. Angl. Reg. p. 214.　　　† De Commines, tome ii. pp. 243-4.
‡ Fabyan's Chronicles, p. 670.　　§ Polydore Virgil, lib. xxv. p. 694.
‖ "Clam ferro feriri jussit."—*Vita Henr. Sept.* p. 24.

two writers were courtiers, and that Polydore
Virgil wrote his history expressly at the desire of
Henry VII., whom it was his object to flatter and
please.   But it must also be remembered that
Polydore Virgil had conversed with many of the
principal persons who were alive at the time of
King Richard's accession, and had every facility of
obtaining the most accurate information.   The
reigning queen, moreover, as the sister of the murdered princes, would naturally take a deep interest
in any historical work which was likely to perpetuate her brothers' melancholy story.   If the story,
then, was merely an idle fiction,—nay, unless it
had been commonly credited by the best informed
persons at the time,—would Polydore Virgil have
confidently published it to the world? or would he
have narrated to the queen a pathetic story of the
fate of her own brothers, which, if false, could
scarcely fail to be most offensive to her?   Is it
likely that the Duke of Buckingham, and the other
noble persons who were associated with him in rebellion, would have risked their lives and estates
in the cause of the Princess Elizabeth, unless they
had been completely satisfied that her brothers had
ceased to exist?   Lastly, unless King Richard had
been convinced beyond all doubt that the work of
murder had been completed, and that consequently
Elizabeth had become the true and indubitable
heiress to the throne, is it likely that so astute a

prince would have sought to strengthen his rule by making her his queen,—a project which, on his becoming a widower, there seems to be little question that he contemplated? Doubtless, so long as history shall be read, the question whether Richard was, or was not, guilty of the murder of his nephews, will continue to be a matter of dispute. Men will interpret the evidence according to their prejudices or their feelings. For our own part, could the coroner hold his inquest over those mouldering relics of humanity which were discovered at the base of the White Tower, we cannot but think that there would be forthcoming a mass of circumstantial evidence, sufficient to convict Richard Plantagenet, King of England, of the crime of wilful murder.

The principal persons, associated with the Duke of Buckingham in the secret conspiracy which was forming against Richard, were Margaret Countess of Richmond, the lineal heiress and representative of the house of Lancaster, and Dr. Morton, Bishop of Ely, afterwards Cardinal and Archbishop of Canterbury. According to Sir Thomas More, who in his youth had been intimately associated with the latter, the bishop was "a man of great natural wit, very well learned, and of a winning behaviour."* He had formerly been chaplain to Henry VI., and had sat at the council-table of that

* Sir T. More's Richard III. p. 138.

unhappy monarch.*   Edward IV., on his accession, found means to attach him to his interests; rewarding his complaisance by retaining him as a privy councillor, and subsequently advancing him to the bishopric of Ely. To King Edward, during his lifetime, and, after the death of that monarch, to his unfortunate sons, the bishop seems to have been sincerely and devotedly attached. This devotion it was which had drawn down on him the hatred and resentment of Richard. The protector, as we have seen, arrested, and, in the first instance, imprisoned him in the Tower, though he subsequently committed him to the milder custody of the Duke of Buckingham.

It was doubtless during the time that the bishop was residing under Buckingham's hospitable roof at Brecknock, that he contrived, by his arguments and persuasions, to wean his powerful host from his allegiance to King Richard. No sooner was Buckingham prevailed upon to turn traitor, than their plans were speedily matured. The line of policy which they resolved to adopt was as simple as it was wise. By the death of her ill-fated brothers, the Princess Elizabeth had become the lineal representative of the house of York. But, however indisputable might have been her title to the throne, her sex, and her close alliance by blood to the unpopular Woodvilles, rendered it improb-

* Sir T. More's Richard III. p. 140.

able that her claims would meet with favour beyond the walls of Brecknock. As Buckingham observed to Bishop Morton,—" I called an old proverb to remembrance, which says, ' Woe to that kingdom where children rule and women govern !' "* The conspirators, therefore, turned their attention to Henry Earl of Richmond, who, by right of his mother, was, in the eyes of the partisans of the house of Lancaster, the head of that fallen house. The project of uniting the princess to the young earl appears to have emanated from the bishop. To the duke he proposed, that, in the event of their obtaining the joint concurrence of the queen-dowager and the Countess of Richmond, the crown should be offered to Henry on the express condition of his guaranteeing to make the princess his wife. Thus, argued the bishop, the rival houses of York and Lancaster will hereafter be united by the closest ties of relationship. Thus a termination will be put to those cruel and unnatural contests, which for so many years have deluged England with blood.

As the secret negotiations, which they proposed to set on foot, must necessarily be attended with imminent peril, it was requisite, for the safety of all concerned, that they should be conducted by a person of singular prudence and foresight. Fortunately the bishop had such a person in his eye.

* Kennet, vol. i. p. 503.

"He had an old friend," he said, "a man sober,
discreet, and well-witted, called Reginald Bray,
whose prudent policy he had known to have compassed things of great importance.*   Bray was of a
good Norman family, which had long attached
itself to the house of Lancaster.   His father had
been of the privy council to Henry VI. ; he himself
had been formerly receiver-general to Buckingham's uncle Sir Henry Stafford, the second husband of the Countess of Richmond, and was, at
this very time, in the service of that illustrious
lady.   As it was deemed prudent by the conspirators that the countess should be the first person
communicated with, Bray's position in her household was rendered of considerable importance.   He
was accordingly summoned to Brecknock, and
forthwith intrusted with the secret designs of the
conspirators.   His services proved of inestimable
value.   Through his agency, secret negotiations
were set on foot, which proved satisfactory to all
parties.   Sir Giles Daubeny, afterwards Lord Daubeny, Sir John Cheney, Sir Richard Guildford, and
other persons of influence, were induced to join the
conspiracy against Richard.†   The queen-dowager
eagerly agreed to the proposals which were made to
her; while the Countess of Richmond naturally
embraced with enthusiasm a project which promised

* Grafton's Chron. vol. ii. p. 129.
† Polydore Virgil, lib. xxv. p. 698.

to restore the fortunes of the house of Lancaster, and to exalt to the throne a son whom she tenderly loved. In the mean time, trustworthy emissaries had been sent to the young earl, then an exile in Brittany, who sent back the most satisfactory replies to his friends in England. A cordial understanding was established between the principal partisans of the rival houses of York and Lancaster. An insurrection was agreed upon. The 18th of October was fixed upon by the Earl of Richmond as the day for his setting foot in England, and on that day Buckingham undertook to raise the standard of insurrection. The greatest promptitude, and the most perfect good faith, appear to have marked the conduct of the leaders of both factions.

But, secretly and ably as the conspiracy had been conducted, it became much too widely spread long to escape the vigilance of Richard. Accordingly, no sooner was he apprized of the peril which threatened his throne, than he issued orders for an immediate levy of troops in the north, and, at the same time, summoned Buckingham to his presence. The summons was couched in friendly terms, but they failed in cajoling the duke. In the mean time, the day for action arrived. The Earl of Richmond set sail from St. Malo with 5000 soldiers on board his transports. The Courtenays rose in formidable numbers in the west of England; the Marquis of Dorset, half-brother to the Princess

Elizabeth, proclaimed the earl at Exeter; her uncle, the Bishop of Salisbury, declared for him in Wiltshire; the gentlemen of Kent assembled, with their retainers, to proclaim him at Maidstone; and the gentlemen of Berkshire met for a similar purpose at Newbury.

An enterprise, so wisely conceived and bravely commenced, seemed to promise, no less than to merit success. Circumstances, however, beyond the control of man destroyed the hopes of the conspirators. A violent tempest drove back the Earl of Richmond and his fleet to the shores of Brittany. The fate of Buckingham was a melancholy one. On the day appointed for the rising, he had unfurled his banner at Brecknock, and was advancing towards Gloucester with the intention of crossing the Severn and marching into the heart of England, when his progress was impeded by rains so heavy and incessant, that no living man remembered so terrible an inundation. The Severn and other rivers were rendered impassable; men, women, and children were drowned in their beds; cradles, with infants in them, were seen floating in the valleys. For a century afterwards it was spoken of as the Great Water, and sometimes as Buckingham's Great Water.* Thus was the duke prevented from keeping his appointment with his friends. His Welsh retainers,—some on account of want of food,

* Hall's Chronicle, p. 394; Holinshed, vol. iii. p. 417.

and some from superstitious feelings,—turned a deaf ear to his entreaties, and insisted on dispersing to their homes. The duke was left alone with a single servant. Having disguised himself in the best manner he could, he made his way towards Shrewsbury, in hopes of finding protection under the roof of an old servant of his family, one Ralph Banister, to whom he had formerly shown kindness. His confidence was met by the cruelest treachery. Whether tempted by the large reward offered for the duke's apprehension, or whether frightened at the hazard which he ran in sheltering so important a rebel, Banister is said to have betrayed his old master to the sheriff of Shropshire, who forthwith carried him to the king at Salisbury. A scaffold was immediately erected in the market-place of that city, on which, on the 2nd of November 1483, was beheaded, without a trial, the wealthiest and most powerful subject in England, the chief hope of the house of Lancaster.

Scarcely waiting till Buckingham's head was off his shoulders, Richard commenced a hurried march to the west of England, where the insurrection had threatened to be most formidable. On the 10th of November he reached Exeter. Not a man opposed his progress; not a blow was struck. , Intimidated by the summary and tragical fate of Buckingham, by the rapidity of the king's advance, and by the vast sums of money which he offered for their heads, the leaders of the late insurrection dispersed in all quarters. The Marquis of Dorset, Lionel Woodville Bishop of Salisbury, Peter Courtenay Bishop of Exeter, Sir John, afterwards Lord Welles, Sir Edward Courtenay, and other persons of rank and influence, found means to escape to Brittany. Others took refuge in sanctuary. Several were tried and executed. Among the latter was the king's own brother-in-law, Sir Thomas St. Leger.* Thus this formidable insurrection, instead of compassing the downfall of Richard, rendered him even more secure on his throne. He was enabled to disband a considerable part of his army, and on the 1st of December, attended by the lord-mayor and aldermen in their robes, he again entered London in triumph.

Richard now ventured to call a parliament, which accordingly assembled at Westminster on the 23rd of January. Overawed, probably, by his masterly policy, and by his recent signal success, the two houses anticipated his wishes with an obsequiousness which could scarcely have failed to afford him the highest satisfaction. They solemnly confirmed the irregular title by which, in the preceding

---

* Sir Thomas St. Leger had married the Lady Anne Plantagenet, daughter of the late Duke of York, and widow of the chivalrous Henry Holland, second Duke of Exeter. "One most noble knight perished, Thomas Saint Leger by name, to save whose life very large sums of money were offered; but all in vain, for he underwent his sentence of capital punishment."—*Croyl. Chron. Cont.* p. 492.

summer, he had been invited to wear the crown. They declared and decreed him to be, as well by right of consanguinity and inheritance, as by *lawful election*, "the very undoubted king of the realm of England." And, lastly, they enacted that, after the king's decease, "the high and excellent Prince Edward, son of our said sovereign lord the king, be heir-apparent to succeed him in the aforesaid crown and royal dignity."* The fact is somewhat a remarkable one, that although this procedure of parliament was virtually an act for deposing Edward V., it nevertheless contains no direct mention of that unhappy prince, either as being alive or dead. It proclaims, indeed, in general terms, that "all the issue and children" of Edward IV. are bastards, and therefore disqualified from inheriting the crown; but of the prince, in whose fate so many thousands of persons were

* An act was passed, the preamble to which set forth that, previously to his consecration and coronation, a roll had been presented to him, on behalf of the three estates of the realm, by divers lords spiritual and temporal, and other notable persons of the commons to the conditions and considerations contained in which he had benignly assented for the public weal and tranquillity of the land; but, forasmuch as the said three estates were not at that time assembled in form of parliament divers doubts and questions had been engendered in the minds of certain persons. For the removal therefore of such doubts and ambiguities, it was enacted by "the said three estates assembled in this present parliament," that all things affirmed and specified in the aforesaid roll be "of the like effect, virtue, and force, as if all the same things had been so said, affirmed, specified, and remembered in full parliament."—*Rot. Parl.* vol. vi. p. 240.

interested, and to whom most of the peers and prelates, who then deposed him, had so recently and so solemnly sworn allegiance, the act makes no direct mention whatever.

Richard had no sooner induced parliament to sanction his usurpation, than he turned his thoughts towards the gloomy sanctuary at Westminster, in which, for nearly twelve months, the widow of his brother Edward, and her five portionless daughters, had been subsisting on the charity of the abbot and monks of Westminster. The pertinacity with which the queen had refused to allow her daughters to quit the protection of the Church, had doubtless occasioned him the greatest annoyance. It amounted, in fact, to a tacit protest against his usurpation; a manifest declaration to the world, that she mistrusted his professions, and apprehended evil at his hands.

By what arguments, or by what pressure of circumstances, Elizabeth was at length induced to surrender herself and her daughters into the hands of her arch-enemy, will probably never be ascertained. Fortunately there is extant the copy of the oath, by which, on the word of a king, and by the Holy Evangelists, Richard solemnly swore, that, on condition of their quitting the sanctuary, he would not only secure to them their lives and liberty, but would provide for their future maintenance. The document is a very curious and interesting one. "I, Richard," it commences, "by the grace of God, King of England and of France, and Lord of Ireland, in the presence of you, my Lords Spiritual and Temporal, and you, Mayor and Aldermen of my city of London, promise and swear *verbo regio*, upon these Holy Evangelists of God, by me personally touched, that if the daughters of Dame Elizabeth Grey, late calling herself Queen of England,—that is to wit, Elizabeth, Cecily, Anne, Katherine, and Bridget,—will come unto me out of the sanctuary at Westminster, and be guided, ruled, and demeaned after me, then I shall see that they shall be in surety of their lives; and also not suffer any manner of hurt by any manner of person or persons to them, or any of them, on their bodies and persons, to be done by way of ravishment or defouling, contrary to their will; nor them nor any of them imprison within the Tower of London or other prison." Richard then proceeds to swear that his nieces shall be supported in a manner becoming his kinswomen; that he will marry them to gentlemen by birth, and endow each of them with "marriage lands and tenements" to the yearly value of 200 marks for the term of their lives; and that such gentlemen, as they may chance to marry, he will "strictly charge, from time to time, lovingly to love and entreat them as their wives and his kinswomen, as they would avoid and eschew his displeasure." To Dame Elizabeth Grey he promises to pay annually 700 marks (266*l.* 13*s.* 4*d.*), for the term of her natural life; and, lastly, he swears to discredit any reports that may be spread to their disadvantage, till they shall have had opportunities for "their lawful defence and answer."* The date of this remarkable document being the 1st of March 1484, the probability is, that the queen and her daughters quitted the sanctuary immediately afterwards.

King Richard was now at the height of his grandeur and power. Treason, indeed, still lay concealed in his path; but it was not from the ill-will nor discontent of the masses of his subjects, but from the intrigues of a restless nobility, and from the treachery of friends whom he had loaded with favours, that he had reason to anticipate peril. If his subjects still remembered, and shuddered at, the one terrible crime which he was more than sus-pected of having committed, they had, on the other hand, every reason to be grateful to him for hav-ing arrested the horrors of civil war, and for hav-ing extended to them a wise and humane adminis-tration. They recognized in him, at all events, an active, wise, temperate, and valiant prince; a prince sensitively jealous of the honour of the English nation, and an anxious well-wisher for its prosper-ity. They beheld in him a prince, who sought to win their suffrages and their affections; not by the

* Ellis's Orig. Letters, Second Series, vol. i. p. 149.

low arts with which those who have suddenly achieved greatness too often pander for popularity, but by reforming immemorial abuses, by introducing laws calculated to secure the safety and welfare of his subjects; by insisting on an equal administration of justice; by taking measures for the suppression of vice and immorality; by removing restrictions from trade, and encouraging commerce and the arts of industry and peace. His patronage of learning, and the encouragement which he extended to architecture, merit especial commendation. He released the University of Oxford of twenty marks of the fee due to him in the first year of his reign; and endowed Queen's College, Cambridge, with five hundred marks a year. He encouraged the newly-discovered art of printing, and, in order to extend learning in the Universities, caused an act to be passed, which was afterwards repealed by Henry VIII., permitting printed books to be brought into, and sold by retail in England.*

Moreover, so far from Richard having been the moody and morose tyrant, such as the venal writers who wrote under the Tudor dynasty delight to describe him, we have evidence from contemporary records that he followed the manly amusements which are popular with Englishmen, and enjoyed those tastes which throw a grace over human

* Wood's Hist. of Oxford, by Gutch, vol. i. pp. 639–40; Rous, p. 216; Sandf. Gen. Hist. book v. p. 434.

nature. His grants to the master of his hawks and the keepers of his mews by Charing Cross, and his payments to the keeper of his hart-hounds, tend to the presumption that he was no less the keen sportsman than the redoubted warrior and accomplished statesman. Lastly, that he delighted in music, is shown by the number of minstrels who came to his court from foreign lands, as well as by the annuities which he settled on musicians born on English soil.*

That Richard's nature was originally a compassionate one, there seems to be every reason for believing. His kindness to the female sex has been especially commented upon. To the Countess of Oxford, the wife of his arch-enemy, he granted a pension of one hundred pounds a year. To the widow of Earl Rivers, he secured the jointure which had been settled on her in the lifetime of her lord; and, notwithstanding the ingratitude which he had encountered from the late Duke of Buckingham, he settled on his widow an annuity of two hundred marks, and further relieved her necessities by the payment of Buckingham's debts.† His kindness to Lady Hastings, in releasing the estates of her lord, which had been forfeited by his attainder, we have already recorded.‡

* MSS. quoted in S. Turner's Middle Ages, vol. iv. pp. 31–2.
† Ibid. vol. iv. pp. 27–9.
‡ See Appendix C.

Considering the terrible crimes which Richard is said to have committed, it might have been expected that the clergy would have held him in especial abhorrence. On the contrary, we find them not only reconciled to his usurpation, but even addressing him in language of enthusiastic admiration. For instance, at a great assemblage of the clergy, convoked in the month of February 1484, about six months after the presumed murder of the young princes, we are not a little surprised at discovering the high dignitaries of the Church not only addressing Richard as a most catholic prince, but actually bearing solemn record to his "most noble and blessed disposition."* Either, then, the best informed persons of the day discredited the monstrous crimes which were laid to his charge, or else flattery and hypocrisy could scarcely be carried to more blasphemous lengths. If Richard was desirous to win the favour of the priesthood, the clergy seem to have been quite as eager on their part to secure Richard as their patron.

Richard, as we have remarked, was now at the height of his grandeur and power. Parliament had, in the most solemn manner, settled the crown upon him, and entailed it upon his heirs. The powerful foes, who had conspired to thwart him in his ambitious designs, had either perished on the scaffold, or were in exile. Their attainder had en-

* MSS. quoted in S. Turner's Middle Ages, vol. iv. p. 24.

abled him to reward his friends and followers without any drain on the royal coffers. According to Polydore Virgil,* he had "attained the type of glory and promotion, and in the eye of the people was accounted a happy man." But though, as Philip de Commines informs us, he reigned with a splendour and authority such as, for a hundred years past, no sovereign of England had achieved,† his mind is said to have been constantly harassed by a sense of the insecurity of his position, and by the tortures of remorse. Above all things, he is said to have reproached himself for having compassed the deaths of his innocent nephews. According to Sir Thomas More, his life was "spent in much pain and trouble outward; in much fear, anguish, and sorrow within; for I have heard, by credible report, of such as were secret with his chamberers, that, after this abominable deed done, he never had quiet in his mind; he never thought himself sure. When he went abroad, his eyes whirled about; his body was privily fenced; his hand ever on his dagger; his countenance and manner like one always ready to strike again. He took ill rest at night, lay long waking and musing. Sore wearied with care and watch, he rather slumbered than slept. Troubled with fearful dreams, he would sometimes suddenly start up, leap out of his bed,

* Camd. Soc. Trans. p. 191.
† Mémoires de Commines, tome ii. p. 158.

and run about the chamber. So was his restless heart continually tossed and tumbled, with the tedious impression and stormy remembrance of his abominable deed."*

An instance of his superstitious frame of mind, and morbid depression of spirits, is mentioned as having occurred during his recent visit to Exeter. Being much struck with the strength and elevation of the castle, he inquired its name. The reply was "Rougemont," a word which he mistook for Richmond, and was evidently startled. An idle prediction, it seems, had reached his ears, that he would not long survive a visit to that place. "Then," he exclaimed, in a tone of alarm, "I see my days will not be long;" and accordingly he hastily quitted Exeter, and returned to London.†

Other peculiarities, we think, might be detected in Richard's conduct at this period, tending to the presumption that his mind was ill at ease with itself, and that he was endeavouring, by good deeds performed in the service of his Maker, to expiate the commission of some terrible crime. Not that Richard can be accused of having been remiss, at any time of his life, in a respect for religion, or in the performance of charitable deeds. The large offerings which he made to religious houses, and the large sums which he subscribed towards the

* Sir T. More's Richard III. pp. 133, 134.
† Holinshed's Chronicles, vol. iii. p. 421.

building and repair of churches, afford sufficient
evidence to the contrary. Among other devo-
tional acts, he subscribed liberal sums to the monks
of Cowsham, and to the parish of Skipton, for the
repair of their several churches.* He rebuilt
the chapel of the Holy Virgin, in the church of
Allhallows, Barking, near the Tower of London,
and founded there a college consisting of a dean
and six canons.† He commenced the erection of a
chapel at Towton, over the bodies of the Yorkists
who fell in the sanguinary battle at that place.‡
He converted the rectory church of Middleham into
a college;§ and founded, within Barnard Castle
in the county of Durham, a college consisting of a
dean, twelve secular priests, ten chaplains, and six
choristers.‖ He subscribed 500*l.*, then a considerable sum, towards the completion of the beautiful
chapel of King's College, Cambridge;¶ he is said to
have been a considerable benefactor to Clare Hall,
Cambridge,** and on Queen's College, in that university, he conferred a large portion of the lands of
John de Vere, Earl of Oxford, which had been for-

* Whitaker's Richmondshire, vol. i. p. 335.
† Stow's Survey of London, book ii. p. 32; Rossi Hist. Reg. Ang.
p. 216.
‡ Drake's Eboracum, p. 111.
§ Rossi Hist. Reg. Ang. p. 215.
‖ Surtees' Hist. of Durham, vol. iv. p. 67.
¶ Hist. of Cambridge, vol. i. p. 197. Ackerman, London, 1815.
** Dyer's Hist. of the University of Cambridge, vol. ii. p. 39.

feited by his attainder. In gratitude for these benefits, the latter college formerly used as their coat of arms a crozier and a pastoral staff piercing the head of a boar, the cognizance of Richard of Gloucester. In the days of Fuller, however, the college had ''waived the wearing of this coat, laying it up in her wardrobe,'' and making use only of the arms assigned to them by their foundress, Margaret of Anjou.*

But, towards the close of his career, his religious offerings and endowments seem not only to have been more numerous, but to have been characterized by an uneasiness in respect to the future welfare of his soul, which is not without its significance. For instance, on the 16th of December 1483, we find him granting an annuity of 10*l.* to John Bray, clerk, for performing divine service, for the welfare of his soul, and the souls of his consort and of Prince Edward their son, in the chapel of St. George, in the castle of Southampton. Again, on the 2nd of March following, we find him endowing his princely foundation, the Herald's College, with lands and tenements for the support of a chaplain, whose duty it was to pray and sing service every day for the good estate of the king, the queen, and Edward their son.† Between the 9th and 10th of the same month, we find the king a

* Fuller's Hist. of the University of Cambridge, pp. 122, 123.
† Rymer's Fœdera, vol. xii. p. 215.

visitor at Cambridge, on which occasion he "devoutly founded" an exhibition at Queen's College for four priests,—the university, at the same time (March 10), decreeing him an annual mass; and, by a second decree, ordaining that service should be annually performed on the 2nd of May "for the happy state of the said most renowned prince, and his dearest consort Anne."*

One or two other instances may be cursorily mentioned. At Sheriff-Hutton, where he had imprisoned the ill-fated Rivers, he added ten pounds a year to the salary of the chantry priest of "our lady chapel." At Pomfret, the town in which he had caused Rivers to be beheaded, he rebuilt the chapel and house of a pious anchoress.† On the 28th of March we find him issuing an order for the annual payment of ten marks to a chaplain, whose duty it was "to sing for the king in a chapel before the holy rood at Northampton."‡ Again, on the 27th of May, we find him signing a second warrant for the payment of twelve marks to the friars of Richmond, in Yorkshire, "for the saying of 1000 masses for the soul of King Edward IV."§ And lastly, apparently about the same time, he founded a college at York for the support of one

---

* Dyer's Privileges of the University of Cambridge, vol. i. p. 41.

† Harl. MSS. quoted in S. Turner's Middle Ages, vol. iv. p. 10.

‡ Ibid.

§ Ibid.   Whitaker's Richmond, vol. i. p. 99.

hundred singing priests, to chant for mercy to his soul.*

These princely endowments and charities have been adduced by the apologists of Richard as proofs that he was innately and sincerely pious. In having adopted, therefore, a different, and we hope not an uncharitable view, of his motives, there are one or two points which we should bear in mind. We must recollect that the usurper lived in an age in which men hesitated not to commit evil, provided, in their own fallacious judgment, good might result from it; that it was an age in which men contrived to reconcile to themselves a strict outward observance of their religious obligations with the perpetration of atrocious crimes; an age in which the Church of Rome authorized the sale of indulgences to a very inordinate extent, and when the purchase of masses, and the endowment of charities, were considered as the infallible means of securing centuries of, if not plenary, exemption from the torments of a future state. Lastly, in estimating the motives and actions of such men as Richard III., we should never lose sight of the necessity of judging them according to the standard of morals and the state of society which existed in their time, and not according to the standard of our own.

But the days were fast approaching when real

* Rossi Hist. Reg. Ang. p. 215.

misfortunes, in addition to the compunctions of conscience, were destined to bow the usurper to the earth. We have already recorded how tenderly and entirely his ambitious hopes, as well as his parental feelings, were centred in his only legitimate child, the young Prince of Wales. We have already stated, that to transmit the crown of England to his child and to his child's posterity, was apparently the mainspring of all his actions, the occasion of all his crimes. We have seen the three estates of the realm solemnly decreeing and declaring that beloved child to be heir-apparent to the crown and royal dignity. But even this authoritative and emphatic admission of his rights had been insufficient to satisfy the doubts and lull the fears of the usurper. Accordingly, in the middle of February, about three weeks after the meeting of parliament, we find him assembling "nearly all the lords of the realm, both spiritual and temporal," at his palace of Westminster; where, "in a certain lower room, near the passage which leads to the queen's apartments, each subscribed his name to a kind of new oath of adherence to Edward, the king's only son, as their supreme lord, in case anything should happen to his father."*

Some six weeks only from this period passed away, when the fair child, in whom hopes so high were centred, and who had been the inno-

* Croyl. Chron. Cont. p. 496.

cent cause of so much crime and misery, was seized
by an illness which hurried him to the grave. The
chronicler Rous tells us that "he died an unhappy
death."* He was apparently only in his eleventh
year. The event took place at Middleham Castle,
that favourite residence of Richard, in which, in
his boyhood, he had first become enamoured of
Anne Neville, which had witnessed his bridal
happiness, and under the roof of which his beloved
child first saw the light. At the time when the
melancholy event took place, the king and queen
were holding their court in Nottingham Castle, and
were consequently denied the mournful satisfaction
of watching over their child in his last moments.
Their grief at his loss is described as having been
excessive. "On hearing the news of this at Nottingham, where they were then residing," writes
the Croyland chronicler, "you might have seen his
father and mother in a state almost bordering on mad-
ness, by reason of their sudden grief."† It was probably from the circumstance of Nottingham Castle
having witnessed his great affliction, that he subsequently gave it the name of the "Castle of Care."‡
The day on which the young prince expired was
the 9th of April, the same day of the same month
on which, in the preceding year, his uncle, King

* "Morte infaustâ."—*Hist. Angl. Reg.* p. 217.
† Croyl. Chron. Cont. p. 497.
‡ Hutton's Bosworth, p. 40.

Edward IV., had breathed his last. The coincidence was certainly a remarkable one. Let us take it for granted, for the sake of argument, that Richard put to death the children of his brother chiefly for the purpose of aggrandizing his own, and where shall we find retributive justice exemplified by a more striking instance? Some three months afterwards, when Richard was called upon at York to put his signature to a warrant for the payment of the last expenses incurred by his late "most dear son," he touchingly added to those words, in his own handwriting, "*whom God pardon.*"*

The remainder of the year passed away without any extraordinary event occurring to chequer the career of King Richard. He kept his Christmas at Westminster with great magnificence, enlivening the old palace of the Confessor with a succession of banquets and balls. At the festival of the Epiphany, he is especially mentioned as presiding at a splendid feast in the great hall of Rufus, wearing a crown on his head.† On these occasions, the presence of the Princess Elizabeth, now a beautiful girl verging on her nineteenth year, appears to have attracted extraordinary attention. It was remarked that, although the law of the land had reduced her to the condition of a private gentle-

* Harl. MSS. 433, p. 183, quoted in Halsted's Richard III. vol. i. p. 325 ; Buck in Kennet, vol. i. p. 525, note.
† Croyl. Chron. Cont. p. 498.

woman, she was not only treated by the king with marked consideration, but that he caused her to be arrayed in royal robes, and, further, that they corresponded in shape and colour with those worn by the queen. "Too much attention," writes the Croyland chronicler, "was given to dancing and gaiety, and vain change of apparel given to Queen Anne and the Lady Elizabeth, the eldest daughter of the late king, being of similiar colour and shape; a thing that caused the people to murmur, and the nobles and prelates greatly to wonder thereat." These circumstances naturally created suspicion and alarm. The king's anxiety to bequeath an heir to the throne was sufficiently well known. It was remembered that the queen had been barren for nearly eleven years, and that the delicacy of her constitution rendered it little likely that she would again become a mother. Richard himself gave out that the physicians had enjoined him to shun her bed. From these circumstances, as well as from their knowledge of his determined and unscrupulous character, his subjects naturally drew inferences in the highest degree unfavourable to their sovereign. In a word, it was more than whispered that his intention was to get rid of his queen, either by poison or a divorce, and to make his beautiful niece the partaker of his throne.*

* Croyland Chron. Cont. pp. 498-9; Polydore Virgil, p. 215; Rous, Hist. Reg. Ang. p. 215 ; Mémoires de Commines, tome ii. p. 160.

A few days after Christmas, while the world was still discussing this delicate topic, it was suddenly announced that the queen had been seized with a serious indisposition. On the 16th of March she died in Westminster Palace, at the early age of twenty-eight.* Her husband honoured her by a magnificent funeral in the neighbouring abbey, and is said to have been so affected as to shed tears.† That his subjects should have attributed those tears to hypocrisy, and the death of his queen to poison, may, under all the circumstances, be readily imagined. The charges, however, which have been brought against Richard of having shortened her life, we believe to be alike unfounded and unjust. Not only is there a want of evidence to convict him of so heinous a crime, but, on the contrary, there is every reason to believe that he loved her sincerely, that they lived happily together, and that she died a natural death. As far as is known, she was the sharer of his anxious and solitary hours; while history proves that, so far from his having neglected her, she constantly sat with him at the banquet, or walked side by side with him in procession in the season of his splendour. Prejudiced as were the chroniclers of the fifteenth century against Richard, not only do they prefer no charge

* She was born on the 11th of June 1456. Rous Roll. Art. 62, Duke of Manchester's copy.

† Baker's Chronicle, p. 232.

against him of cruelty or neglect, but no hint, we believe, is to be found in their pages of the married life of the king and queen having been disturbed by domestic dissensions, by incompatibility of temper, or by jealousy on the part of Anne. But supposing it be true that he secretly wished to supplant her by a younger and lovelier bride, he had only to wait till nature had performed its part. For many weeks, it would seem, her days on earth had been numbered. At an early stage of her illness, her physicians had expressed their conviction that it was unlikely that she would survive till the spring. Her constitution, like that of her sister, the Duchess of Clarence, seems to have had a tendency to consumption; and when, in addition to these circumstances, we learn that her health and spirits were sensibly affected by the death of her only child, can there be a more probable conclusion than that Anne Neville died a natural death? She languished, we are told, "in weakness and extremity of sorrow, until she seemed rather to overtake death, than death her."* Moreover, if Richard really murdered the wife of his choice, not only would the crime seem to have been an unnecessary one, but to have been also opposed to his interests. When we call to mind the remarkable manner in which popular suspicion had been awakened by the gallant appearance of the young Princess Elizabeth

* Buck in Kennet, vol. i. p. 534.

at court, we naturally ask ourselves whether it is probable that so politic a prince as Richard would have invited the detestation of his subjects, by putting his wife out of the way at the very moment when he knew that they were charging him with the foul intention, and actually expecting the event. Richard himself not only saw the question in this light, but is said to have expressed apprehensions lest the death of his queen, in this state of the public mind, might prove fatal to his popularity.

It seems to have been during the queen's last illness, and probably after the physicians had expressed their opinion that her case was a hopeless one, that Richard first confided to his friends his project of marrying his niece. That he seriously conceived that project, there cannot, we think, exist any doubt. The fact is asserted by a contemporary writer, the chronicler of Croyland, as well as by Polydore Virgil and Grafton.* Even Richard's apologist, Buck, admits that "it was entertained and well-liked by the king and his friends *a good while.*"† It has been argued, indeed, that it was directly opposed to Richard's interests to marry Elizabeth; since by so doing he would have shown himself capable of inconsistency so great, and of a change of tactics so flagrant, as to have en-

---

* Croyl. Cont. p. 499 ; Grafton's Chronicle, vol. ii. p. 144 ; Polydore Virgil, lib. xxv. p. 707.

† Buck in Kennet, vol. i. p. 567.

dangered his political existence. His only title to
the throne, it has been insisted, was derived from
the fact of the children of his brother Edward having been declared by parliament to be illegitimate,
and, consequently, had he married the Princess
Elizabeth, he would have reversed the act which
stigmatized her with bastardy; thus tacitly acknowledging her claims to the crown, and pro-
claiming himself an usurper. " His worst enemies,"
it has been said, "have contented themselves with
representing him as an atrocious villain, but not
one of them has described him as a fool."*

But Richard had already been guilty of a similar
act of inconsistency, by nominating as his successor
the attainted Earl of Warwick, the son of his
elder brother the Duke of Clarence.† Richard's
title to the sceptre rested quite as much on the circumstance of the issue of Clarence having been de-
barred by parliament from the succession, as on
the fact that the issue of his brother Edward had
been declared illegitimate. By nominating, therefore, the Earl of Warwick to be his successor, he
virtually admitted the injustice of that attainder,

* Privy Purse Expenses of Elizabeth of York; Memoir prefixed
to, by Sir Harris Nicolas, p. 49.

† Richard subsequently altered the succession in favour of another
nephew, John Earl of Lincoln, the eldest son of his sister Elizabeth,
Duchess of Suffolk. In the following reign, the Earl of Lincoln raised
the standard of revolt against Henry VII., and fell, in the lifetime of
his father, at the battle of Stoke, 16th of June 1487.

and tacitly acknowledged the superior claims of his nephew to the sovereign power. Moreover, there occur to us more than one weighty reason why Richard should have been desirous of making Elizabeth his wife. "It appeared," says the Croyland chronicler, "that in no other way could his kingly power be established, or the hopes of his rival be put an end to."* This rival, it is needless to remark, was Henry Earl of Richmond, who had pledged his troth to Elizabeth, and whose union with her, should it take place, must necessarily combine against Richard the two houses of York and Lancaster. What could be more natural, then, than that Richard, by marrying Elizabeth himself, should have sought to wrest from Henry the only weapon which rendered him formidable? The partisans of the house of York might at any time rise in revolt to raise Elizabeth to the throne. But let Elizabeth once ascend the throne of England as the consort of Richard, and the crown be secured to her children, and the motives for rebellion would cease to exist, the peril which threatened him be at an end. So convinced does Henry appear to have been that it was Richard's intention to marry his niece, and that their union was inevitable, that we find him seeking in marriage the Lady Catherine Herbert, daughter of the late William Earl of Pembroke. Surely he must have been fully satisfied

* Croyl. Chron. Cont. p. 499.

that his betrothed was irrevocably engaged to another, and that all further pursuit was hopeless, or he would never have broken a troth which he had so selemnly pledged, nor have ceased to prosecute an alliance by means of which he had fondly hoped to raise himself to a throne.*

Historians, hostile to the memory and character of Richard III., delight in stigmatizing his project of marrying his niece as a wicked and incestuous act. But surely there is much injustice in the charge. The marriage of an uncle with a niece was, doubtless, in the fifteenth century, as it has been in our time, an event of very unusual occurrence. Moreover, being forbidden by the canon law, such an union was little likely to be regarded with favour by the people of England. But, on the other hand, not only is a dispensing power vested in the pope, which he is empowered to exercise whenever he thinks proper, but it must have been notorious at the time that marriages between uncle and nieces had often before been permitted. Surely, therefore, if Richard sought to make his niece Elizabeth his wife, the fault, if fault there

* That Richard paid his addresses to his niece is not denied by Lord Orford, though he is of opinion that it was not with any intention to make her his wife. "I should suppose," writes the noble historian, "that Richard, learning the projected marriage of Elizabeth and the Earl of Richmond, amused the young princess with the hopes of making her his queen."—*Historic Doubts*, Lord Orford's Works, vol. ii. p. 151.

existed, lay not in himself, but in the church on whose infallibility, as one of its disciples, he was bound to place reliance.*

According to the Croyland chronicler, the persons from whom Richard encountered the most strenuous opposition in this delicate matter were his creatures, Sir Richard Ratcliffe and Sir William Catesby. These persons had been very instrumental in bringing Earl Rivers and Sir Richard Grey to the block, and consequently, as, in the event of her being raised to the throne, Elizabeth would naturally seek to punish the instigators of the deaths of her uncle and brother, they had every reason to prevent the marriage. Accordingly, they are said to have represented to their royal master how entirely the English clergy were prejudiced against such marriages; and further, that, as the majority of his subjects regarded them as incestuous, they might be induced to rise in open rebellion against his authority. They even went so far, we are told, as to produce before him certain doctors of divinity, who denied that the pontiff had any power of granting a dispensation where the degree of consanguinity was so near.† Already,

---

* "In our time," writes Buck, "the daughter and heir of Duke Infantasgo, in Spain, was married to his brother Don Alde Mendoza; and more lately, the Earl of Miranda married his brother's daughter. In the house of Austria, marriages of this kind have been very usual and thought lawful."—*Buck in Kennet*, vol. i. p. 568.

† Croyl. Chron. Cont. p. 499.

argued his confidants, suspicions—idle and in-
famous, no doubt—were current that his late queen
had met with an untimely end ; and, consequently,
his marriage with his niece would unquestionably
endue them with a painful and dangerous importance. There were men still living, they said—and
among them some of his most faithful partisans—
who still held in affectionate veneration the memory
of the great Earl of Warwick, and who would ill
brook the suspicion that his gentle daughter had
been consigned to an early grave for the purpose of
making room for a more eligible rival.*

Richard was the least likely of all living men to
be diverted from his purpose by the arguments or
solicitations of others. But whether convinced by
the soundness of the reasoning of Ratcliffe and
Catesby, or whether, as is probable, his own strong
sense suggested still weightier grounds for breaking
off his projected marriage, he resolved not only on
relinquishing his purpose, but to repair as much as
possible the injury which his reputation had suffered, by boldly declaring to his subjects that no
such project had ever entered his head. Accordingly, in the great hall in the priory of St. John's,
Clerkenwell, in the presence of the lord-mayor and
the principal citizens of London, he rose, and, " in
a loud and distinct voice," solemnly declared that
a marriage with his niece had never entered into his

* Croyl. Chron. Cont. p. 499.

contemplation.* At the same time he addressed a letter to the citizens of York, in which he not only exhorted them to give no credit to the " false and abominable language and lies " which were presumptuously circulated to his disadvantage, but enjoined them to bring to condign punishment the " authors and makers " of such unwarrantable slanders.†

This especial appeal to the citizens of York is curious and interesting. Evil times, Richard was aware, were threatening him. He knew not how soon he might require the aid of that important city. From the days in which he held high office among them, it had ever been the policy of Richard to secure the confidence and attachment of the people of the north. It was the north which had sent him up the levies which kept the Woodvilles in awe at the time of his usurpation.‡ It was on his

* Croyl. Chron. Cont. p. 500.

† Drake's Ebor. p. 119.

‡ "Soon after, for fear of the queen's blood, and other, which he had in jealousy, he sent for a strength of men out of the north, the which came shortly to London a little before his coronation, and mustered in the Moorfields, well upon 4000 men."—*Fabyan*, p. 516. According to Sir Thomas More, these northern levies presented but a sorry appearance : "To be sure of his enemies, he sent for 5000 men out of the north, who came up to town ill clothed and worse harnessed, their horses poor and their arms rusty, who, being mustered in Finsbury Fields, were the contempt of the spectators."—*Sir T. More in Kennet*, vol. i. p. 500. When Richard subsequently visited York, in the month of September 1483, we find him hanging some of these rude men-at-arms on account of certain lawless proceedings of which they had been guilty on their march back to their native city. Drake's Ebor. p. 116.

friends in the north that he had almost exclusively conferred the possessions which lapsed to the crown by the attainder of Buckingham and his associates;* and lastly, when Ratcliffe and Catesby sought to divert him from marrying the Princess Elizabeth, the stress which we find them laying on the risk which he ran of forfeiting the allegiance of " the people of the north," proves how great was the importance which he attached to their loyalty.†

In the mean time, not only were secret conspiracies forming against the usurper's government at home, but abroad, the Earl of Richmond and his partisans were making active preparations for a second invasion of his kingdom. So far back, indeed, as the preceding Christmas, when Richard was enlivening the old palace of Westminster with " dancing and gaiety," his spies in Brittany had secretly advised him that, in the course of the ensuing summer, a descent would unquestionably be attempted on the shores of England. If guilt be usually the parent of fear, Richard of Gloucester at least was an exception to the rule. To him, as to his brother Edward, the approach of danger and the hour of battle are said to have been sources of pleasurable excitement. Instead of betraying any apprehension at the threatened invasion of his king-

*Croyl. Chron. Cont. p. 496.   † Ibid. p. 499.

dom, he is said to have looked forward with positive satisfaction to the day which was destined to settle for ever the dispute between him and the heir of Lancaster. The danger, however, was not as yet so imminent as to require his presence in the field; and accordingly, with the exception of three brief residences at Windsor, we find him continuing to hold his court at Westminster till the month of May. In the mean time he energetically set to work to defend the shores of England from foreign invasion, as well as to prevent popular commotions at home. So admirable were his arrangements, that when eventually the Earl of Richmond effected his memorable landing, no single town in England or Wales rose in insurrection. To prevent the Princess Elizabeth falling into the hands of his enemies, he sent her to Sheriff-Hutton, a "stately mansion" of his own in Yorkshire, where his northern friends were all-powerful, and where her cousin, the young Earl of Warwick, was already detained in safe though honourable durance. An oak, called the "Warwick oak," was formerly, and perhaps may still be, pointed out in the park, as the boundary tree which limited the walks of the heir of the ill-fated Clarence during his imprisonment at Sheriff-Hutton. When, subsequently, the two cousins were conducted from their prison-house, very different was their destiny. Elizabeth was led forth to ascend a throne; the unfortunate earl to perish, a few years afterwards, on the scaffold.*

No sooner did the hour of danger draw near than Richard prepared to leave London, which city he quitted "shortly before the feast of Pentecost."† About the end of May we find him at Coventry, and on the 6th of June at Kenilworth. Nottingham, on account of its central position, he selected for his headquarters. From hence he might readily march to the part of the kingdom where his presence was most required or where danger was most imminent. In due time he had completed his preparations for defence. Large bodies of armed men marched from place to place; the king's cruisers and vessels of war commanded the entire southern coast; every port, at which there seemed a probability of Henry attempting to land, was

---

* The fate of the Earl of Warwick has been already alluded to. This unhappy prince, the last male heir of the royal line of Plantagenet, was a prisoner in the Tower in the year 1499, when its gates opened to admit the famous adventurer, Perkin Warbeck. The two youths, having found means to confer with each other in secret, contrived a plan for escaping from the gloomy fortress. Their project, however, unfortunately was discovered, and the Earl of Warwick, whose only known offence had been a natural longing for life and liberty, was brought to his trial, on the 21st of November, before the Earl of Oxford, as High Steward of England. He was condemned to death, and, on the 28th of the same month, was beheaded on Tower Hill. Forty-four years afterwards, his only sister, the Lady Margaret Plantagenet, Countess of Salisbury, was beheaded on the same spot, at the advanced age of seventy. Such was the tragical termination of the great house of Plantagenet!

† Croyl. Chron. Cont. p. 500.

closed. Mandates were issued, calling upon every man in England, who had been born to the inheritance of landed property, to join the king's standard without fail, and threatening death, and the forfeiture of their possessions, in the event of disobedience.*   Lastly, single horsemen were stationed at distances of twenty miles from one another, who, being instructed to ride at their utmost speed, but on no account to pass their restricted limits, were thus enabled to forward a letter from one to another at the rate of two hundred miles in forty-eight hours.†

Richard had recourse also to the pen as well as to the sword.   In a proclamation, dated Westminster, the 23rd of June, he artfully appeals to the fears and interests of his subjects.   He denounces Henry's adherents as rebels and traitors—men disabled and attainted by the high court of parliament, and many of them notoriously murderers, adulterers, and extortioners.   Henry himself he stigmatizes as one Henry Tudor, of bastard blood both on his father's and his mother's side, and possessing no title whatever to the royal dignity. The Earl is further charged with having entered into a covenant with the French king to give up, on the part of England, all title and claim to the crown and realm of France, together with the duchies of Normandy, Anjou, and Maine; to surrender Gas-

* Croyl. Chron. Cont. p. 501.   † Ibid. p. 497.

cony, Guienne, and Calais, and to remove for ever
the arms of France from those of England. "And,"
the proclamation proceeds, "in more proof and
showing of his said purpose of conquest, the said
Henry Tudor hath given, as well to diverse of the
said king's enemies as to his said rebels and traitors, archbishoprics, bishoprics, and other dignities
spiritual; and also the duchies, earldoms, baronies,
and other possessions and inheritances of knights,
esquires, gentlemen, and other the king's true subjects within the realm;" the intention of the
invaders being "to do the most cruel murders,
slaughters, robberies, and disherisons, that were
ever seen in any Christian realm." Under these
circumstances, the king entreats and commands all
true Englishmen to furnish themselves with arms
for the defence of their wives, goods, and heredita-
ments; assuring his "true and faithful liegemen"
that he himself will expose his royal person, as
becomes a courageous prince, to all hazard and
labour, for the purpose of subduing the said enemies, rebels, and traitors, and establishing the welfare and safety of his subjects.*

While the people of England were still engaged
in discussing the merits of this remarkable document, information reached Richard from France
that the Earl of Richmond had taken his departure
for Harfleur, and that his ships had assembled at

* Paston Letters, vol. ii. p. 152.

the mouth of the Seine. On the 6th of August they reached Milford Haven. "On hearing of their arrival," says the Croyland chronicler, "the king rejoiced, or at least seemed to rejoice; writing to his adherents in every quarter that now the long wished-for day had arrived for him to triumph over so contemptible a faction."* At all events, if he failed to conquer, he was resolved to die as became a hero and a king.

* Croyl. Chron. Cont. p. 501.

CHAPTER VII.

THE DESOLATION AND DEATH OF RICHARD OF GLOUCESTER.

ON Tuesday, the 16th of August 1485, King Richard marched out of the town of Nottingham at the head of twelve thousand men. Clad in armour of burnished steel, and seated on a magnificent snow-white charger, the famous "white Surrey" of the poet, his appearance, attended by his glittering body-guard, is said to have been eminently striking. His armour was the same which he had worn at the battle of Tewkesbury.* A kingly diadem encircled his helmet. Above him floated the royal banner, while around him waved a variety of standards, radiant with the "silver boar," his peculiar cognizance, and other insignia of the house of Plantagenet. About sunset he entered Leicester.

On the following day Richard led his army from Leicester to Elmsthorpe, where he encamped for the night. On Thursday, the 18th, he advanced to Stableton, about a mile and a half from the field of Bosworth. Here he pitched his camp upon some

* Hutton's Bosworth, Nichols' ed. p. 82.

ground called the Bradshaws, and here he remained during the two following days, employed in throwing up breastworks and making other preparations for the approaching battle.

In the mean time, the Earl of Richmond had broken up his camp at Atherstone, and had advanced his army, amounting to about seven thousand men, to the field of Bosworth, then called Redmore Plain, from the red colour of its soil.* The same evening, Richard pushed forward his army to a spot called Ambeame, or Anbein Hill, where "he pitched his field." Thus, on the evening of the 21st, the day immediately before the battle, the two armies lay encamped in full view of each other. The forces of the usurper were posted to the northeast, those of the Earl of Richmond faced them on the southwest. Lord Stanley, and his brother Sir William Stanley, took up independent and menacing positions. On the south, "myddeway betwixt the two battaylles,"† Lord Stanley pitched his camp, somewhat nearer to the left of the king than to the right of Richmond, as if with the intention of supporting his sovereign. Sir William Stanley faced him on the north. The former having married Margaret Countess of Richmond, was consequently stepfather to the invader. This, and apparently other circumstances, having

* Hutton's Bosworth, Nichols' ed. p. 68.
† Polydore Virgil, p. 222, Camd. Soc. Trans

aroused suspicions of Stanley's fidelity in the mind of Richard, he had, some days since, seized the person of his eldest son, Lord Strange, whom he now retained in his camp as a hostage for his father's good behaviour. Thus, suspicious of one of the most powerful of his subjects, and apprehensive lest the evident disaffection of the Stanleys might extend to others, Richard, doubtless, would only too willingly have compelled Richmond to join issue in an immediate encounter, and thus have emancipated himself from a suspense which must have been almost intolerable. It was Sunday, however, and a feeling of veneration or superstition, such as had forbidden him to march from Nottingham on the preceding Monday, the " Assumption of our Lady,"* probably prevented his attacking his enemy and shedding blood on the Sabbath.

Though wearing the kingly crown, and at the head of a magnificent army, there was probably not one of his subjects whose heart was so comfortless; not one who was more entirely alienated from the sympathies of his fellow-creatures, than at this period was Richard of Gloucester. The death of his nephews had estranged from him all who were nearest allied to him in blood. The fair boy, in whom all his ambitious hopes had centred, had suddenly been hurried to the tomb. The wife of his choice had speedily followed him. Treason was

* Paston Letters, vol. ii. p. 156.

rife among those whom he had sought to love, and on whom he had conferred the greatest favours. In this, then, the hour of his desolation—yearning, perhaps, for the presence of some human being on whose affections he had a claim—he is said to have recalled to mind an illegitimate son, for whom he had hitherto shown no particular predilection, and to have sent for him to his camp. The circumstances connected with their interview have their peculiar interest, and will be presently related.

The night before the battle of Bosworth was the last of Richard's existence: it was probably also the most terrible.

> "To the guilty king, that black fore-running night,
>   Appeared the dreadful ghosts of Henry and his son,
>   Of his own brother George, and his two nephews done
>   Most cruelly to death; and of his wife and friend
>   Lord Hastings, with pale hands prepared as they would rend
>   Him piecemeal; at which oft he roared in his sleep."
>
> DRAYTON.

That Richard passed a perturbed and miserable night, we have good evidence for believing. We learn, from high authority, that of late he had been an habitually restless sleeper; "that he took ill rest a-nights; lay long wakening and musing, sore wearied with care and watch, rather slumbered than slept."* He was evidently constitutionally nervous and irritable. Fits of abstraction, in which

* Sir T. More's Hist. of Richard III. p. 134.

it was his habit to bite his under lip, and to draw his dagger hurriedly up and down in its scabbard, were not unfrequent with him.* That a man, therefore, of a morbid and excitable temperament, —surrounded, moreover, as he was by secret traitors, and with his life and crown dependent on the issue of the morrow's conflict,—should have passed an uneasy night, and have been troubled with distressing dreams, may be readily comprehended. But, on the other hand, that he was visited, or believed himself to have been visited, by the apparitions of those whom it was assumed that he had cruelly murdered, rests on no sounder foundation than the poetic flights of Drayton and Shakspeare. The old chroniclers, though they dwell on the night of horrors which he spent, make no mention of his having been haunted by the spectres of his imaginary victims. "The fame went," writes Polydore Virgil, "that he had the same night a dreadful and a terrible dream; for it seemed to him, *being asleep*, that he saw divers images, like terrible devils, which pulled and haled him, not suffering him to take any quiet or rest."† Again, according to the most faithful chronicler of the period, "As it is generally stated, in the morn-

* Kennet, vol. i. p. 513.

† Grafton, vol. ii. p. 150. "It is reported," writes Polydore Virgil, "that King Richard had that night a terrible dream; for he thought, *in his sleep*, that he saw horrible images, as it were, of evil spectres haunting evidently about him."—*P. Virgil*, p. 221, Camd. Soc. Trans.

ing he declared that he had seen dreadful visions, and had imagined himself surrounded by a multitude of demons."*

> "By the Apostle Paul, shadows to-night
> Have struck more terror to the soul of Richard,
> Than can the substance of ten thousand soldiers,
> Armed in proof, and led by shallow Richmond."
>
> *King Richard III.* Act. v. Sc. 3.

It was in the grey dawn of the morning that Richard started from his troubled slumbers. So early was the hour, that his chaplains were still asleep in their tents. His attendants were unprepared with his breakfast.† Attended by Lord Lovel, his lord-chamberlain; by Sir William Catesby, his attorney-general; and by another privy councillor, Sir Richard Ratcliffe, the usurper passed from his tent into the silent camp, which lay stretched around him in the twilight. Perceiving a sentinel asleep at his post, he is said to have stabbed him, exclaiming, as he pursued his rounds, "I found him asleep, and I have left him as I found him."‡ The depression of his spirits, occasioned by the horrors of the preceding night, is said to have been visibly depicted on his pallid countenance. A painful thought occurred to him, that his agitation might be attributed to cowardice; and accordingly we are told he "recited and declared to his particular friends his wonderful vision

* Croyl. Chron. Cont. p. 503.   † Ibid.   ‡ Hutton's Bosworth, p. 79.

and terrible dream.''* On all former occasions, on
the eve of a deadly encounter, it had been remarked that, as the hour of peril drew near, his
eye had grown brighter, and his spirits apparently
more light. But now, dreading ''that the event
of the battle would be grievous, he did not buckle
himself to the conflict with such liveliness of courage and countenance as before.''†

But Richard had graver causes for anxiety and
alarm than from mere superstitious fantasies. The
well-known warning which, on the preceding night,
had been appended to the tent of the Duke of Norfolk, was only too significant of the general treachery which surrounded him :—

> " Jock of Norfolk, be not too bold,
>   For Dickon, thy master, is bought and sold."‡

Splendid, indeed, as was the appearance of his
army, more than two-thirds of his followers were
probably traitors in their hearts. Already more than
one gallant and distinguished warrior,—such men as
Sir John Savage, Sir Simon Digby, Sir Brian Sandford, Sir John Cheney, Sir Walter Hungerford,
and Sir Thomas Bourchier,—had deserted his service for that of the invader. Of these persons more

* Grafton, vol. ii. p. 150.

† Polydore Virgil, p. 222, Camd. Soc. Ed. No longer, according to
another old chronicler, he exhibited that "alacrity and mirth of mind
and countenance, as he was accustomed to do before he came toward the
battle."—*Holinshed*, vol. iii. p. 438.

‡ Grafton, vol. i. p. 154. ,

than one had been high in favour with Richard. Hungerford and Bourchier had been esquires of his body; Savage had received grants of land from him, and was one of the knights of his body; Hungerford "was keeper of parks in Wells."* There can be no stronger evidence how widely treason had spread among Richard's followers, than the fact that during the preceding night Sir Simon Digby had been allowed to penetrate as a spy into the heart of his camp, and to return, unquestioned, with such information as he could collect, to the Earl of Richmond.

But it was the imposing positions taken up by the Stanleys, and their more questionable fidelity, which doubtless occasioned Richard the greatest anxiety. Lord Stanley, who was in secret communication with the Earl of Richmond, was compelled to pursue the most cautious policy. He was placed in a most painful situation. His word was pledged to his royal master; his wishes were with his stepson; all his fears were with his son. A single imprudent move might have sent the latter to the block. When, therefore, on the morning of the battle of Bosworth, the king and the Earl of Richmond severally sent messengers to exhort him to join them forthwith, he returned an equivocal answer to each. To the latter he replied that he was engaged in putting his

* Harl. MSS. quoted in Turner's Middle Ages, vol. iii. p. 522.

own troops in battle array; that he would "join him at supper-time."* Richmond, though he could scarcely have doubted the good intentions of his stepfather, listened to the answer with emotion. He was "no little vexed," we are told, "and began to be somewhat alarmed."†

The reply which Lord Stanley sent back to the king's more peremptory command, savoured more of the spirit of the Roman. Richard, it seems, had sent him word by a pursuivant-at-arms that, by Christ's passion, he would cut off Lord Strange's head, if he dared to disobey his orders. "Tell the king," was Stanley's reply, "that it is inconvenient for me to go to him at present: tell him also," he added, "that I have other sons."‡ These words so exasperated the king, that he ordered Lord Strange to be instantly executed. Fortunately, however, Lord Stanley had friends in the usurper's camp. Lord Ferrers of Chartley, and others, represented to Richard that he was about to commit not only a cruel, but also an impolitic action. Lord Stanley, they argued, had hitherto committed no overt act of treason. They represented that were any blood to be shed that day, except by the sword, it would fix an indelible stain

* Buck's Richard III. in Kennet, vol. i. p. 510 ; Grafton, vol. ii. p. 151.

† Polydore Virgil, p. 223, Camd. Soc. Ed.

‡ Grafton, vol. ii. p. 156.

upon their cause. Lord Stanley, they said, was so nearly allied by family ties to the earl, that he probably wished to avoid coming to blows with him if possible; whereas the execution of his son would impel him to make common cause with the earl, and might not impossibly change the fortunes of the day. These arguments convinced the usurper. Accordingly, delivering back Lord Strange to the custody of the "keepers of his tents," he consented to defer the execution to a more convenient opportunity.*

When, on the morning of the 22nd of August, King Richard placed himself at the head of his army, the paleness of his face and a tremor of his frame are said to have been observable by all. Yet, from whatever cause his disturbance arose, whether from evil dreams or from the treachery of his friends, it effected no change in his conduct as a general, or in his valour as a man. His military arrangements were completed with his accustomed precision and skill. His archers, under the command of the Duke of Norfolk and his son, the Earl of Surrey, he placed in front. Next came a dense square, composed of bombards, morris-pikes, and arquebuses, commanded by the king in person. Still clad in the magnificent suit of armour which he had worn at Tewkesbury, and mounted on his

* Hutton's Bosworth, pp. 92, 93; Croyland Chron. p. 503; Kennet, vol. i. p. 512; Hall, pp. 412, 420; Holinshed, vol. iii. pp. 431, 435.

celebrated milk-white charger, he addressed his chieftains in an animated speech, the purport of which his contemporaries have bequeathed to us: "Advance forth your standards," he exclaimed, "and every one give but one sure stroke, and surely the journey is ours. And as for me, I assure you this day I will triumph for victory, or suffer death for immortal fame."*

In the mean time, the Earl of Richmond had also arranged his forces in battle array. His front, composed of archers like that of the king, was commanded by the Earl of Oxford. The right wing was intrusted to Sir Gilbert Talbot; Sir John Savage led the left. Richmond himself, assisted by the military skill and experience of his uncle, the veteran Jasper Tudor, Earl of Pembroke, assumed the supreme command. He, too, addressed a spirited appeal to his followers. Arrayed in complete armour, with the exception of his helmet, of which he had modestly divested himself, he rode from rank to rank, descanting, "with a loud voice and bold speech," on the justness of his cause and on the crimes of the usurper. His trust, he said, was in the God of justice and of battles. Victory, he insisted, was decided not by numbers but by valour; the smaller the numbers, the greater the fame which would reward the vanquishers. For himself, he continued, he would

* Grafton, vol. ii. p. 152.

rather lie a corpse on the cold ground, than recline a free prisoner on a carpet in a lady's chamber. One choice only was theirs—that of winning the victory, and exulting as conquerors; or losing the battle, and being branded as slaves. "Therefore," he concluded, "in the name of God and St. George, let every man courageously advance forth his standard."*

The accounts which the old chroniclers have bequeathed to us of the battle of Bosworth are highly spirited and graphic. "Lord!" says Grafton, "how hastily the soldiers buckled their helms! How quickly the archers bent their bows, and frushed their feathers! How readily the billmen shook their bills and proved their staves, ready to approach and join when the terrible trumpet should sound the bloody blast to victory or death!" And anon, after that terrible pause, "the trumpets blew, and the soldiers shouted, and the king's archers courageously let fly their arrows. The earl's bowmen stood not still, but paid them home again; and, the terrible shot once passed, the armies joined and came to hand-strokes."†

For some time, the brunt of the battle was borne by the Duke of Norfolk on the side of the king, and by the Earl of Oxford on the part of Richmond. Having expended their arrows, the archers on each side laid aside their bows, and fought,

* Grafton, vol. ii. p. 153.   † Ibid. vol. ii. p. 154.

sword in hand, in a close and desperate struggle. In the midst of the *mélée*, Norfolk chanced to recognize Oxford by his device—a star with rays, which was glittering on his standard. In like manner, Oxford discovered the duke by his cognizance, the silver lion. These gallant men were nearly allied to each other by the ties of blood. Formerly they had been united by the ties of friendship. In that hour of deadly conflict, however, friendship and relationship were alike disregarded. The lances of the two chieftains crossed, and each shivered on the armour of the other. Renewing the combat with their swords, Norfolk wounded Oxford in the left arm, a stroke which the earl paid back by cleaving the beaver from Norfolk's helmet. The duke's face being thus exposed, Oxford chivalrously declined to continue the combat with so great an advantage on his side. His generosity, however, was of no avail to Norfolk. An arrow, shot by an obscure hand, struck him in the face, and laid him a corpse at Oxford's feet. Lord Surrey, who beheld his father fall, now made a furious onset to revenge his death. He was encountered, however, by superior numbers, and, notwithstanding the chivalrous valour with which he fought, his own position soon became a critical one. A generous effort to rescue him was made by Sir Richard Clarendon and Sir William Conyers. Those gallant knights, however, were in their turn surrounded by

Sir John Savage and his retainers, and cut to pieces. In the mean time, Surrey was singly opposed by the veteran Sir Gilbert Talbot, who would willingly have spared the life of one so chivalrous and so young. Surrey, however, refused to accept quarter, and, when an attempt was made to take him prisoner, dealt death among those who approached him. One last endeavor to capture him was made by a private soldier. Surrey, however, turning furiously on him, collected his remaining strength, and severed the man's arm from his body.

> "Young Howard single with an army fights;
> When, moved with pity, two renownèd knights,
> Strong Clarendon and valiant Conyers, try
> To rescue him, in which attempt they die.
> Now Surrey, fainting, scarce his sword can hold,
> Which made a common soldier grow so bold,
> To lay rude hands upon that noble flower,
> Which he disdaining,—anger gives him power,—
> Erects his weapon with a nimble round,
> And sends the peasant's arm to kiss the ground."*

By this time he was completely exhausted. Accordingly, presenting the hilt of his sword to Talbot, he requested him to take his life, in order to prevent his dying by an ignoble hand. "The maxim of our family," he said, "is to support the crown of England, and I would fight for it, though

---

* Bosworth Field, by Sir John Beaumont, Bart., in Weever's Funeral Monuments, p. 554.

it were placed on a hedge-stick." Talbot, it is needless to observe, spared his life.*

Had the Earl of Northumberland remained true to his sovereign, or even if the Stanleys had continued neuter, victory would, in all probability, have declared for Richard. But Northumberland, instead of hastening to the aid of his royal master, withdrew his troops to a convenient distance, where he remained a passive spectator of the combat. This glaring act of disloyalty manifested how widespread was the defection in Richard's army, and may not improbably have induced Lord Stanley to throw off the mask. Suddenly he gave orders for his troops to advance to the left, thus uniting them with the right of Richmond's army. The king beheld the movement with astonishment and rage. Victory was evidently on the point of deciding for his adversary; and accordingly, his faithful knights, "perceiving the soldiers faintly, and nothing cour-

* Hutton's Bosworth, pp. 100–106. Lord Surrey was committed to the Tower, where he remained a prisoner about three years and a half; but, says Grafton (vol. ii. p. 154), "for his truth and fidelity he was afterwards promoted to high honours, offices, and dignities." On the 9th of September 1513, he defeated and slew King James IV. of Scotland at the battle of Flodden, for which distinguished service he was restored to the dukedom of Norfolk, of which he had been deprived by attainder after the battle of Bosworth. In 1521, he presided, as Lord High Steward, at the trial of Edward Stafford, Duke of Buckingham, and, on passing sentence of death on him, is said to have been so much affected as to shed tears. The duke died at Framlingham Castle, May 21, 1524.

ageously, to set on their enemies," brought him a fresh and fleet charger, and entreated him to seek safety in flight.* Richard, however, indignantly repelled their advice. "Bring me my battle-axe," he is said to have exclaimed, "and fix my crown of gold on my head; for, by Him that shaped both sea and land, king of England this day will I die!"†

The situation of the usurper had indeed become a critical one. The gallant Norfolk was no more; Surrey was a prisoner; Northumberland had turned traitor. Stanley's followers were already dealing "sore dints" among his troops, and Sir William Stanley might at any moment follow the example set him by his brother. One chance only remained to the undaunted monarch. Descrying Richmond on a neighbouring eminence, with only a few men-at-arms for his personal guard, he resolved either to fight his way to him and terminate their differences by a personal encounter, or to perish in the gallant attempt.‡ With a voice and mien inspired by indomitable resolution and courage, he called upon all true knights to imitate the intrepid example which he proposed to set them. "If none will follow me," he exclaimed, "I will try the

* Polydore Virgil, p. 225, Camd. Soc. Trans.; Grafton, vol. ii. p. 155.
† Harl. MSS. 542, fol. 34, quoted in Hutton's Bosworth, by Nichols, p. 217; Grafton, vol. ii. p. 155; Polydore Virgil, p. 225.
‡ Grafton, vol. ii. p. 154; Polydore Virgil, lib. xxv. p. 714.

cause alone." But the gallant men to whom he appealed responded in a manner such as should gladden the ear of a king on such an occasion. One and all, they prepared to triumph with their sovereign, or die by his side. Of the names of those devoted men only a few have been handed down to us. They included, however, Francis Viscount Lovel, Walter Lord Ferrers of Chartley, Sir Gervoise Clifton, Sir Richard Ratcliffe, and Sir Robert Brakenbury—names to which the historian delights to do honour. Lastly, there rode by the side of the king Sir William Catesby, "learned in the laws of the realm," who, false as he had been to Hastings and others, remained true to his sovereign in his hour of imminent peril. The reflection is a melancholy one, that, of that heroic band, Lord Lovel alone survived to mourn the fate of his king and comrades, and to relate the tale of their prowess. Catesby, indeed, quitted the field alive, but it was to perish, two days afterwards, by the hands of the headsman.

Then it was that King Richard headed and led on that memorable charge, on the success or failure of which the sceptre of an ancient dynasty depended. Fixing his spear in its rest, and calling on his knights to follow him, he set spurs to his noble charger, and from the right flank of his army rode directly and impetuously towards his adversary. Only for a few seconds he paused in his desperate course. It was to quench his thirst at a fountain, which still bears the name of "King Richard's well." Then recommenced that glorious onset of the hero-king and his brother warriors. Four of them were knights of the Garter.* Flinging themselves into the thickest of the battle, onward and furiously they fought their way. At their head,— "making open passage by dint of sword,"—rode the last king who was destined to wear the crown of the Plantagenets. The nearer he advanced to his detested rival, the greater became his impetuosity and rage. In the words of the old chronicler, "he put spurs to his horse, and like a hungry lion ran with spear in rest towards him."† In the course of that terrible onslaught, more than one affecting incident occurred. Sir Robert Brakenbury happened to cross Sir Walter Hungerford, who, only a few hours previously, had deserted the cause of Richard for that of Henry. The word traitor escaped the lips of Brakenbury, on which Hungerford dealt a blow at him which shivered his shield. Stroke after stroke was then exchanged between them; but Brakenbury had survived the vigour of youth, and was ill matched against a younger adversary. At length a blow from Hungerford's sword crushed the helmet of the veteran

* King Richard, Lord Ferrers of Chartley, Lord Lovel, and Sir Richard Ratcliffe.

† Grafton, p. 154.

knight, and exposed his silvery hairs to the light. "Spare his life, brave Hungerford," exclaimed Sir Thomas Bourchier; but the generous entreaty came too late. Before the words could escape his lips, the arm of Hungerford had descended, and the old warrior lay stretched, with the life-blood flowing from him, at their feet.

In that exciting hour, friend was arrayed against friend, and neighbour encountered neighbour. Sir Gervoise Clifton and Sir John Byron * were not only neighbours in Nottinghamshire, but were intimate friends. Clifton fought in the ranks of the king; Byron on the side of Richmond. Previously to their departure from their several homes, they had exchanged a solemn oath, that whoever of the two might prove to be on the victorious side, he should exert all his influence to prevent the confiscation of the estates of his friend, and the consequent ruin of his wife and children. It so happened, that while Clifton was charging with his royal master, he received a blow which felled him to the ground. Byron chanced to be at hand, and saw him fall. Deeply affected by the incident, he dashed through the ranks to his assistance, and, covering him with his shield, exhorted him to surrender. Clifton, however, had received his death-

---

* Sir John Byron, constable of Nottingham Castle, was knighted by Henry shortly after his landing at Milford-Haven. He died 3rd May 1488, and was buried at Colwick in Nottinghamshire.

wound.   Faintly murmuring that all was over with him, he collected sufficient strength to be able to remind his friend of his engagement, and then expired.*   The interesting fact that, after the lapse of nearly four centuries, the descendants of Sir Gervoise Clifton still enjoy the lands possessed by their ancestor, attest that the injunctions of the dying hero were not disregarded by his friend.

In the mean time, King Richard and the survivors of his warrior band continued to fight their way towards Richmond.   One and all, as they swept onward, they dealt death and havoc round them.   The nearer Richard approached to the person of his adversary, the more he seemed to be fortified by an almost superhuman resolution and strength.   Not far in advance of Richmond, he encountered and unhorsed Sir John Cheney, a gallant knight of colossal stature.   By a desperate effort, he fought his way to the standard of his adversary.   Richmond was now almost within his grasp.   With one stroke he slew Sir William Brandon, who was waving the banner over the head of his master, and, seizing it from the grasp of the falling warrior, flung it contemptuously on the ground.

The moment was unquestionably a critical one for Richmond.   His followers are said to have been

* Hutton's Bosworth, p. 117, &c.

"almost in despair of victory."* His life was in imminent peril. It was at this conjuncture that Sir William Stanley, following the example of his brother, came to Richmond's assistance with "three thousand tall men."† "He came time enough," afterwards observed Henry, "to save my life; but he stayed long enough to endanger it."‡ The object of Sir William Stanley was to surround Richard, and he completely succeeded. Bitterly was this last act of treachery felt by the usurper. The last words which he was heard to mutter were, "Treason, treason, treason!"§ But, though separated from his army, and gradually hemmed in by overpowering numbers, his intrepidity never for a moment deserted him. When Catesby urged him to fly, he retorted by taxing him with cowardice. The hope of reaching his adversary, and dying with his grasp round his throat, seems to have animated him to the last. But, by this time, his knights, with the exception of Lord Lovel and his faithful standard-bearer, had all fallen lifeless around him. The latter continued to wave the royal banner over the head of his sovereign to the last. Resolved to sell his life as dearly as possible, the warrior king still stood at bay, "manfully

* Grafton, vol ii. p. 154.
† Ibid.
‡ Lord Bacon's Henry VII. in Kennet, vol. i. p. 611.
§ Rous's Hist. Reg. Ang p. 218.

fighting in the middle of his enemies,''* till, covered
with wounds and exhausted by loss of blood and
fatigue, he either staggered or was struck down
from his horse. Thus, as the old chronicler observes, '' while fighting, and not in the act of flight,
the said King Richard was pierced with numerous
deadly wounds, and fell in the field like a brave
and most valiant prince.''† The death of the king
decided the fate of the day. A third of his followers are said to have fallen in battle. The remainder sought safety by a precipitate flight.‡

The first act of the Earl of Richmond, on finding himself master of the field, was to fall upon his
knees and return thanks to the Almighty for the
great victory which He had vouchsafed to him.§
This pious act of gratitude having been discharged,
he was conducted by Lord Stanley and the Earls of

* Grafton, vol. ii. p. 154. "Fighting manfully in the thickest press
of his enemies."—*Polydore Virgil*, p. 224, Camd. Soc. Trans.

† Croyland Chron. Cont. p. 304.

‡ "The blood of the slain tinged the little brook long after the battle,
particularly in rain. The battle being fought in a dry season, much of
the blood would lodge upon the ground, become baked with the sun,
and be the longer in washing off; which inspired a belief in the
country people, that the rivulet runs blood to this day, and they frequently examine it. Possessed with this opinion, they refuse to drink
it."—*Hutton's Bosworth*, p. 127. According to Hutton's calculation,
King Richard lost no more than nine hundred men at the battle of
Bosworth, and Richmond only one hundred. This estimate nearly
agrees with Grafton's statement, that one thousand men fell on the side
of the king, and one hundred on the side of the earl. Vol. ii. pp.
154, 155.

§ Grafton, vol. ii. p. 155 ; Polydore Virgil, lib. xxv. p. 715.

Pembroke and Oxford to a neighboring eminence, on which the *Te Deum* was solemnly chanted. In an energetic speech he thanked his army for the great service which it had rendered him, extolling the valour of his followers, and promising them adequate rewards. In the mean time, the battered crown, which had been reft from the helmet of Richard during his death-struggle, had been discovered concealed under a hawthorn bush, and was carried by Sir Reginald Bray to Lord Stanley. This opportune circumstance, added to the favourable effect produced by the speech of the victor, seems to have suggested to the Stanleys and their friends the policy of seizing advantage of the general enthusiasm, by at once offering the crown to Richmond, and calling upon the assembled army to acknowledge him as their sovereign. The armed multitude listened to the proposal with rapture, and, amidst their cheers and acclamations, Lord Stanley placed the crown of the Plantagenets on the head of the first king of the house of Tudor. The same day Richmond entered Leicester in triumph, where, "by sound of trumpets," he was proclaimed King of England, by the title of Henry VII.*

At each end and side of the magnificent tomb of Henry VII. in Westminster Abbey, may be seen the device of a crown in a hawthorn bush, an interest-

* Hutton's Bosworth, pp. 132, 133; Grafton, vol. ii. p. 155; Polydore Virgil, lib. xxv. p. 715.

ing memento of his military coronation on the field of Bosworth. The eminence on which Lord Stanley placed the royal diadem on the brow of Henry, still retains the name of Crown Hill.

The death of Richard III. took place on the 22nd of August 1485. He had reigned only two years and two months; his age was only thirty-two. Whatever may have been his faults or his crimes, he certainly died not unlamented. In the register of the city of York, there is an entry, dated the day after his death, which is the more touching inasmuch as it was inserted at a time when flattery was unserviceable to the dead, and might have been perilous to the living. "It was shown by divers persons," proceeds the register, "especially by John Spon, sent unto the field of Redmore to bring tidings from the same to the city, that King Richard, late *lawfully* reigning over us, was, through great treason of the Duke of Norfolk,* and many others that turned against him, with many other lords and nobility of the north parts, *piteously slain and murdered*, to the great heaviness of this city." It was therefore determined, at that "wofull season," to apply to the Earl of Northumberland for advice.†

---

* Norfolk, as we have seen, had been true to Richard, and was slain on the field. Apparently authentic accounts of the battle had not as yet been received at York.

† Drake's Ebor. p. 120. That Richard was cruelly betrayed at the battle of Bosworth, there can be no question. Many of his followers,

The corpse of Richard was treated with the grossest indignities.* Having been dragged from under a heap of the slain, it was flung across the back of a horse, entirely stripped to the skin, and thus conveyed into Leicester. In front of the dead body sat a pursuivant-at-arms, "Blanc Sanglier;" his tabard, as if in mockery, glittering with the silver boar, the famous cognizance of the deceased. Thus, "naked and despoiled to the skin," covered with wounds, and besmeared with dust and blood,— a halter round his neck, his head hanging down on one side of the horse, and his legs dangling on the other, was the corpse of Richard carried into Leicester,—into that very town from which he had so recently ridden forth a mighty warrior and a sceptred king! His body, in order to satisfy the most sceptical that the dreaded usurper had ceased to exist, was exposed to the public gaze at one of the fortified gates of Leicester, so that "every man might see and look upon him." Eventually his remains met with decent, if not honourable sepulture. His body, we are told, was "begged" by the monks of the society of Grey Friars, who interred it in the church of St. Mary belonging to

according to Grafton, " came not thither in hope to see the king prosper and prevail, but to hear that he should be shamefully confounded and brought to ruin."—*Grafton*, vol. ii. p. 154.

* Croyl. Chron. Cont. p. 504; Grrfton, vol. ii. p. 156; Fabyan, p. 673; Hutton, pp. 141, 142.

their order, then the principal place of worship in Leicester.*

Feeling that some respect was due to the memory of the last monarch of a mighty line and the uncle of his queen, Henry VII., some years after the death of his rival, caused a tomb of many-coloured marble, surmounted by a marble effigy of Richard, to be erected over the spot of his interment.†   Unfortunately, the dissolution of the religious houses

---

* Hutton, p. 142.

† The following lines were engraved on Richard's tomb :—

> "Hic ego, quem vario tellus sub marmore claudit,
>   Tertius à multâ voce Ricardus eram ;
> Nam patriæ tutor, patruus pro jure nepotis,
>   Diruptâ tenui Regna Britanna fide ;
> Sexaginta dies, binis duntaxat ademptis,
>   Æstatesque tuli non mea sceptra duas.
> Fortiter in bello, merito desertus ab Anglis,
>   Rex Henrice, tibi, septime, succubui :
> At sumptu, pius ipse, tuo, sic ossa decoras,
>   Regem olimque facis Regis honore coli.
> Quatuor exceptis jam tantum, quinque bis annis
>   Acta tricenta quidem, lustra salutis erant,
> Anteque Septembris undenâ luce kalendas,
>   Reddideram rubræ debita jura rosæ.
> At mea, quisquis eris, propter commissa precare
>   Sit minor ut precibus pœna fienda tuis."   ·

From a MS. in the College of Arms. Sandford, Gen. Hist. book v. p. 435. Sandford justly remarks that these lines " differ not much " from those inserted by Buck in his " Life and Reign of Richard III." Those differences, however, trifling as they at first appear to be, seem to the author not a little curious, as manifesting Buck's unscrupulous partiality for Richard's memory. For instance, in the second line, *justâ* is substituted for *multâ ;* in the seventh line, *certans* for *merito ;* and in the fourteenth line, *jura petita* for *debita jura.* See Buck, in Kennet, vol. i. p. 577.

in the reign of Henry VIII. occasioned the demolition of St. Mary's Church and the defacement of its most interesting memorial. When, in the reign of James I., the spot was visited by Dr. Christopher Wren, afterwards Dean of Windsor, the ancient tomb had ceased to exist. The ground on which the monastery of Grey Friars had stood he found in the possession of an influential citizen of Leicester, Mr. Robert Hayrick, who over the grave of the usurper had erected a handsome pillar of stone, with the inscription, "Here lies the body of Richard III., sometime king of England." "This," says Dr. Wren, "he shewed me walking in the garden, 1612." * But the pillar of stone has shared the fate of the alabaster effigy. No vestige of it remains. Even local gossip has ceased to point to the spot which covered the dust of the warrior-king. In the days of Charles I., his grave, "overgrown with nettles and weeds," was not to be traced.†

There exists a tradition at Leicester, that, at the dissolution of the monasteries, the coffin of Richard was removed from its resting-place, and that his ashes were flung into the Soar.‡ The rumour seems not to be altogether without foundation. Long

* Wren's Parentalia, p. 144.

† Baker's Chronicle, p. 235; Sandford, Gen. Hist. book v. p. 434, ed. 1707.

‡ Nichols, vol. ii. p. 298.

ago, a stone coffin, said to have been that of King Richard, was used as a drinking-trough for horses at the White Horse Inn at Leicester.* But even this apocryphal memorial of the usurper no longer exists. When, in 1722, it was seen by the Rev. Samuel Carte, the father of the historian,—although there was still discernible "some appearance of the hollow fitted for containing the head and shoulders."—the greater portion of it had yielded to the ravages of time. Thirty-six years afterwards Hutton searched for it, and searched in vain.†

During three centuries and a half there stood in the town of Leicester the venerable hostelry in which King Richard passed the night on his march from Nottingham to Bosworth. Hutton describes it as "a large, handsome half-timber house, with one story projecting over the other." In the days

* Sandford, Gen. Hist. book v. p. 434; Hutton's Bosworth, p. 143; Speed's Description of England, anno 1627.

† "I took a journey to Leicester in 1758," writes Hutton, "to see a trough which had been the repository of one of the most singular bodies that ever existed, but found it had not withstood the ravages of time. The best intelligence I could obtain was, that it was destroyed about the latter end of the reign of George I., and some of the pieces placed as steps in a cellar, in the same inn where it had served as a trough."— *Hutton's Bosworth,* p. 143. With respect to the "appearance of hollow" remarked upon by Mr. Carte, either he must have been mistaken in supposing that it was constructed for the purpose of receiving the head and shoulders of the dead, or else the coffin could scarcely have been that of King Richard. The custom of shaping coffins with such concavities, had been discontinued for centuries previously to the death of that monarch.

of King Richard it was styled, in compliment to
him, the "White Boar." To have retained the
name, however, after the accession of King Henry,
might have exposed the landlord to a rebuke from
the authorities, or perhaps an attack by the rabble.*

Accordingly, the name of the "Blue Boar" was
substituted for the "White." This name the old
hostelry retained so late as the year 1836, when,
notwithstanding it was uninjured by the lapse of
ages, and unaltered by the hand of man, it was
sacrilegiously razed to the ground. "Blue Boar
Lane" still denotes the site from which Richard
III. marched to his death upon Bosworth Field.

Another, and no less interesting relic,—the camp-
bedstead which Richard carried about with him,
and on which he slept at Leicester,—is, fortunately,
still in existence. It appears also to have contained his treasure-chest. The material of which it
is constructed is oak, being ornamented with panels
of different coloured wood, two of which are carved
with designs representing apparently the Holy
Sepulchre. For nearly two centuries after the battle of Bosworth, the old bedstead was allowed to
remain, an object of interest and curiosity, at the
old hostelry. When Hutton, however, visited
Leicester in 1758, it had come into the possession

* "The proud bragging white boar, which was his badge, was violently razed and plucked down from every sign and place where it
might be espied."—*Grafton*, vol. ii. p. 166.

of Alderman Drake, of that city, from whom it descended to his grandson, the Rev. Matthew Babington. Massive and cumbrous though it be, this curious piece of furniture is so fashioned that it may easily be taken to pieces and reconstructed in the form of a chest. This circumstance, added to the unquestionable fact of its having formerly been gilt, and its being profusely ornamented with fleurs-de-lis, a favourite emblem of the house of Plantagenet, seems to afford almost incontestable evidence of the authenticity of this remarkable relic.*

King Richard III. was the father of at least two illegitimate children, a son and a daughter, to each of whom he gave the surname of Plantagenet. Like his brother, King Edward IV., he had been a watch-

---

* See Hutton's Bosworth, p. 48; Halsted's Richard III. vol. ii. pp. 491—494; Notes and Queries, vol. iv. pp. 102, 153, 154, New Series. In some verses prefixed to Tom Coryate's "Crudities," published in 1611, King Richard's bedstead is recorded as one of the "sights" of Leicester. With reference to the surmise that it concealed his military treasure, a tragical story is related. No suspicion of its having been used for such a purpose appears to have been entertained till the reign of James 1., when a man of the name of Clark happened to be the landlord of the Blue Boar. The wife of this person was one day engaged in arranging the bed, when her curiosity was excited by a piece of gold dropping from it on the floor. The probability that more gold lay concealed in it, led to a close examination of the old bedstead, when there was discovered—between what they had always supposed to be the bottom of the bed and a false bottom beneath it—a large amount of gold, the coinage either of the reign of Richard III. or of his predecessors. Clark carefully kept his good fortune a secret. To the surprise of his neighbours, he suddenly became transformed from a poor to a rich man, and eventually rose to be mayor of Leicester. After the death of Clark, his widow became possessed of what remained of the royal treas-

ful and an affectionate parent.   John of Gloucester, or, as he was sometimes styled, John of Pomfret, was knighted by his father on the occasion of his second coronation at York in 1483.   Eighteen months afterwards,* few as his years must have been, he found the king appointing him governor of Calais; the royal patent styling him "our beloved son John of Gloucester," and expressing "undoubted hope" that, from his singular gifts of mind and body, he was destined to perform good service to the State.† The fate of a youth whose career had promised to be so brilliant, has, we believe, been left unrecorded.   Presuming that he survived his father, the probability is that he either courted safety by changing his name and

ure ; but, unhappily for her, she allowed the secret to transpire. The desire of possessing themselves of such wealth excited the worst passions of one of the housemaids and her sweetheart ; and accordingly, in the night-time, the former, stealing into the bedroom of her mistress, either strangled or suffocated her in her sleep. Both offenders were subsequently brought to justice, and suffered the penalty awarded to their crime. The woman was burned to death ; the man was hanged. Extraordinary as this story may appear, there are reasonable grounds for giving it credit. Certain it is—for the existing archives of the city of Leicester attest the fact—that, in the year 1605, a man and woman were executed there for the murder of the landlady of the Blue Boar. Moreover, Sir Roger Twysden, writing in 1653, informs us that he heard the story vouched for by two " very good, true, and worthy persons,"—Sir Basil Brooke and a Mrs. Cumber, both of whom would seem to have lived contemporaneously with the facts which they related. The latter was brought up at Leicester, and actually saw the murderess burned at the stake. Notes and Queries, vol. iv. pp. 102, 153, 154, New Series ; Hutton, p. 49 ; Halsted, vol. ii. pp. 491, 492.

* 11th March 1485.   † Rymer's Fœdera, vol. xii. p. 265.

living in obscurity, or that he obtained military service in a foreign land.

Richard's only daughter, "Dame Katherine Plantagenet," was married, apparently almost in childhood, to William Herbert, Earl of Huntingdon. In the deed of settlement, which still exists, the king guarantees to defray the expenses of their nuptials, and to endow her with a fortune of 400 marks a year. The earl, on his part, engages to make her "a fair and efficient estate of certain of his manors in England, to the yearly value of 200*l.* over all charges."* Richard received her husband into high favour, selecting him to fill more than one office of importance, and conferring on him the stewardship of several rich domains. The Countess of Huntingdon died young; so young, indeed, that it seems questionable whether the marriage was ever consummated.

In addition to John of Gloucester, King Richard is said to have been the father of another illegitimate son, Richard Plantagenet, of whose chequered fortunes some romantic particulars have been recorded. About the latter part of the reign of Henry VIII., when Sir Thomas Moyle, the maternal ancestor of the Earls of Winchilsea, was erecting his noble mansion, Eastwell Place, in Kent, his curiosity was excited by observing the recluse and studious habits of the principal stonemason

* Sandford, Gen. Hist. book v. p. 435.

employed on the works. Avoiding the society of his fellows, no sooner was the task of the day completed, than the old man—for he must have been considerably advanced in years—drew a book from his pocket, and retired to peruse it in private. One of his peculiarities was a disinclination to disclose the nature of his studies. Whenever any one approached, he closed the volume. The circumstance excited the curiosity of Sir Thomas, who, one day surprising him at his studies, discovered that the book which he was reading was in Latin. Some remarks, which Sir Thomas ventured to make, induced the old man to open his heart, and to narrate to him the story of his life. He had received, he said, much kindness from Sir Thomas, and would therefore reveal to him a secret which he had intrusted to no other living being. His story was as follows:—

Until he had attained the age, he said, of fifteen or sixteen, he had been boarded and educated in the house of a "Latin schoolmaster," ignorant of the names of the authors of his being, or to whom he was indebted for his maintenance. Once in each quarter of the year he was visited by a gentleman, who, though he seemed to take an interest in his welfare, and regularly defrayed the expense of his board and instruction, took care to impress on his mind that no relationship existed between them. Once only, there seemed to be a chance of his discovering the secret of his birth; but it was destined to end in disappointment. On that occasion he was unexpectedly visited by his mysterious benefactor, who, taking him with him, "carried him to a fine great house, where he passed through several stately rooms, in one of which he left him, bidding him stay there." Then there came to him one "finely dressed with a star and garter," who, after having put some questions to him, dismissed him with a present of money. That person, if there be any truth in this singular tradition, was King Richard. "Then the forementioned gentleman returned, and carried him back to school."

Once more, and for the last time, he was visited by his friend, who, furnishing him with a horse and a proper equipment, intimated that he must take a journey with him into the country. Their destination was the field of Bosworth, where they arrived on the eve of the memorable battle. On reaching the royal camp, the boy was conducted to the tent of King Richard, who embraced him and bade him welcome. He then disclosed to him the startling fact of his being his father, promising, at the same time, that, in the event of his winning the approaching battle, he would openly acknowledge him as his son.

"But, child," he said, "to-morrow I must fight for my crown, and assure yourself that if I lose that I will also lose my life." He then pointed out a particular spot, which overlooked the battle-field, where he desired the boy to station himself on the following day. " If I should be so unfortunate as to lose the battle," said the king, " take care to let nobody know that I am your father, for no mercy will be shown to any one so nearly related to me." The king then presented him with a purse of gold, and bade him farewell.

The boy witnessed the memorable battle, and beheld the death of his heroic father. The result of the conflict, of course, was fatal to his future prospects. Accordingly, hurrying to London, he sold his horse and fine clothes, and, as soon as these resources were expended, bound himself apprentice to a bricklayer. Fortunately, with the excellent education he had received, he had imbibed a taste for literature, which served to solace him in adversity, and to throw a refinement over poverty. He was unwilling, as he told Sir Thomas Moyle, to forget his knowledge of Latin; and as the conversation of his fellow-workmen was uncongenial to him, books became his only companions, and reading his favourite amusement.*

Of so romantic a character is the story of Richard Plantagenet, that we are naturally disposed to treat it with incredulity. And yet all the evidence seems to us to be in favour of its being genuine.

* Peck's Desiderata Curiosa, lib. vii. pp. 249—251.

That it was believed by Sir Thomas Moyle, who, as
a contemporary of the narrator, must have had excellent opportunities of testing its truth, is proved
by his having erected a cottage near Eastwell Place
for the old man, in which he comfortably passed the
remainder of his days.   Moreover, having held the
important office of Chancellor of the Court of Aug-
mentation, Sir Thomas must have been a man of
business and of the world, and therefore most unlikely to have been duped by a story which, if un-
corroborated, would scarcely have found credence
out of a nursery.   Not many years have passed by,
since the foundations of Richard Plantagenet's cottage were still pointed out by the inhabitants of
Eastwell and of the neighbourhood; nor was it till
the middle of the seventeenth century that the cottage itself was razed to the ground, in the time of
Thomas third Earl of Winchilsea.   His son, Earl
Heneage, told Dr. Brett that he would almost as
soon have pulled down Eastwell Place itself.
When, in 1720, Dr. Brett called upon the Earl at
Eastwell, " I found him," he writes, " sitting with
the register of the parish of Eastwell lying open
before him.   He told me that he had been looking
there to see who of his own family were mentioned
in it; but, says he, ' I have a curiosity here to
show you.'   The earl then pointed to the entry of
the burial of Richard Plantagenet.   ' This is all,'
said Lord Winchilsea, ' that we can glean of his

history, except the tradition which exists in our family, and some little marks where his house stood.'" The remarkable entry in the parish register, to which the lord of Eastwell pointed, appears "*sub anno Domini* 1550," and runs as follows :—

"Rychard Plantagenet was buried the **xxii** day of Decembre.
Anno di supra."

Anciently, when any person of noble family was interred at Eastwell, it was the custom to affix this mark, V, against the name of the deceased in the register of burials. The fact is a significant one, that this aristocratic symbol is prefixed to the name of Richard Plantagenet.* At Eastwell his story still excites curiosity and interest. Although eleven generations have passed away since the death of the humble stonemason, more than one interesting local memorial continues to perpetuate his memory. A well in Eastwell Park still bears his name; tradition points to an uninscribed tomb in Eastwell churchyard as his resting-place; and, lastly, the very handwriting, which more than three centuries ago recorded his interment, is still in existence.†

* Letter from the Rev. T. Parsons, Rector of Eastwell, 10th August 1767, Gentleman's Magazine, vol. xxxvii. p. 408; Peck's Desiderata Curiosa, lib. vii. p. 249.

† From information kindly furnished to the author by the present Earl of Winchilsea and Nottingham. (1861.)

CHAPTER VIII.

THIS volume had nearly passed the press, when there appeared, under the auspices of the Master of the Rolls, two historical works of considerable value, each of which contains a point bearing on the disputed criminality of Richard III. The works alluded to are " Letters and Papers illustrative of the Reigns of Richard III. and Henry VII.," edited by James Gairdner, Esq.; and " Political Poems and Songs, composed between the Accession of Edward III. and that of Richard III.," edited by Thomas Wright, Esq.

Previously to the appearance of the former of these works, some doubts had been entertained by the author of this volume whether parliament can properly be said to have assembled during the brief reign of Edward V.; a point involving the weighty question as to how far the usurpation of Richard III. was sanctioned by the legislature. Certainly, strong evidence of such a parliamentary meeting having taken place had been adduced by the late Mr. Sharon Turner, although he admits that it may have been irregularly convened, and merely for

" present exigencies."* But the validity of these arguments has since been impugned by Mr. Nichols;† and thus the question stood when Mr. Gairdner, with whose views on the subject the author ventures to express his humble concurrence, thus steps forward as arbiter between the two. " Mr. Nichol's Historical Introduction," he says, " contains some important remarks in correction of Lingard and Sharon Turner, which show how difficult it is to avoid rash assumptions in dealing with this obscure portion of our history. It is my desire in these pages to avoid, as far as possible, making statements the truth of which is open to controversy, but one important fact relating to the accession of Richard III. appears to me to have been misunderstood even by Mr. Nichols. It is known that writs were sent out on the 13th of May for a parliament to meet on the 25th of June. On the 21st of June, however, a writ of *supersedeas* was received in the city of York to prevent its assembling; and Mr. Nichols considers that the parliament did not actually meet, a fact which he says is further declared in the Act of Settlement of the first year of Richard III. Now the words of that act do indeed declare that there was no true and legal parliament, but they appear no less distinctly

* History of England during the Middle Ages, vol. iii. pp. 383—395, ed. 1830.

† Grants, &c. from the Crown during the Reign of Edward V. Hist. Introduction by John G. Nichols, Esq., pp. 387—395.

to show that there was the semblance of such a thing. In plain ordinary language, the parliament really did meet, but the meeting was an informal one, and what was done was of a doubtful validity until confirmed by a parliament regularly assembled. Parliament did meet, and the petition to Richard to assume the crown was presented by a deputation of the Lords and Commons of England, accompanied by another from the city of London, on the very day that had been originally appointed for the meeting."*

But, whatever may have been the constitution of the assembly which invited Richard to assume the sovereign dignity, certain it is that the legal parliament, which met seven months afterwards, fully acquiesced in its procedures, and confirmed Richard's title as King of England. Neither, as might be conjectured, was that parliament a packed or a venal one. On the contrary, as Lord Chancellor Campbell writes,—"we have no difficulty in pronouncing it the most meritorious national assembly for protecting the liberty of the subject and putting down abuses in the administration of justice, that had sat since the reign of Edward I."† And yet, according to Hume, "never was there in any country a usurpation more flagrant than that of

---

* Letters and Papers illustrative of the Reigns of Richard III. and Henry VII., Preface, pp. xvii and xviii.

† Lord Campbell's Lives of the Chancellors, vol. i. p. 407.

Richard, or more repugnant to every principle of justice and public interest." Again, writes the great historian, "his title was never acknowledged by any national assembly; scarcely even by the lowest populace to whom he appealed." But what was really the state of the case? Assuming, for instance, that the bench of bishops may be selected as having fairly represented property and rank, as well as the integrity and intelligence of the age, let us ask what was the conduct of the majority of them when Richard set forth his claims to the sovereign power. Thomas Bourchier, Archbishop of Canterbury, and formerly Lord Chancellor, placed the crown on his head in Westminster Abbey. A few weeks afterwards, Thomas Rotheram, Archbishop of York, also formerly Lord Chancellor and " considered to be the greatest equity lawyer of the age,"* crowned him at York. John Russell, Bishop of Lincoln,—"a wise man and good,"† and one of the executors of Edward IV.,—not only consented to retain the Great Seal, but held it till within about three weeks of Richard's death. At Richard's first coronation there walked in procession Peter Courtenay, Bishop of Exeter; James Goldwell, Bishop of Norwich; William Dudley, Bishop of Durham; Robert Still-

* Lord Campbell's Lives of the Chancellors, vol. i. p. 397.

† Lord Bacon's Richard III. Lord Campbell also speaks of Bishop Russell as distinguished for " uncommon learning, piety, and wisdom.' —*Lives of the Chroniclers*, p. 404.

ington, Bishop of Bath and Wells; and Edmund Audley, Bishop of Rochester. Again, when, seventeen days after his coronation, Richard visited the University of Cambridge, he was met in procession and congratulated, by William Waynflete, Bishop of Winchester and formerly Lord Chancellor; Richard Redman, Bishop of St. Asaph; Thomas Langton, Bishop of St. David's; and, lastly, by the accomplished Master of the Rolls, architect, and ambassador, John Alcock, Bishop of Worcester,— the same prelate who had been selected to be preceptor to Edward V., and who, less than three months previously, had been arrested, in company with Earl Rivers and Sir Richard Grey, by Richard's orders, at Stony Stratford.*   Surely, after perusing this list of reverend prelates, including no fewer than four who had held the appointment of Lord Chancellor of England, we can scarcely be called upon to believe that the usurpation of Rich-

---

* The names of the prelates, recorded in the text as having directly sanctioned the deposition of Edward V., are merely those which recur at the moment to the author. Among the remaining ten, a curious inquirer would probably discover several others who sent in their allegiance to Richard III. Their names are:—Lionel Woodville, Bishop of Salisbury, brother to the Queen Dowager; John Morton, Bishop of Ely, in custody; Thomas Milling Bishop of Hereford; Thomas Ednam, Bishop of Bangor; Edward Story, Bishop of Chichester; John Halse or Hales, Bishop of Litchfield; John Marshal, Bishop of Llandaff; Thomas Kemp, Bishop of London ; Richard Bell, Bishop of Carlisle; and Richard Oldham, Bishop of Man. The sees of Bristol, Chester, Gloucester, Oxford, Peterborough, Manchester, and Ripon, were not then in existence.

ard of Gloucester was so utterly unauthorized, so flagrant, so abhorrent to the feelings of his fellow-countrymen, as it is usually represented by the historian. Let it not be forgotten, moreover, that the learned and venerable Bishop of Winchester, had previously invited Richard to be his guest at his new foundation, Magdalen College; that he honourably entertained him there, and, that, at his departure, he caused to be entered on the college register,—

"VIVAT REX IN ÆTERNUM."

We will now venture to say a few words in reference to the favourable manner in which we find Richard occasionally spoken of by his contemporaries, compared with the virulent abuse too often heaped upon him by the succeeding Tudor chroniclers. Thus, in a very interesting contemporary poem, entitled "On the Recovery of the Throne by Edward IV.,"* for which we are indebted to Mr. Wright, occurs the following stanza :—

> "The Duke of Gloucester, that noble prince,
>   Young of age and victorious in battle,
> To the honour of Hector that he might come.
>   Grace him followeth, fortune and good speed.
>   I suppose he is the same that clerks read of.
> Fortune hath him chosen, and forth with him will go,
>   Her husband to be ; the will of God is so."

---

* Political Poems and Songs, p. 380.

But, doubtless, among the most remarkable encomiums which were lavished on Richard in his lifetime, were those which emanated from the mercurial priest and antiquary, John Rous. This person had not only been often in the presence of Richard, but probably had also often actually conversed with him. Rous, who was born about the year 1411, was one of the chaplains of a chantry at Guy's Cliff, about a mile and a half from Warwick Castle. His principal duties were to pray for the good estate of the Earls of Warwick: his principal occupation was studying and writing about antiquities. Of the many years which he spent at Guy's Cliff, twenty were passed while the great "Kingmaker" lorded it over the neighbouring castle. Among other works, Rous was the author and artist of two pictorial Rolls of the Earls of Warwick, of which one is preserved in the College of Arms at London, and the other in the possession of the Duke of Manchester. Both of these Rolls were executed before the death of Richard III., and, no doubt, both originally contained passages highly laudatory of the husband of the surviving heiress of the great earl. But, in due time, the period arrived when it was no longer safe to eulogize the house of York, and when it had become gainful to extol the house of Lancaster. Henry Earl of Richmond ascended the throne as Henry VII., and the recluse of Guy's Cliff hastened to

salute the rising sun.   Forgetting the praises which
he had formerly lavished on Richard III. he dedi-
cated to the new Tudor sovereign a work, in which
he accused Richard of the most frightful crimes,
and heaped on him the most virulent abuse.*   He
went even further.   Unfortunately, one of the two
rolls which he had executed was, at the time of the
accession of Henry VII., either in his own possession or within his reach, and accordingly he proceeded to mutilate and extract from it all that
might have reflected honour on the memory of a
dead king, or give offence to a living one.   This is
the roll which is preserved in the College of Arms.
The portraits of two of the Yorkist kings are ex-
tracted; Anne Neville is despoiled of her royal
insignia as Queen of England; while her son,
Edward Prince of Wales, instead of the crown
which he had formerly worn on his head, and the
sceptre which he had held in his hand, is represented in a tabard, wearing merely a ducal cap and
circlet.   King Richard himself is merely introduced as the "*infelix maritus*" of Anne
Neville.

But, fortunately, the other, or "Manchester
Roll," had passed, as it would seem, into other,
and probably Yorkist hands, and thus was preserved from Rous's mutilations.   There, then, we
find touches of Richard's character, such as it had

* Historia Regum Angliæ.   See ante, pp. 66, 75.

originally, and probably conscientiously, been sketched by the antiquary. There he is the "mighty prince in his day, special good lord to the town and lordship of Warwick." Again, he is "the most victorious prince, King Richard III.;" and, lastly, he is described, almost enthusiastically, as,—"In his realm [ruling] full commendably; punishing offenders of his laws, especially extortioners and oppressors of his commons, and cherishing those that were virtuous; by the which discreet guiding he got great thanks of God, and love of all his subjects rich and poor, and great laud of the people of all other lands about him."* Such, let us hope, was the true light in which Richard's kingly character was viewed by the priestly antiquary of Guy's Cliff. Rous's treatment of the memory of the hero-king was, after all, probably not very different from that of other writers of the age on suddenly finding themselves transferred from the rule of a Plantagenet to that of a Tudor. Of these two houses, the former was unquestionably the more popular. It was, therefore, obviously the object of Henry and his friends to depreciate and revile, as much as possible, the character of Richard, for the purpose of preventing commiseration attaching itself to his

---

* See Rous's biographical notices, Nos. 17, 62, 63, in the Duke of Manchester's copy of the Rous Roll, edited, with an interesting introduction, by William Courthope, Esq., Somerset Herald.

memory, and also to bring his line into disfavour and contempt. Had Richard proved victorious on the field of Bosworth; had he quietly transmitted his crown to one of the princes of his race, we should probably find, in the chronicles and records of the past, little to his discredit, and possibly much fulsome panegyric in his favour.

We may mention that in Mr. Gairdner's recent work, to which we have previously alluded, there is a remarkable document* tending to give fearful force to a suspicion which has long existed, that the concession, by which Henry VII. induced King Ferdinand of Spain to consent to the marriage of his daughter Katherine with Arthur Prince of Wales, was the blood of the unfortunate heir of the house of York, Edward Earl of Warwick, son of the late Duke of Clarence. If such be the case, surely the worst sin of the last king of the house of Plantagenet was not greater than that of the first sovereign of the house of Tudor. From what we know of the character of Richard III. in his public capacity, we may fairly presume that, if he murdered his nephews, he was at least patriotic enough to have had in view the prosperity of his subjects and the tranquillity of his kingdom, as well as the selfish object of personal aggrandizement. Henry, on the contrary, would seem to

* Page 113. Letter from De Puebla, the Spanish ambassador in England to King Ferdinand and Queen Isabella.

have been actuated by no more generous motive than that of securing an illustrious alliance for his son, in order more securely to establish his mushroom race on the throne.

Appendix

APPENDIX.

A.

KING RICHARD'S PERSONAL APPEARANCE.

(See p. 105.)

"THE old Countess of Desmond, who had danced with Richard," writes Walpole, "declared he was the handsomest man in the room except his brother Edward, and very well made."—*Historic Doubts*, Lord Orford's Works, vol. ii. p. 166.

"As I have just received, through another channel," writes Sharon Turner, "a traditional statement of what the Countess of Desmond mentioned on this subject, I will subjoin it, and the series of authorities for it. Mr. Paynter, the magistrate, related to my son, the Rev. Sydney Turner, the following particulars:—When a boy, about the year 1810, he heard the old Lord Glastonbury, then at least ninety years of age, declare that, when he was a young lad, he saw, and was often with, the Countess of Desmond, then living, an aged woman. She told him that when she was a girl she had known familiarly, and frequently seen, an old lady who had been brought up by the former Countess of Desmond, who became noted for her remarkable longevity, as she lived to be one hundred and twenty years of age. This lady mentioned that this aged Countess of Desmond had declared that she had been at a court banquet where Richard was present, and that he was in no way personally deformed or crooked. Edward IV. was deemed, in his day, the handsomest man of his court."—*Sharon Turner's Richard the Third, a Poem*, p. 277, *note*.

The reader, who may be interested in the story of the "old Countess of Desmond" and her remarkable recollections of Richard III., is referred to "An Enquiry into the Person and Age of the Countess of Desmond," Lord Orford's Works, vol. i. p. 210; Sharon Turner's Hist. of the Middle Ages, vol. iii. p. 443; Quarterly Review, vol. ii. p. 329; and Notes and Queries, vols. ii. iii. iv. and v. passim.

329

B.

MURDER OF EDWARD V. AND THE DUKE OF YORK.

(See p. 219.)

The details of the murder of the young princes, as recounted in the text, are derived almost entirely from the narrative of Sir Thomas More, whose account has been followed by every subsequent historian. That there may be discovered occasional inconsistencies and improbabilities in his narrative, can scarcely be denied. It must be remembered, however, that More himself claims no greater weight for the truth of his statements, than that he learned them from well-informed and trustworthy persons who had no motive to falsify or mislead. For instance, in the account which he gives of the confessions said to have been made by Sir James Tyrrell and Dighton in the reign of Henry VII., we find Sir Thomas cautiously introducing such expressions as "they say," and "I have heard." But, though even More himself hesitates to vouch for the entire truth of all he relates, his narrative is nevertheless entitled to the highest respect. It should be borne in mind how near he lived to the times of which he wrote; that his position in society enabled him to converse with and interrogate many persons who had excellent means of knowing the truth; that, as a man learned in the law, he was eminently well qualified to weigh, and decide on the value of the evidence which he had collected; and, lastly, how great is the improbability that a man of high honour and integrity, such as was Sir Thomas More, should have deliberately falsified or garbled facts.

That there were current, in the days of Sir Thomas More, many and contradictory versions of the tragical story of the young princes, we can readily understand. "Of the manner of the death of this young king and of his brother," writes the chronicler Rastell, "there were *diverse opinions;* but the most common opinion was, that they were smothered between two feather-beds, and that, in the doing, the younger brother escaped from under the feather-beds, and crept under the bedstead, and there lay naked awhile, till they had smothered the young king so that he was surely dead; and, after that, one of them took his brother from under the bedstead, and held his face down to the ground with his one hand, and with the other hand cut his throat asunder with a dagger. It is a marvel that any man could have so hard a heart to do so cruel a deed, save only that necessity compelled them; for they were so charged by the duke, the protector, that if they showed not to him the bodies of both those children dead, on the morrow after they were so commanded. that then they themselves should be put to death. Wherefore they that were so commanded to do it, were compelled to fulfil the protector's will.

"And after that, the bodies of these two children, as the opinion ran, were both closed in a great heavy chest, and, by the means of one that was secret with the protector, they were put in a ship going to Flanders; and, when the ship was in the black deeps, this man threw both those dead bodies so closed in the chest, over the hatches into the sea; and yet none of the mariners, nor none in the ship save only the said man, wist what things it was that were there so enclosed. Which saying diverse men conjectured to be true, because that the bones of the said children could never be found buried, neither in the Tower nor in any other place.

"Another opinion there is, that they which had the charge to put them to death, caused one to cry suddenly, 'Treason, treason!' Wherewith the children, being afraid, desired to know what was best for them to do. And then they bade them hide themselves in a great chest, that no man should find them, and if anybody came into the chamber they would say they were not there. And, according as they counselled them, they crept both into the chest, which, anon after, they locked. And then anon they buried that chest in a great pit *under a stair*, which they before had made therefor, and anon cast earth thereon, and so buried them quick [alive]. Which chest was after cast into the black deeps, as is before said."—*Rastell's Chronicles* (A.D. 1529), pp. 292, 293.

C.

JANE SHORE.
(See p. 251.)

It may be argued, that the cruel treatment, which the too-celebrated Jane Shore encountered during the protectorate of Richard, tends to weaken the evidence which has been adduced in support of his sympathy with female suffering. But Walpole has suggested, and his conjecture is probably correct, that it was at the instigation of the priesthood, and not of Richard, that this frail but tender-hearted woman suffered her celebrated persecution. Certain it is, that the punishment to which she was subjected was not on account of the crime of treason with which she was charged, but for her notorious adultery.* Moreover, when, some time afterwards, Richard was afforded the opportunity of increasing the severity of her punishment, so far was he from playing the tyrant, that he behaved towards her with the most considerate kindness. The facts of the case are curious. While a prisoner in Ludgate, to which stronghold she had been committed after having performed her penance, Jane Shore had the good fortune to fascinate the king's solicitor-general, Sir Thomas Lynom, who had been employed to interrogate her while under restraint, and who became so enamoured of her as to make her an offer of his hand. Richard naturally regarded the conduct of his solicitor as indecent and reprehensible; nor probably, in those days, would the conduct of the sovereign have been considered over-harsh, had he dismissed Sir Thomas from his post, or even committed him to prison. But, so far from acting with severity, his behaviour, on being apprized of the unseemly courtship, was alike that of a lenient prince and a kind-hearted man. To Russell, Bishop of Lincoln, then lord-chancellor, he writes:—"We, for many causes, should be sorry that he (the solicitor-general) so should be disposed. Pray you therefore to send for him, and in that ye goodly may exhort and stir him to the contrary. And if ye find him utterly set for to marry her, and none otherwise will be advised, then (if it may stand with the law of the church) we be content, (the time of marriage deferred to our coming next to London) that, upon sufficient surety found of her good abering, ye do send for her keeper, and discharge him of our said commandment by warrant of these, committing her to the rule and guidance of her father, or any other by your discretion, in the mean season.

" *To the right reverend father in God, &c., the Bishop of Lincoln.*"†

The popular story of Richard forbidding the citizens of London to relieve the unfortunate woman during her penance, and of her dying, in consequence of hunger and fatigue, in Shoreditch, is manifestly apocryphal.

> "I could not get one bit of bread,
> Whereby my hunger might be fed;
> Nor drink, but such as channels yield,
> Or stinking ditches in the field.

---

* Hist. Doubts, Lord Orford's Works, vol. ii. p. 174; S. Turner's Middle Ages, vol. iii. p. 449, ed. 1825.

† Harl. MS. 433, fol. 340, quoted in Lord Orford's Works, vol. ii. p. 174; Campbell's Chancellors, vol. i. p. 409, where Lord Orford's inaccurate reference to the Harl. MS. is corrected.

> " Thus, weary of my life, at length
> I yielded up my vital strength
> Within a ditch of loathsome scent,
> Where carrion dogs did much frequent.

> " The which now, since my dying day,
> Is Shoreditch called, as writers say,
> Which is a witness of my sin,
> For being concubine to a king." *

To Sir Thomas More we are indebted for the following quaint and graphic description of Jane Shore undergoing her penance at Paul's Cross :—" He " [Richard] " caused the Bishop of London to put her to open penance, going before the cross in procession upon a Sunday with a taper in her hand. In which she went in countenance, and pace demure, so womanly, and albeit she was out of all array save her kirtle [petticoat] only; yet went she so fair and lovely, namely, while the wondering of the people cast a comely red in her cheeks,—of which she before had most miss,—that her great shame won her much praise among those that were more amorous of her body, than curious of her soul. And many good folk also, that hated her living, and glad were to see sin corrected, yet pitied they more her penance than rejoiced therein."†

How charming is Michael Drayton's portrait of the once adored and envied mistress of the mighty Edward !—" Her hair was of a dark yellow; her face round and full; her eye grey, delicate harmony being betwixt each part's proportion, and each proportion's colour; her body fat, white, and smooth ; her countenance cheerful and like to her condition. That picture which I have seen of her ‡ was such as she rose out of her bed in the morning, having nothing on but a rich mantle cast under one arm over her shoulder, and sitting on a chair, on which her naked arm did lie. What her father's name was, or where she was born, is

* " The woefull Lamentation of Jane Shore, a goldsmith's wife in London," &c. Percy's Reliques, vol. ii. p. 279, ed. 1847. That Shoreditch derived its name from Jane Shore is, of course, a popular error. Stow informs us that the name existed at least as early as 1440. Survey, Book v. p. 53.

† More's Richard III. p. 82.

‡ There is an original picture of Jane Shore in the provost's lodgings at Eton, and another in the provost's lodge at King's College, Cambridge, to both of which foundations she is presumed to have been a benefactress. Granger mentions another original picture of her, which, in his day, was " at Dr. Peckard's of Magdalen College, Cambridge," and was formerly in the posession of Dean Colet. Granger also informs us that a lock of her hair, " which looked as if it had been powdered with gold dust," was in the possession of the Duchess of Montagu. Biog. Illst. vol. i p. 87.

not certainly known. But Shore, a young man of right goodly person, wealth, and behaviour, abandoned her bed after the king had made her his concubine." * Drayton and Sir Thomas More agree that a want of stature was a drawback to her otherwise singular loveliness. " Proper she was," says the latter, "and fair; nothing in her body that you would have changed, but if you would have wished her somewhat higher. Thus they say that knew her in her youth."—" Yet," continues the future lord-chancellor, " delighted not men so much in her beauty as in her pleasant behaviour. For a proper wit had she, and could both read well and write; merry in company, ready and quick of answer, neither mute nor full of babble, somewhat taunting, without displeasure and not without disport. The king would say that he had three concubines, which in three diverse properties diversely excelled. One the merriest, another the wiliest, the third the holiest harlot in his realm, as one whom no man could get out of the church lightly to any place, but it were to his bed. The other two were somewhat greater personages, and natheless of their humility content to be nameless, and to forbear the praise of those properties. But the merriest was this Shore's wife, in whom the king therefore took special pleasure. For many he had but her he loved, whose favours, to say the truth (for sin it were to belie the devil), she never abused to any man's hurt, but to many a man's comfort and relief. Where the king took displeasure, she would mitigate and appease his mind. Where men were out of favour, she would bring them in his grace. For many that had highly offended, she obtained pardon. Of great forfeitures she got men remission. And finally, in many weighty suits, she stood many men in great stead, either for none or very small rewards, and those rather gay than rich; either for that she was content with the deed itself well done, or for that she delighted to be sued unto, and show what she was able to do with the king, or for that wanton women and wealthy be not always covetous.

" I doubt not some shall think this woman so slight a thing, to be written of and set among the remembrances of great matters; which they shall specially think, that haply shall esteem her only by that they now see her. But meseemeth the chance so much the more worthy to be remembered, in how much she is now in the more beggarly condition, unfriended and worn out of acquaintance, after good substance, after as great favour with the prince, after as great suit and seeking to with all those that those days had business to speed." †

Jane Shore survived to the reign of Henry VIII., dying, apparently,

<hr>

* Drayton's Works, p. 121. Ed. 1748.   † More's Richard III. pp. 83—86.

in great distress and at an advanced age. "At this day," writes Sir Thomas More, "she beggeth of many, at this day living, that at this day had begged if she had not been."* Of the beauty which had captivated the voluptuous Edward, not a vestige remained. "Albeit," writes Sir Thomas, "some that now see her deem her never to have been well-visaged. Whose judgment seemeth me somewhat like as though men should guess the beauty of one long before departed, by her scalp, taken out of the charnel house; for now she is old, lean, withered and dried up, nothing left but shrivelled skin and hard bone. And yet, being even such, whoso will advise her visage, might guess and devise which parts how filled, would make it a fair face." †

NOTE.

The author takes this opportunity of pointing out an error into which not only he himself has fallen, but which has long been universally prevalent. He refers to an allusion which he has made ‡ to a painting, said to be by Mabuse, at Hampton Court, which is still described in the catalogue of royal pictures as representing "The Children of Henry VII." The charm, however, which so long attached itself to that venerable picture, has been recently dispelled. It has been shown, on high authority, that it represents, not the children of Henry VII., but of Christian II. King of Denmark. As such the picture is described in a catalogue contemporary with the reign of Henry VIII., and as such, we presume, it will be transmitted to posterity.

* More's Richard III. p. 86. † Ibid. p. 84. ‡ Ante, p. 206.

END OF VOL. I.